Richard Cumberland

The Observer

Being a Collection of Moral, Literary and Familiar Essays. Vol. IV

Richard Cumberland

The Observer

Being a Collection of Moral, Literary and Familiar Essays. Vol. IV

ISBN/EAN: 9783744767712

Printed in Europe, USA, Canada, Australia, Japan

Cover: Foto ©Andreas Hilbeck / pixelio.de

More available books at **www.hansebooks.com**

THE

OBSERVER:

BEING A COLLECTION OF

MORAL, LITERARY AND FAMILIAR

ESSAYS.

——MULTORUM PROVIDUS URBES
ET MORES HOMINUM INSPEXIT——— (HORAT;)

By *RICHARD CUMBERLAND*, Esq.

THE FIFTH EDITION, NEWLY ARRANGED.

TO WHICH IS ADDED,

AN ENTIRE TRANSLATION OF THE COMEDY OF THE CLOUDS.

IN SIX VOLUMES.

VOL. IV.

LONDON:
Printed for C. DILLY, in the Poultry.

1798.

CONTENTS

OF THE

FOURTH VOLUME.

NUMBER

LXXXVII. WRITTEN on the laſt day of the year 1789. Short review of the remarkable events within the period of that year, with ſome elegiac lines applicable to its hiſtory and character - - - 1

LXXXVIII. The hiſtory of Nicolas' Pedroſa, and his eſcape from the inquiſition in Madrid - - 8

LXXXIX. The hiſtory of Nicolas Pedroſa continued - - - - 21

XC. The hiſtory concluded - - 33

XCI. A review of the preſent ſtate of ſociety in this country, as dependent upon laws, religion, manners, and arts. The ſame compared with antecedent periods, and murmurs againſt the preſent times reprehended and confuted - 44

XCII. Letter from Poſthumous, complaining of a certain writer, who had publiſhed a collection of his memoirs and remarkable ſayings, with an account of his laſt will and teſtament; alſo a letter from H. B. to the author, offering to ſupply him with a collection of witty ſayings, for poſthumous publication - - - 56

CONTENTS.

NUMBER

XCIII. Kit Cracker, a great dealer in the marvellous, describes himself and his adventures, in a letter to the Observer - - 66

XCIV. Walter Wormwood, an envious defamer, gives his own history, in a letter to the Observer. Remarks thereupon, and a few lines on the passion of envy - - - - 77

XCV. Letter from Simon Sapling, describing his own character, the incidents that befel him on the death of his father, his marriages, and the characters of both his wives. 89

XCVI. On the topic of procrastination. A letter from Tom Tortoise. The supposed form of a deed of conveyance, to be signed by To-day, for making over sundry engagements to its successor To-morrow - - - 100

XCVII. Letter from Benevolus, giving an account of a damper. Also one signed Pro bono publico, describing a club of dampers and puffers, with their invention of an instrument, called the thermometer of merit - - - 111

XCVIII. Letters from various correspondents, particularly from Gorgon, a self-conceited painter of the deformed and terrible - - 119

XCIX. Discovery of a curious Greek fragment, describing the paintings of Apelles, Parrhasius, and Timanthes, taken from certain dramas of Æschylus - - - - 129

C. Athenian vision - - - 137

CI. Athenian vision concluded - - 148

CII. Remarks

CONTENTS.

NUMBER

CII. Remarks upon the prefent tafte for acting private plays. A fhort poem, annexed, founded upon reflections refulting from that fubject 160

CIII. Anecdotes of Jack Gaylefs - - 178

CIV. Memoirs of a fentimentalift, exemplified in the adventures of Sappho and Mufidorus 191

CV. Conclufion of the above - - 205

CVI. Obfervations on the paffions, addreffed to the ladies - - - 215

CVII. The character of a flatterer pourtrayed in the adventures of Billy Simper - - 226

CVIII. The adventures of Billy Simper concluded, and the flatterer reformed - - 239

CIX. Sketches of various characters in a populous country town - - - 252

CX. Remarks upon anger. The character of Tom Tinder delineated and contrafted with that of Major Manlove - - 264

CXI. Upon the effects of jealoufy exemplified in the occurrences that happened in the family of Sir Paul Tefty - - - 276

CXII. The author's explanation of his motives in an addrefs to his readers upon the conclufion of this volume - - - 291

CXIII. The ftory of Adelifa and Leander. Conclufion of the work, with a fhort addrefs from the author to his readers - - 300.

THE

OBSERVER.

No. LXXXVII.

Jam te premit nox.　　　HORAT.

I AM fitting down to begin the tafk of
adding a new volume to thefe effays, when
the laft day of the year 1789 is within a
few hours of its conclufion, and I fhall bid
farewell to this eventful period with a grateful mind for its having paffed lightly over
my head without any extraordinary pertur-
bation or misfortune on my part fuffered,
gently leading me towards that deftined and
not far diftant hour, when I, like it, fhall be
no more.

I have accompanied it through all thofe
changes and fucceffions of feafons, which in
our climate are fo ftrongly difcriminated;

have

have fhared in the pleafures and productions of each, and if any little idle jars or bickerings may occafionally have ftarted up betwixt us, as will fometimes happen to the beft of friends, I willingly confign them to oblivion, and keep in mind only thofe kind and good offices, which will pleafe on reflection, and ferve to endear the memory of the deceafed.

All days in twelve months will not be days of funfhine; but I will fay this for *my friend in his laft moments*, that I cannot put my finger upon one in the fame century, that hath given birth to more interefting events, been a warmer advocate for the liberties and rights of mankind in general, or a kinder patron to this country in particular: I could name a day (if there was any need to point out what is fo ftrongly impreffed on our hearts) a day of gratulation and thankfgiving which will ever ftand forth amongft the whiteft in our calendar.

> *Hic dies verè mihi feftus atras*
> *Eximet curas: ego nec tumultum,*
> *Nec mori per vim metuam, tenente*
>   *Cæfare terras.* HORAT.

         " This

" This is indeed a feſtal day,
" A day that heals my cares and pains,
" Drives death and danger far away,
" And tells me—Cæſar lives and reigns."

Though *my friend in his laſt moments* hath
in this and other inſtances been ſo conſiderate
of our happineſs, I am afraid he is not likely
to leave our morals much better than he
found them : I cannot ſay that in the courſe
of my duty as an *Obſerver* any very ſtriking
inſtance of amendment hath come under
my notice; and though I have all the diſ-
poſition in life to ſpeak as favourably in my
friend's behalf as truth will let me, I am
bound to confeſs he was not apt to think
ſo ſeriouſly of his latter end as I could have
wiſhed; there was a levity in his conduĉt,
which he took no pains to conceal; he did
not ſeem to reflect upon the lapſe of time,
how ſpeedily his *ſpring, ſummer,* and *autumn*
would paſs away, and the *winter* of his days
come upon him; like *Wolſey* he was not
aware how ſoon the *froſt, the killing froſt
would nip his root :* he was however a
gay conviyial fellow, loved his bottle
and his friend, paſſed his time peaceably
amongſt us, and certainly merits the good

word of every loyal fubject in this kingdom.

As for his proceedings in other countries,
it is not here the reader muft look for an
account of them ; politics have no place in
thefe volumes ; but it cannot be denied
that he has made many widows and orphans
in Europe, been an active agent for the
court of death, and dipped his hands deep
in Chriftian and Mahometan blood.   By
the friends of freedom he will be celebrated
to the lateft time. He has begun a bufinefs,
which if followed up by his fucceffor with
equal zeal, lefs ferocity and more difcretion,
may lead to wonderful revolutions : there
are indeed fome inftances of cruelty, which
bear hard upon his character ; if feparately
viewed, they admit of no palliation; in a general light allowances may be made for that
phrenfy, which feizes the mind, when im-
pelled to great and arduous undertakings ;
when the wound is gangrened the incifion
muft be deep, and if that is to be done by
coarfe inftruments and unfkilful hands, who
can wonder if the gafh more refembles the
ftab of an affaffin than the operation of a
furgeon? An æra is now open, awful, interefting

terefting and fo involved in myftery, that
the acuteft fpeculation cannot penetrate to
the iffue of it : In fhort, *my friend in his laft
moments* hath put a vaft machine in motion,
and left a tafk to futurity, that will demand
the ftrongeft hands and ableft heads to compleat : in the mean time I fhall hope that
my countrymen, who have all ·thofe bleffings by inheritance, which lefs-favoured nations are now ftruggling to obtain by force,
will fo ufe their liberty, that the reft of the
world, who are not fo happy, may think it an
object worth contending for, and quote our
peace and our profperity as the beft proofs
exifting of its real value.

Whilft my thoughts have been thus employed in reflecting upon the laft day of an
ever-memorable year, I have compofed a few
elegiac lines to be thrown into the grave, which
time is now opening to receive his reliques.

" The year's gay verdure, all its charms are gone,
" And now comes old December chill and drear,
" Dragging a darkling length of evening on,
" Whilft all things droop, as Nature's death were near.

" Time flies amain with broad-expanded wings,
" Whence never yet a fingle feather fell,
" But holds his fpeed, and through the welkin rings
" Of all that breathe the inexorable knell.

" Oh!

" Oh! for a moment ſtop—a moment's ſpace
" For recollection mercy might concede,
" A little pauſe for man's unthinking race
" To ponder on that world, to which they ſpeed.

" But 'tis in vain; old Time diſdains to reſt,
" And moment after moment flits along,
" Each with a ſting to pierce the idler's breaſt,
" And vindicate its predeceſſor's wrong.

" Though the new-dawning year in its advance
" With hope's gay promiſe may entrap the mind,
" Let memory give one retroſpective glance
" Through the bright period, which it leaves behind.

" Æra of mercies! my wrapt boſom ſprings
" To meet the tranſport recollection gives:
" Heaven's angel comes with healing on his wings;
" He ſhakes his plumes, my country's father lives.

" The joyful tidings o'er the diſtant round
" Of Britain's empire the four winds proclaim,
" Her ſun-burnt iſlands ſwell the exulting ſound,
" And fartheſt Ganges echoes George's name.

" Period of bliſs! can any Britiſh muſe
" Bid thee farewell without a parting tear?
" Shall the hiſtorians's gratitude refuſe
" His brighteſt page to this recorded year?

" Thou Freedom's nurſing mother ſhall be ſtil'd,
" The glories of its birth are all thine own,
" Upon thy breaſts hung the Herculean child,
" And tyrants trembled at its baby frown.

                              " A ſanguine

" A sanguine mantle the dread infant wore,
" Before it roll'd a stream of human blood;
" Smiling it stood, and, pointing to the shore,
" Beckon'd the nations from across the flood.

" Then at that awful sight, as with a spell,
" The everlasting doors of death gave way,
" Prone to the dust Oppression's fortress fell,
" And rescu'd captives hail'd the light of day.

" Meanwhile Ambition chac'd its fairy prize
" With moonstruck madness down the Danube's stream,
" The Turkish crescent glittering in its eyes,
" And lost an empire to pursue a dream.

" The trampled serpent (Superstition) wreath'd
" Her fest'ring scales with anguish to and fro,
" Torpid she lay, then darting forward sheath'd
" Her deadly fangs in the unguarded foe.

" Oh Austria! why so prompt to venture forth,
" When fate now hurries thee to life's last goal?
" Thee too, thou crowned eagle of the north,
" Death's dart arrests, though tow'ring to the pole.

" Down then, Ambition; drop into the grave!
" And by thy follies be this maxim shewn—
" 'Tis not the monarch's glory to enslave
" His neighbour's empire, but to bless his own.

" Come then, sweet Peace! in Britain fix thy reign,
" Bid Plenty smile, and Commerce croud her coast;
" And may this ever blessed year remain
" Her king's, her people's, and her muse's boast.

No. LXXXVIII.

NICOLAS PEDROSA, a bufy little being, who followed the trades of fhaver, furgeon and man-midwife in the town of Madrid, mounted his mule at the door of his fhop in the Plazuela de los Affligidos, and pufhed through the gate of San Bernardino, being called to a patient in the neighbouring village of Foncarral, upon a preffing occafion. Every body knows that the ladies in Spain in certain cafes do not give long warning to practitioners of a certain defcription, and no body knew it better than Nicolas, who was refolved not to lofe an inch of his way, nor of his mule's beft fpeed by the way, if cudgelling could beat it out of her. · It was plain to Nicolas's conviction as plain could be, that his road laid ftrait forward to the little convent in front ; the mule was of opinion, that the turning on the left down the hill towards the Prado was the road of all roads moft familiar and agreeable to herfelf, and accordingly began to difpute the point of topography with Nicolas by fixing her fore feet refolutely in

the

the ground, dipping her head at the same time between them, and launching heels and crupper furiously into the air in the way of argument.   Little Pedrofa, who was armed at heel with one maffy filver fpur of ftout, though antient, workmanfhip, refolutely applied the rufty rowel to the fhoulder of his beaft, driving it with all the good will in the world to the very butt, and at the fame time adroitly tucking his blue cloth capa under his right arm, and flinging the fkirt over the left fhoulder *en cavalier*, began to lay about him with a ftout afhen fapling upon the ears, pole and cheeks of the recreánt mule.   The fire now flafhed from a pair of Andalufian eyes, as black as charcoal and not lefs inflammable, and taking the fegara from his mouth, with which he had vainly hoped to have regaled his noftrils in a fharp winter's evening by the way, raifed fuch a thundering troop of angels, faints and martyrs, from St. Michael downwards, not forgetting his own namefake Saint Nicolas de Tolentino by the way, that if curfes could have made the mule to go, the difpute would have been foon ended, but not a faint could make her ftir any other ways than

B 5   upwards

upwards and downwards at a ſtand.   A
ſmall troop of mendicant friars were at this
moment conducting the hoſt to a dying
man.—" Nicolas Pedroſa," ſays an old
friar, " be patient with your beaſt and ſpare
" your blaſphemies; remember Balaam."
—" Ah father," replied Pedroſa, " Balaam
" cudgelled his beaſt till ſhe ſpoke, ſo will I
" mine till ſhe roars." —" Fie, fie, prophane
" fellow," cries another of the fraternity.
" Go about your work, friend," quoth Nicolas, " and let me go about mine; I war-
" rant it is the more preſſing of the two;
" your patient is going out of the world,
" mine is coming into it."—" Hear him,"
cries a third, " hear the vile wretch, how
" he blaſphemes the body of God."—And
then the troop paſt ſlowly on to the tinkling of the bell.

. A man muſt know nothing of a mule's
ears who does not know what a paſſion they
have for the tinkling of a bell, and no
ſooner had the jingling cords vibrated in the
ſympathetic organs of Pedroſa's beaſt, than
boulting forward with a ſudden ſpring ſhe
ran roaring into the throng of friars, tramp-
ling on ſome and ſhouldering others at a
                                    moſt

moſt prophane rate; when Nicolas availing himſelf of the impetus, and perhaps not able to controul it, broke away and was out of ſight in a moment. "All the devils, "in hell blow fire into thy tail, thou beaſt "of Babylon," muttered Nicolas to himſelf as he ſcampered along, never once looking behind him or ſtopping to apologize for the miſchief he had done to the bare feet and ſhirtleſs ribs of the holy brotherhood.

Whether Nicolas ſaved his diſtance, as likewiſe, if he did, whether it was a male or female Caſtilian he uſhered into the world, we will not juſt now enquire, contented to wait his return in the firſt of the morning next day, when he had no ſooner diſmounted at his ſhop and delivered his mule to a ſturdy Arragoneſe wench, when Don Ignacio de Santos Aparicio, alguazil mayor of the ſupreme and general inquiſition, put an order into his hand, ſigned and ſealed by the inquiſidor general, for the conveying his body to the Caſa, whoſe formidable door preſents itſelf in the ſtreet adjoining to the ſquare in which Nicolas's brazen baſin hung forth the emblem of his trade.

The poor little fellow, trembling in every

B 6   joint,

joint, and with a face as yellow as faffron,
dropt a knee to the altar, which fronts the
entrance, and croffed himfelf moft devout-
ly; as foon as he had afcended the firft
flight of ftairs, a porter habited in black
opened the tremendous barricade, and Nicolas with horror heard the grating of the
heavy bolts that fhut him in.   He was led
through paffages and vaults and melancholy cells, till he was delivered into the
dungeon, where he was finally left to his folitary meditations.   Haplefs being! what
a fcene of horror.——Nicolas felt all the terrors of his condition, but being an Andalufian, and like his countrymen of a lively
imagination, he began to turn over all the
refources of his invention for fome happy
fetch, if any fuch might occur, for helping
him out of the difmal limbo he was in:
He was not long to feek for the caufe of his
misfortune: his adventure with the barefooted friars was a ready folution of all difficulties of that nature, had there been any;
there was however another thing, which
might have troubled a ftouter heart than
Nicolas's——He was a Jew.——This of a certain would have been a ftaggering item in a

poor

poor devil's confeffion, but then it was a fecret to all the world but Nicolas, and Nicolas's confcience did not juft then urge him to reveal it : He now began to overhaul the inventory of his perfonals about him, and with fome fatisfaction counted three little medals of the Bleffed Virgin, two Agnus Deis, a Saint Nicolas de Tolentino and a formidable ftring of beads all pendant from his neck and within his fhirt; in his pockets he had a paper of dried figs, a fmall bundle of fegaras, a cafe of lancets, fquirt and forceps, and two old razors in a leathern envelope; thefe he had delivered one by one to the alguazil, who firft arrefted him,—" and let him make the moft " of them," faid he to himfelf, " they can " never prove me an Ifraelite by a cafe of " razors."—Upon a clofer rummage however he difcovered in a fecret pocket a letter, which the alguazil had overlooked, and which his patient Donna Leonora de Cafafonda had given him in charge to deliver as directed—" Well, well," cried he, " let " it pafs; there can be no myftery in this " harmlefs fcrawl; a letter of advice to fome " friend or relation, I'll not break the feal;

" let

" let the fathers read it, if they like, 'twill
" prove the truth of my depofition, and help
" out my excufe for the hurry of my errand,
" and the unfortunate adventure of my
" damned refractory mule."—And now no
fooner had the recollection of the wayward
mule croffed the brain of poor Nicolas Pedrofa, than he began to blaft her at a furious-
rate.—" The fcratches and the fcab to boot
" confound thy fcurvy hide," quoth he,
" thou afs-begotten baftard, whom Noah.
" never let into his ark! The vengeance
" take thee for an uncreated barren beaft of
" promifcuous generation! What devil's
" crotchet got into thy capricious noddle,
" that thou fhouldft fall in love with that
" Nazaritifh bell, and run bellowing like
" Lucifer into the midft of thofe barefooted
" vermin, who are more malicious and'
" more greedy than the locufts of Egypt?
" Oh! that I had the art of Simon Magus
" to conjure thee into this dungeon in my
" ftead; but I warrant thou art chewing
" thy barley ftraw without any pity for thy
" wretched mafter, whom thy jade's tricks
" have delivered bodily to the tormentors,
" to be fport of thefe uncircumcifed fons of
                                        " Dagon."

"Dagon." And now the cell door opened, when a favage figure entered, carrying a huge parcel of clanking fetters, with a collar of iron, which he put round the neck of poor Pedrofa, telling him with a truly diabolic grin, whilft he was rivetting it on, that it was a proper cravat for the throat of a blaf-phemer.—" Jefu-Maria," quoth Pedrofa, " is all this fallen upon me for only cudgel-" ling a reftive mule?" "Aye," cried the demon, " and this is only a tafte of what " is to come," at the fame time flipping his pincers from the fcrew he was forcing to the head, he caught a piece of flefh in the forceps and wrenched it out of his cheek, laughing at poor Nicolas, whilft he roared aloud with the pain, telling him it was a juft reward for the torture he had put him to awhile ago, when he tugged at a tooth, till he broke it in his jaw. " Ah, for the love " of Heaven," cried Pedrofa, " have more " pity on me ; for the fake of Saint Nicolas " de Tolentino, my holy patron, be not fo " unmerciful to a poor barber-furgeon, and " I will fhave your worfhip's beard for no-" thing as long as I have life." One of the meffengers of the auditory now came in, and

and bade the fellow ftrike off the prifoner's
fetters, for that the holy fathers were in
council and demanded him for examination.
" This is fomething extraordinary," quoth
the tormentor, " I fhould not have expected
" it this twelvemonth to come." Pedrofa's
fetters were ftruck off; fome brandy was applied to ftaunch the bleeding of his cheeks;
his hands and face were wafhed, and a fhort
jacket of coarfe ticking thrown over him,
and the meffenger with an affiftant taking
him each under an arm led him into a fpacious chamber, where at the head of a long
table fate his excellency the inquifidor general with fix of his affeffors, three on each
fide the chair of ftate: the alguazil mayor,
a fecretary and two notaries with other
officers of the holy council were attending
in their places.

The prifoner was placed behind a bar at
the foot of the table between the meffengers
who brought him in, and having made his
obeifance to the awful prefence in the moft
fupplicating manner, he was called upon according to the ufual form of queftions by one
of the junior judges to declare his name,
parentage, profeffion, age, place of abode,
and

and to anfwer various interrogatories of the
like trifling nature: His excellency the inquifidor general now opened his reverend
lips, and in a folemn tone of voice, that penetrated to the heart of the poor trembling
prifoner, interrogated him as follows—

" Nicolas Pedrofa, we have liftened to
" the account you give of yourfelf, your bu-
" finefs and connections, now tell us for
" what offence, or offences, you are here
" ftanding a prifoner before us : Examine
" your own heart, and fpeak the truth from
" your confcience without prevarication or
" difguife." " May it pleafe your excel-
" lency," replied Pedrofa, " with all due
" fubmiffion to your holinefs and this re-
" verend affembly, my moft equitable
" judges, I conceive I ftand here before you
" for no worfe a crime, than that of cudgel-
" ling a refractory mule; an animal fo ref-
" tive in its nature, (under correction of
" your holinefs be it fpoken) that although
" I were bleft with the forbearance of holy
" Job, (for like him too I am married and
" my patience hath been exercifed by a wife)
" yet could I not forbear to fmite my beaft
" for her obftinacy, and the rather becaufe I

" was

" was fummoned in the way of my profef-
" fion, as I have already made known to
" your moft merciful ears, upon a certain
" crying occafion, which would not admit
" of a moment's delay."

" Recollect 'yourfelf, Nicolas," faid his
Excellency the inquifidor general, " was
" there nothing elfe you did, fave fmiting
" your beaft."

" I take faint Nicolas de Tolentino to
" witnefs," replied he, " that I know of no
" other crime, for which I can be refponfible
" at this righteous tribunal, fave fmiting
" my unruly beaft."

" Take notice, brethren," exclaimed the
inquifidor, " this unholy wretch holds tramp-
" ling over friars to be no crime."

" Pardon me, holy father," replied Nico-
" las, I hold it for the worft of crimes, and
" therefore willingly furrender my refractory
" mule to be dealt with as you fee fit, and if
" you impale her alive it will not be more
" than fhe deferves."

" Your wits are too nimble, Nicolas,"
cried the judge ; " have a care they do not
" run away with your difcretion : Recollect
" the

" the blasphemies you uttered in the hearing
" of those pious people."

"I humbly pray your excellency," answered the prisoner, " to recollect that
" anger is a short madness, and I hope al-
" lowances will be made by your holy coun-
" cil for words spoke in haste to a rebellious
" mule: The prophet Balaam was thrown
" off his guard with a simple afs, and what
" is an afs compared to a mule: If your
" excellency had seen the lovely creature
" that was screaming in an agony till I came
" to her relief, and how fine a boy I ushered
" into the world, which would have been
" loft but for my affistance, I am sure I
" should not be condemned for a few hasty
" words spoke in passion."

" Sirrah!" cried one of the puisny judges,
" respect the decency of the court."

" Produce the contents of this fellow's
" pockets before the court," said the presi-
dent, " lay them on the table."

" Monster," resumed the aforesaid puisny
judge, taking up the forceps, " what is the
" use of this diabolical machine?"

" Please your reverence," replied Pedrosa,
" *aptum eft ad extrahendos fœtus.*"—" Unna-
" tural

" tural wretch," again exclaimed the judge,
" you have murdered the mother."

" The mother of God forbid," exclaimed
Pedrofa, " I believe I have a proof in my
" pocket, that will acquit me of that
" charge;" and fo faying, he tendered the
letter we have before made mention of:
The fecretary took it, and by command of
the court read as follows :

Senor Don Manuel de Herrera,

*When this letter, which I fend by Nicolas
Pedrofa, fhall reach your hands, you fhall know
that I am fafely delivered of a lovely boy after
a dangerous labour, in confideration of which I
pray you to pay to the faid Nicolas Pedrofa the
fum of twenty gold piftoles, which fum his excellency*——

" Hold," cried the inquifidor general,
ftarting haftily from his feat, and fnatching
away the letter, " there is more in this than
" meets the eye: Break up the court; I
" muft take an examination of this prifoner
" in private."

No. LXXXIX.

As foon as the room was cleared, the inquifidor general beckoning to the prifoner
to follow him, retired into a private clofet,
where throwing himfelf carelefsly in an arm
chair, he turned a gracious countenance
upon the poor affrighted accoucheur, and
bidding him fit down upon a low ftool by
his fide, thus accofted him :—"Take heart,
"fenor Pedrofa, your imprifonment is not
"likely to be very tedious, for I have a
"commiffion you muft execute without
"lofs of time : you have too much confi-
"deration for yourfelf to betray a truft, the
"violation of which muft involve you in in-
"evitable ruin, and can in no degree attaint
"my character, which is far enough beyond
"the reach of malice : Be attentive therefore
"to my orders; execute them punctually,
"and keep my fecret as you tender your
"own life : Doft thou know the name and
"condition of the lady, whom thou haft de-
"livered ?" Nicolas affured him he did not,
and his excellency proceeded as follows—
"Then I tell thee, Nicolas, it is the illuf-
                                    "trious

" trious Donna Leonora de Cafafonda : her
" hufband is the prefident of Quito, and
" daily expected with the next arrivals from
" the South Seas; now, though meafures
" have been taken for detaining him at the
" port, wherever he fhall land, till he fhall
" receive further orders, yet you muft be
" fenfible Donna Leonora's fituation is
" fomewhat delicate : It will be your bu-
" finefs to take the fpeedieft meafures for hei
" recovery, but as it feems fhe has had a
" dangerous and painful labour, this may be
" a work of more time than could be wifhed,
" unlefs fome medicines more efficacious
" than common are adminiftered : Art thou
" acquainted with any fuch, friend Nicolas ?"
—" So pleafe your excellency," quoth Nicolas, " my proceffes have been tolerably fuc-
" cefsful; I have bandages and cataplafms
" with oils and conferves, that I have no
" caufe to complain of: they will reftore
" nature to its proper ftate in all decent
" time."—" Thou talkeft like a fool, friend
" Nicolas," interrupting him, faid the inquifidor ; " What telleft thou me of thy fwath-
" ings and fwadlings? quick work muft
" be wrought by quick medicines: Haft
                                " thou

" thou none such in thy botica ? I'll answer
" for it thou hast not ; therefore look you,
" sirrah, here is a little vial compounded by
" a famous chymist; see that you mix it in
" the next apozem you administer to Donna
" Leonora ; it is the most capital sedative in
" nature; give her the whole of it, and let her
" husband return when he will, depend upon
" it he will make no discoveries from her."
—" Humph !" quoth Nicolas within himself, " Well said, inquisidor !" He took the
vial with all possible respect, and was not
wanting in professions of the most inviolable
fidelity and secrecy—" No more words,
" friend Nicolas," quoth the inquisidor,
" upon that score; I do not believe thee
" one jot the more for all thy promises; my
" dependance is upon thy fears and not thy
" faith; I fancy thou hast seen enough of
" this place not to be willing to return to it
" once for all."—Having so said, he rang a
bell, and ordered Nicolas to be forthwith liberated, bidding the messenger return his
clothes instantly to him with all that be-
longed to him, and having slipped a purse
into his hand well filled with doubloons, he
bade him begone about his business, and not

fee his face again till he had executed his
commands.

Nicolas boulted out of the porch without
taking leave of the altar, and never checked
his fpeed till he found himfelf fairly houfed
under fhelter of his own beloved brafs bafin.
—" Aha !" quoth Nicolas, " my lord in-
" quifidor, I fee the king is not likely to
" gain a fubject more by your intrigues :
" A pretty job you have fet me about; and
" fo, when I have put the poor lady to reft
" with your damned fedative, my tongue
" muft be ftopt next to prevent its blabbing :
" But I'll fhow you I was not born in An-
" dalufia for nothing." Nicolas now opened
a fecret drawer and took out a few pieces
of money, which in fact was his whole ftock
of cafh in the world ; he loaded and primed
his piftols, and carefully lodged them in the
houfers of his faddle, he buckled to his fide
his trufty fpada, and haftened to caparifon
his mule.　" Ah, thou imp of the old one,"
quoth he as he entered the ftable, " art not
" afhamed to look me in the face ? But
" come, huffey, thou oweft me a good turn
" methinks, ftand by me this once, and be
" friends for ever ! thou art in good cafe,
　　　　　　　　　　　" and

" and if thou wilt put thy beſt foot fore-
" moſt, like a faithful beaſt, thou ſhalt not
" want for barley by the way." The bargain
was ſoon ſtruck between Nicolas and his
mule, he mounted her in the happy moment, and pointing his courſe towards the
bridge of Toledo, which proudly ſtrides with
half a dozen lofty arches over a ſtream
ſcarce three feet wide, he found himſelf as
completely in a deſart in half a mile's riding,
as if he had been dropt in the center of Ara-
bia petræa.   As Nicolas's journey was not
a tour of curioſity, he did not amuſe himſelf with a peep at Toledo, or Talavera, or
even Merida by the way ; for the ſame reaſon he took a *circumbendibus* round the
frontier town of Badajoz, and croſſing a little brook refreſhed his mule with the laſt
draught of Spaniſh water, and inſtantly con-
gratulated himſelf upon entering the terri-
tory of Portugal. " Brava !" quoth he, pat-
ting the neck of his mule, " thou ſhalt have
" a ſupper this night of the beſt ſieve-meat
" that Eſtramadura can furniſh : We are
" now in a country where the ſcattered
" flock of Iſrael fold thick and fare well,"

He now began to chaunt the fong of Solomon, and gently ambled on in the joy of his heart.

When Nicolas at length reached the city of Lifbon, he hugged himfelf in his good fortune; ftill he recollected that the inquifition has long arms, and he was yet in a place of no perfect fecurity. Our adventurer had in early life acted as affiftant furgeon in a Spanifh frigate bound to Buenos Ayres, and being captured by a Britifh man of war, and carried into Jamaica, had very quietly paffed fome years in that place as journeyman apothecary, in which time he had acquired a tolerable acquaintance with the Englifh language: No fooner then did he difcover the Britifh enfign flying on the poop of an Englifh frigate then lying in the Tagus, than he eagerly caught the opportunity of paying a vifit to the furgeon, and finding he was in want of a mate, offered himfelf, and was entered in that capacity for a cruize againft the French and Spaniards, with whom Great Britain was then at war. In this fecure afylum Nicolas enjoyed the firft happy moments he had experienced for a long time paft,

paft, and being a lively good-humoured little fellow, and one that touched the guitar
and fung fequidillas with a tolerable grace,
he foon recommended himfelf to his fhip-
mates, and grew in favour with every body
on board from the captain to the cook's
mate.

When they were out upon their cruife
hovering on the Spanifh coaft, it occurred
to Nicolas that the inquifidor general at Madrid had told him of the expected arrival of
the prefident of Quito, and having imparted
this to one of the lieutenants, he reported it
to the captain, and as the intelligence feemed
of importance, he availed himfelf of it by
hawling into the track of the homeward-
bound galleons, and great was the joy, when
at the break of the morning the man at the
maft-head announced a fquare rigged veffel
in view : The ardor of a chace now fet all
hands at work, and a few hours brought
them near enough to difcern that fhe was a
Spanifh frigate, and feemingly from a long
voyage : Little Pedrofa, as alert as the reft,
ftript himfelf for his work, and repaired to
his poft in the cock-pit, whilft the thunder
of the guns rolled inceffantly overhead ; three

cheers

cheers from the whole crew at length announced the moment of victory, and a few
more minutes afcertained the good news
that the prize was a frigate richly laden from
the South Seas, with the governor of Quito
and his fuite on board.

Pedrofa was now called upon deck, and
fent on board the prize as interpreter to the
firft lieutenant, who was to take poffeffion
of her.   He found every thing in confufion,
a deck covered with the flain, and the whole
crew in confternation at an event they were
in no degree prepared for, not having received any intimation of a war.   He found
the officers in general, and the paffengers without exception, under the moft
horrid impreffions of the Englifh, and ex-
pecting to be plundered, and perhaps but-
chered without mercy.   Don Manuel de
Cafafonda the governor, whofe countenance
befpoke a conftitution far gone in a decline,
had thrown himfelf on a fopha in the laft
ftate of defpair, and given way to an effufion
of tears; when the lieutenant entered the
cabin he rofe trembling from his couch, and
with the moft fupplicating action prefented
to him his fword, and with it a cafket
which

which he carried in his other hand; as he
tendered thefe fpoils to his conqueror, whether through weaknefs or of his own will, he
made a motion of bending his knee : the generous Briton, fhocked at the unmanly overture, caught him fuddenly with both hands,
and turning to Pedrofa, faid aloud—" Con-
" vince this gentleman he is fallen into the
" hands of an honourable enemy."—" Is it
" poffible !" cried Don Manuel, and lifting
up his ftreaming eyes to the countenance
of the Britifh officer, faw humanity, valour,
and generous pity fo ftrongly charactered in
his youthful features, that the conviction
was irrefiftible.   " Will he not accept my
" fword ?" cried the Spaniard. " He defires
" you to wear it, till he has the honour of
" prefenting you to his captain."—"Ah then
" he has a captain," exclaimed Don Manuel, " his fuperior will be of another way of
" thinking; tell him this cafket contains my
" jewels; they are valuable; let him pre-
" fent them as a lawful prize, which will
" enrich the captor; his fuperior will not
" hefitate to take them from me."—" If
" they are your excellency's private pro-
" perty," replied Pedrofa, " I am ordered

C 3   " to

" to affure you, that if your fhip was load-
" ed with jewels, no Britifh officer, in the
" fervice of his king, will take them at your
" hands; the fhip and effects of his Catho-
" lic Majefty are the only prize of the cap-
" tors; the perfonals of the paffengers are
" inviolate."—" Generous nation !" exclaimed Don Manuel, " how greatly have
" I wronged thee !"—The boats of the Britifh frigate now came alongfide, and part of
the crew were fhifted out of the prize, taking
their clothes and trunks along with them,
in which they were very cordially affifted by
their conquerors. The barge foon after
came aboard with an officer in the ftern-
fheets, and the crew in their white fhirts
and velvet caps, to efcort the governor and
the fhip's captain on board the frigate, which
lay with her fails to the maft awaiting their
arrival; the accommodation ladder was
flung over the fide, and manned for the prifoners, who were received on the gang-way
by the fecond lieutenant, whilft perfect
filence and the ftricteft difcipline reigned in
the fhip, where all were under the decks, and
no inquifitive curious eyes were fuffered to
wound the feelings of the conquered even
                                        with

with a glance; in the door of his cabin ftood
the captain, who received them with that modeft complaifance, which does not revolt the
unfortunate by an overftrained poli﹡nefs; he
was a man of high birth and elegant manners, with a heart as benevolent as it was
brave: Such an addrefs, fet off with a perfon
finely formed and perfectly engaging, could
not fail to imprefs the prifoners with the
moft favourable ideas; and as Don Manuel
fpoke French fluently, he could converfe
with the Britifh captain without the help of
an interpreter: As he expreffed an impatient defire of being admitted to his parole,
that he might revifit friends and connections,
from which he had been long feparated, he
was overjoyed to hear that the Englifh fhip
would carry her prize into Lifbon; and that
he would be there fet on fhore, and permitted to make the beft of his way from thence
to Madrid; he talked of his wife with all
the ardor of the moft impaffioned lover, and
apologized for his tears, by imputing them
to the agony of his mind, and the infirmity
of his health, under the dread of being longer
feparated from an object fo dear to his heart,
and on whom he doated with the fondeft

　affection.

affection. The generous captor indulged him in thefe converfations, and, being a hufband himfelf, knew how to allow for all the tendernefs of his fenfations. " Ah, fir," cried Don Manuel, " would to Heaven it " were in my power to have the honour of " prefenting my beloved Leonora to you " on our landing at Lifbon—Perhaps," added he, turning to Pedrofa, who at that moment entered the cabin, " this gentle- " man, whom I take to be a Spaniard, may " have heard the name of Donna Leonora de " Cafafonda; if he has been at Madrid, it " is poffible he may have feen her; fhould " that be the cafe, he can teftify to her " external charms; I alone can witnefs to " the exquifite perfection of her mind." —" Senor Don Manuel," replied Pedrofa, " I have feen Donna Leonora, and your " excellency is warranted in all you can fay " in her praife; fhe is of incomparable " beauty." Thefe words threw the uxorious Spaniard into raptures; his eyes fparkled with delight; the blood rufhed into his emaciated cheeks, and every feature glowed with unutterable joy : He preffed Pedrofa with a variety of rapid enquiries,

ries, all which he evaded by pleading ignorance, faying, that he had only had a cafual
glance of her, as fhe paffed along the Pár-
do.   The embarraffment however which
accompanied thefe anfwers, did not efcape
the Englifh captain, who fhortly after
drawing Pedrofa afide into the furgeon's cabin, was by him made acquainted with the
melancholy fituation of that unfortunate
lady, and every particular of the ftory as
before related; nay the very vial was produced with it's contents, as put into the
hands of Pedrofa by the inquifidor.

No. XC.

" CAN there be fuch villainy in man?"
    cried the Britifh captain, when Pe-
drofa had concluded his detail: " Alas! my
" heart bleeds for this unhappy hufband:
" affuredly that monfter has deftroyed Leo-
" nora: as for thee, Pedrofa, whilft the
" Britifh flag flies over thy head, neither
" Spain, nor Portugal, nor Inquifitors, nor
" Devils fhall annoy thee under it's protec-
" tion;

" tion; but if thou ever venturest over the
" side of this ship, and rashly settest one foot
" upon Catholic soil, when we arrive at
" Lisbon, thou art a lost man."—" I were
" worse than a madman," replied Nicolas,
" should I attempt it."—" Keep close in
" this asylum then," resumed the captain,
" and fear nothing: Had it been our fate
" to have been captured by the Spaniard,
" what would have become of thee?"—
" In the worst of extremities," replied
Nicolas, " I should have applied to the in-
" quisidor's vial; but I confess I had no fears
" of that sort; a ship so commanded and
" so manned is in little danger of being car-
" ried into a Spanish port."—" I hope
" not," said the captain, " and I promise
" thee thou shalt take thy chance in her, so
" long as she is afloat under my command,
" and if we live to conduct her to England,
" thou shalt have thy proper share of prize
" money, which, if the galleon breaks up
" according to her entries, will be some-
" thing towards enabling thee to shift, and
" if thou art as diligent in thy duty, as I
" am persuaded thou wilt be, whilst I live
" thou shalt never want a seaman's friend."

—At

*

—At thefe chearing words, little Nicolas threw himfelf at the feet of his generous preferver, and with ftreaming eyes poured out his thanks from a heart animated with joy and gratitude.—The captain raifing him by the hand, forbade him, as he prized his friendfhip, ever to addrefs him in that pofture any more: " Thank me, if you will," added he, " but thank me as one man " fhould another; let no knees bend in this " fhip but to the name of God.—But now," continued he, " let us turn our thoughts to " the fituation of our unhappy Cafafonda ; " we are now drawing near to Lifbon, where " he will look to be liberated on his parole." " By no means let him venture into Spain," faid Pedrofa ; " I am well affured, there are " orders to arreft him in every port or fron- " tier town, where he may prefent him- " felf."—" I can well believe it," replied the captain ; " his piteous cafe will require " further deliberation ; in the mean time let " nothing tranfpire on your part, and keep " yourfelf out of his fight as carefully as " you can."—This faid, the captain left the cabin, and both parties repaired to their feveral occupations.

As

As foon as the frigate and her prize caft anchor in the Tagus, Don Manuel de Cafafonda impatiently reminded our captain of his promifed parole.   The painful moment was now come, when an explanation of fome fort became unavoidable: The generous Englifhman, with a countenance ..expreffive of the tendereft pity, took the Spaniard's hand in his, and feating him on a couch befide him, ordered the centinel to keep the cabin private, and delivered himfelf as follows—

" Senor Don Manuel, I muft now im-
" part to you an anxiety which I labour un-
" der on your account; I have ftrong rea-
" fon to fufpect you have enemies in your
" own country, who are upon the watch to
" arreft you on your landing : when I have
" told you this, I expect you will repofe
" fuch truft in my honour, and the fincerity
" of my regard for you, as not to demand
" a further explanation of the particulars,
" on which my intelligence is founded."—
" Heaven and Earth!" cried the aftonifhed Spaniard, " who can be thofe enemies I have
" to fear, and what can I have done to de-
" ferve them ?"— " So far I will open my-
" felf to you," anfwered the captain, " as to
" point

"" point out the principal to you, the inqui-
" fidor general."—" The beft friend I have
" in Spain," exclaimed the governor, " my
" fworn protector, the patron of my fortune.
" He my enemy! impoffible."—" Well,
" Sir," replied the captain, " if my advice
" does not meet belief, I muft fo far exert
" my authority for your fake, as to make this
" fhip your prifon till I have waited on our
" minifter at Lifbon, and made the enquiries
" neceffary for your fafety ; fufpend your
" judgment upon the feeming harfhnefs of
" this meafure till I return to you again ;"
and at the fame time rifing from his feat, he
gave orders for the barge, and leaving ftrict
injunctions with the firft lieutenant not to
allow of the governor's quitting the frigate,
he put off for the fhore, and left the melancholy Spaniard buried in profound and
filent meditation.

The emiffaries of the Inqufition having at
laft traced Pedrofa to Lifbon, and there gained
intelligence of his having entered on board the
frigate, our captain had no fooner turned into
the porch of the hotel at Buenos-Ayres, than
he was accofted by a meffenger of ftate, with
a requifition from the prime minifter's office
for

for the surrender of one Nicolas Pedrofa, a
fubject of Spain and a criminal, who had
efcaped out of the prifon of the Inquifition
in Madrid, where he. ftood charged with
high crimes and mifdemeanors.—As foon as
this requifition was explained to our worthy
captain, without condefcending to a word in
reply, he called for pen and ink, and writing
a fhort order to the officer commanding on
board, inftantly difpatched the midfhipman,
who attended him, to the barge, with direc-
tions to make the beft of his way back to the
frigate, and deliver it to the lieutenant: Then
turning to the meffenger, he faid to him in a
refolute tone—" That Spaniard is now borne
" on my. books, and before you fhall take him
." out of the fervice of my King, you muft
" fink his. fhip."—Not waiting for a reply,
he immediately proceeded without ftop to
the houfe of the Britifh Minifter at the far-
ther end of the city: Here he found Pedrofa's intelligence, with regard to the Governor of Quito, exprefsly verified, for the order
had come down even to Lifbon, upon the
chance of the Spanifh frigate's taking fhelter
in that port: To this Minifter he related the
horrid tale, which Pedrofa had delivered to
                                        him,

him, and with his concurrence it was determined to forward letters into Spain, which
Don Manuel ſhould be adviſed to write to
his lady and friends at Madrid, and to wait
their anſwer before any further diſcoveries
were imparted to him reſpecting the blacker
circumſtances of the caſe: In the mean
time it was reſolved to keep the priſoner ſafe
in his aſylum.

The generous Captain loſt no time in returning to his frigate, where he immediately
imparted to Don Manuel the intelligence he
had obtained at the Britiſh Miniſter's—
" This, indeed," cried the afflicted Spaniard, " is a ſtroke I was in no reſpect pre-
" pared for; I had fondly perſuaded myſelf
" there was not in the whole empire of Spain,
" a more friendly heart than that of the In-
" quiſidor's; to my beloved Leonora he had
" ever ſhewn the tenderneſs of a paternal
" affection from her very childhood; by him
" our hands were joined; his lips pronounc-
" ed the nuptial benediction, and through
" his favour I was promoted to my govern-
" ment: Grant, Heaven, no misfortune
" hath befallen my Leonora! ſurely ſhe
" cannot have offended him, and forfeited
" his

" his favour."—As I know him not; replied the Captain, " I can form no judg-
" ment of his motives; but this I know,
" that if a man's heart is capable of cruelty,
" the fitteſt ſchool to learn it in, muſt be
" the Inquiſition." The propoſal was now
ſuggeſted of fending letters into Spain, and
the Governor retired to his deſk for the purpoſe of writing them; in the afternoon of
the ſame day the Miniſter paid a viſit to the
Captain, and receiving a packet from the
hands of Don Manuel, promiſed to get it
forwarded by a ſafe conveyance according to
direction.

In due courſe of time this fatal letter from
Leonora, opened all the horrible tranſaction
to the wretched huſband:—

*The guilty hand of an expiring wife, under
the agonizing operation of a mortal poiſon,
traces theſe few trembling lines to an injured
wretched huſband. If thou haſt any pity for my
parting ſpirit fly the ruin that awaits thee, and
avoid this ſcene of villainy and horror. When
I tell thee I have borne a child to the monſter,
whoſe poiſon runs in my veins, thou wilt abhor
thy faithleſs Leonora; had I ſtrength to relate*

*to thee the subtle machinations, which betrayed
me to disgrace, thou wouldst pity and perhaps
forgive me. Oh agony ! can I write his name?
The Inquisidor is my murderer—My pen falls
from my hand—Farewell for ever.*

Had a shot passed through the heart of
Don Manuel, it could not more effectually
have stopt it's motions, than the perusal of
this fatal writing: He dropped lifeless on the
couch, and but for the care and assistance of
the Captain and Pedrosa, in that posture he
had probably expired. Grief like his will
not be described by words, for to words it
gave no utterance; 'twas suffocating, silent
woe.

Let us drop the curtain over this melancholy pause in our narration, and attend
upon the mournful widower now landing
upon English ground, and conveyed by his
humane and generous preserver to the house
of a noble Earl, the father of our amiable
Captain, and a man by his virtues still more
conspicuous than by his rank. Here amidst
the gentle solicitudes of a benevolent family,
in one of the most enchanting spots on earth,
in a climate most salubrious and restorative.

to a conftitution exhaufted by heat, and a
heart near broken with forrow, the reviving
fpirits of the unfortunate Don Manuel gave
the firft fymptoms of a poffible recovery.
At the period of a few tranquillizing weeks
here paffed in the bofom of humanity, letters came to hand from the Britifh Minifter
at Lifbon, in anfwer to a memorial, that I
fhould have ftated to have been drawn up
by the friendly Captain before his departure
from that port, with a detail of facts de-
pofed and fworn to by Nicolas Pedrofa,
which memorial, with the documents attached to it, was forwarded to the Spanifh Court
by fpecial exprefs from the Portuguefe pre-
mier. By thefe letters it appeared, that the
high dignity of the perfon impeached by
this ftatement of facts, had not been fufficient to fcreen him from a very ferious and
complete inveftigation; in the courfe of
which facts had been fo clearly brought
home to him by the confeffion of his feveral
agents, and the teftimony of the deceafed
Leonora's attendants, together with her own
written declarations, whilft the poifon was
in operation, that though no public fentence
had been executed upon the criminal, it was
generally

generally understood he was either no longer in existence, or in a situation never to be heard of any more, till roused by the awakening trump he shall be summoned to his tremendous last account.   As for the unhappy widower, it was fully signified to him from authority, that his return to Spain, whether upon exchange or parole, would be no longer opposed, nor had he any thing to apprehend on the part of government, when he should there arrive.   The same was signified in fewer words to the exculpated Pedrosa.

Whether Don Manuel de Casafonda will in time to come avail himself of these overtures time alone can prove : As for little Nicolas, whose prize money has set him up in a comfortable little shop in Duke's Place, where he breathes the veins and cleanses the bowels of his Israelitish brethren, in a land of freedom and toleration, his merry heart is at rest, save only when with fire in his eyes, and vengeance on his tongue, he anathematizes the Inquisition, and struts into the synagogue every sabbath with as bold a step and as erect a look, as if he was himself High Priest of the Temple, going to perform sacrifice upon the re-assembling of the scattered tribes.

No. XCI.

A GOOD man will live with the world as a wife man lives with his wife; he will not let himfelf down to be a dupe to it's humours, a devotee to it's pleafures, or a flatterer of it's faults; he will make himfelf as happy as he can in the connection for his own fake, reform where he is able, and complain only when he cannot help it. I am fick of that converfation which fpends itfelf in railing at the times we live in; I am apt to think they are not made better by thofe complaints, and I have oftentimes occafion to know they are made worfe by thofe very people who are loudeft to complain of them. If this be really one of the habits of age, it is high time for every man, who grows old, to guard againft it; for there is no occafion to invite more peevifh companions for the laft hours of life, than time and decrepitude will bring in their train: Let us look back upon things paft with what content we can, falute time prefent with the beft grace we are able, and refign ourfelves to futurity

futurity with calmness and a patient mind
If we do not wish to be banished from fociety before death withdraws us from it,
don't let us truft to the world's refpect
only, let us ftrive alfo to conciliate it's love.

But I do not wifh to argue this point with
the feét of *the Murmurers* merely upon the
ground of good policy; I fhould be forry
for the world, if I could give no better reafon for keeping well with it than in felf-defence : I really think it a world very eafy to
live with upon paffable good terms ; I am
free to confefs it has mended me fince I have
lived with it, and I am fully of opinion it has
mended itfelf: I don't deny but it has it's
failings ; it ftill cuts out work for the moralifts, and I am in no fear of finding fubject
matter for three more volumes of effays, before I have exhaufted the duty of an *Obferver*. However, though I have prefumed
upon taking up this charaéter late in life,
yet I feel no provocation from what I *obferve*
in others, or in myfelf, to turn *Murmurer* ;
I can call the time paft under my review,
as far back as my experience will go, and
comfort myfelf by the comparifon of it with
the time prefent ; I can turn to the authors,
who

who have delineated the manners of ages
antecedent to my own, without being
afhamed of my contemporaries, or enter-
taining a fuperior refpect for their's.   I cannot look back to any period of our own
annals, of which I can confcientioufly pronounce, according to fuch judgment as I am
poffeffed of, that the happinefs of fociety
was better fecured, and more completely
provided for, than at the prefent moment.

This may appear fo hardy an affertion,
that if the *Murmurers* take the field againft
me, I fufpect that I fhall find myfelf, as I
frequently have done, in a very decided
minority ; for let the reader take notice, I
know the world too well to think of getting
popularity by defending it ; if ever I make
that my object, I muft run counter to my
own principles, and abufe many, that all may
read me : In the mean time I fhall make a
fhew of fome of my defences, if it be only
to convince the *Murmurers*, that I fhall not
capitulate upon the firft fummons ; and I will
keep fome ftrong pofts mafked from their
view, that if they repeat their affault, I may
ftill have refources in my reach.

Society is cemented by laws, upheld by
religion,

religion, endeared by manners, and adorned by arts.

Let us now enquire what is the prefent ftate of thefe great fundamentals of focial happinefs, and whether any better period can be pointed out, compared to which their prefent ftate may be juftly pronounced a ftate of declenfion.

The conftitution of England has undergone many changes: The monarch, the nobles, and the people, have each in their turn for a time deftroyed that proper balance, in which its excellence confifts. In feudal times the ariftocratic power preponderated, and the kingdom was torn to pieces with civil diftractions. From the acceffion of Henry the Seventh to the breaking out of the great rebellion, the power of the fovereign was all but abfolute; the rapacity of that monarch, the brutality of his fucceffor, the perfecuting fpirit of Mary, and the imperious prerogative of Elizabeth, left fcarce a fhadow of freedom in the people; and, in fpite of all the boafted glories of Elizabeth's golden days, I muft doubt if any nation can be happy, whofe lives and properties were no better fecured than thofe

of

of her fubjects actually were : In all this
period, the moft tranquil moments are to be
found in the peaceful reign of James the
Firft ; yet even then the king's *jus divinum*
was at it's height, and totally overturned
the fcale and equipoife of the conftitution.
What followed in Charles's day I need not
dwell upon; a revolution enfued; monarchy
was fhaken to it's foundations, and in the
general fermentation and concuffion of affairs, the very dregs of the people were thrown
up into power, and all was anarchy, flaughter
and oppreffion. From the Reftoration to the
Revolution we contemplate a period full of
trouble, and, for the moft part, ftained with
the deepeft difgrace ; a penfioned monarch,
an abandoned court, and a licentious people : The abdication, or, more properly, the
expulfion of a royal bigot, fet the conftitution upon it's bottom, but it left the minds
of men in a ferment that could not fpeedily
fubfide; antient loyalty and high monarchical
principles were not to be filenced at once by
the peremptory fiat of an act of parliament ;
men ftill harboured them in their hearts,
and popery, three times expelled, was ftill
upon the watch, and fecretly whetting her
weapons

weapons for a fourth attempt. Was this a period of social happiness ?—The succession of the house of Hanover still left a pretender to the throne ; and though the character of the new sovereign had every requisite of temper and judgment for conciliating his government, yet the old leaven was not exhausted, fresh revolutions were attempted, and the nation felt a painful repetition of it's former sorrows.

So far therefore as the happiness of society depends upon the secure establishment of the constitution, the just administration of the laws, the strict and correct ascertainment of the subjects rights, and those sacred and inviolable privileges as to person and property, which every man amongst us can now define, and no man living dares to dispute, so far we must acknowledge that the times we live in, are happier times than ever fell to the lot of our ancestors, and if we complain of them, it must be on account of something which has not yet come under our review; we will therefore proceed to the next point, and take the present state of religion into our consideration.

Religious feuds are so terrible in their con-

fequences, and the peace of this kingdom
has been fo often deftroyed by the furiouf-
nefs of. zealots and enthufiafts, ftruggling
for church-eftablifhment, and perfecuting in
their turns the fallen party without mercy,
that the tranquillity we now enjoy, (greater,
as I believe, than in any time paft, but certainly as great) is of itfelf fufficient to put
the modern *murmurer* to filence.   To fub-
ftantiate my affertion, let me refer to the
rifing fpirit of toleration ; wherever that
bleffed fpirit prevails, it prevails for the honour of man's nature, for the enlargement of
his heart, and for the augmentation of his
focial happinefs.   Whilft we were contending for our own rights, felf-defence compelled us to keep off the encroachments of others,
that were hoftile to thofe rights ; but thefe
being firmly eftablifhed, we are no longer
warranted to hang the fword of the law over
the head of religion, and opprefs our feced-
ing fellow-fubjects.   Is there any juft reafon to complain of our eftablifhed clergy in
their collective character? If they do not
ftun us with controverfies, it is becaufe they
underftand the fpirit of their religion better
than to engage in them : The publications

H   of

of the pulpit are ftill numerous, and if they have dropt their high inflammatory tone, it is to the honour of Chriftianity that they have fo done, and taken up a milder, meeker language in it's ftead. As for the practice of religion, it is not in my prefent argument to fpeak of that; my bufinefs is only to appeal to it as an eftablifhment, effential to the fupport and happinefs of fociety; and when we reflect how often in times paft it has been made an engine for fubverting that tranquillity and good order in the ftate, which it now peaceably upholds, I think it will be clear to every candid man, that this cannot be one of the caufes of complaint and murmur againft the prefent times.

The *Manners* of the age we live in is the next point I am to review; and if I am to bring this into any decent compafs, I muft reject many things out of the account, that would make for my argument, and fpeak very briefly upon all others.

To compare the manners of one age with thofe of another, we muft begin by calling to remembrance the changes that may have been made in our own time, (if we have lived long enough to be witneffes of any) or we

muft

muſt take them upon tradition, or gueſs at
them by the writings of thoſe who deſcribe
them: The comic poets are in general
good deſcribers of the living manners, and
of all dramatic painters in this claſs Ben
Jonſon is decidedly the beſt. In the mirror
of the ſtage we have the reflection of the
times through all their changes, from the
reign of Elizabeth to that of Anne, with an
exception to the days of Oliver, of which
interval, if there was no other delineation of
the reigning manners than what we find in
the annals of Whitelocke, and Clarendon, we
ſhould be at no loſs to form our judgment
of them. I ſtop at the age of queen Anne,
becauſe it was then that Sir Richard Steele
and Mr. Addiſon began to ſpread their pal-
lets, and when they had compleated *The
Spectator*, nobody will diſpute their having
given a very finiſhed pourtrait of the age
they lived in. Where they ſtop tradition
may begin; ſo that I think an obſerving
man, with all theſe aids, and no ſhort experience of his own to help them out, may
form a pretty cloſe compariſon in his own
thoughts upon the ſubject.

Here I muſt remind the reader that I am

ſpeaking

speaking of manners as they respect society.
Now we can readily refer to certain times
past, when the manners of men in this
country were insufferably boisterous and un-
polished; we can point to the period, when
they were as notoriously reserved, gloomy,
dark and fanatical; we know when profligacy threw off all appearances, and libertinifm
went naked as it were into all societies; we
can tell when pedantry was in general fashion, when duelling was the rage, and the
point of honour was to be defined by a chain
of logic that would have puzzled Ariftotle;
we can turn to the time, when it was repu-
table to get drunk, and when the fine gentleman of the comedy entertains his miftrefs
with his feats over the bottle, and recommends himfelf to her good graces by fwearing,
bluftering, and beating up the watch: We
know there are fuch words in the language as
fop and beau, and fome can remember them
in daily ufe; many are yet living, who have had
their full-bottomed wigs brought home in a
chair, and many an old lady now crouds herfelf into a corner, who once hooped herfelf in a
circle hardly lefs than Arthur's round table:
Here I may be told that drefs is not man-

ners; but I muſt contend that the manners
of a man in a full-bottomed wig muſt par-
take ſomething of the ſtiffneſs of the bar-
ber's buckle; nor do I ſee how he can walk
on foot at his eaſe, when his wig goes in a
chair. How many of us can call to mind
the day, when it was a mark of good-breeding to cram a poor ſurfeited gueſt to the
throat, and the moſt ſocial hours of life
were thrown away in a continual inter-
change of ſolicitations and apologies? What
a ſtroke upon the nerves of a modeſt man
was it then to make his firſt approaches, and
perform his awkward reverences to a ſolemn
circle all riſing on their legs at the aweful
moment of his entry! and what was his
condition at departing, when, after having
performed the ſame tremendous ceremonies,
he ſaw his retreat cut off by a double row
of guards in livery, to every one of whom
he was to pay a toll for free paſſage! A man
will now find his ſuperiors more acceſſible,
his equals more at their eaſe, and his inferiors more mannerly than in any time paſt.
The effects of public education, travel and
a general intercourſe with mankind, the
great influx of foreigners, the variety of
public

public amusements, where all ranks and degrees meet promiscuously, the constant re-
sort to bathing and water-drinking places in
the summer, and above all the company of
the fair sex, who mix so much more in
society than heretofore, have, with many
other conspiring causes, altogether produced
such an ease and suavity of manners throughout the nation, as have totally changed the
face of society, and levelled all those bars
and barriers, which made the approaches to
what was called good company so troublesome, and obstructed the intercourse between man and man. Here then I shall
conclude upon this topic, and pass to the
Arts, which I said were the ornaments of
society.

As I am persuaded my argument will not
be contested in this quarter, I need spend
few words upon so clear a point. If ever
this country saw an age of artists, it is the
present; Italy, Spain, Flanders and France,
have had their turn, but they are now in no
capacity to dispute the palm, and England
stands without a rival; her painters, sculp-
tors and engravers are now the only schools,
properly so called, in Europe; Rome will

D 4   bear

bear witnefs that the Englifh artifts are as fuperior in talents as they are in numbers to thofe of all nations befides. I referve the mention of her architects as a feparate clafs, that I may for once break in upon my general rule, by indulging myfelf in a prediction, (upon which I am willing to ftake all my credit with the reader) that when the modeft genius of a *Harrifon* fhall be brought into fuller difplay, England will have to boaft of a native architect, which the brighteft age of Greece would glory to acknowledge.

No. XCII.

To the OBSERVER.

Etiam mortuus loquitur.

SIR,

IF I am rightly advifed, the laws of England have provided no remedy for an injury, which I have received from a certain gentleman, who fets me at defiance, and whom

whom I am not confcious of having offended in the fmalleft article in life. My cafe is as follows: Some time ago I went into the South of France for the recovery of my health, which (thank God) I have fo far effected, that I fhould think I was at this very moment enjoying as good a ftock of fpirits and ftrength, as I have enjoyed for many years of my life paft, if I was not outfaced by the gentleman in queftion, who fwears I am dead, and has proceeded fo far as to publifh me dead to all the world, with a whole volume of memoirs which I have no remembrance of, and of fayings which I never faid.

I think this is very hard upon me, and if there is no redrefs for fuch proceedings, but that a man muft be printed dead, whenever any fanciful fellow chufes to write a book of memoirs, I muft take the freedom to fay this is no country to live in; and let my ingenious biographer take it how he will, I fhall ftill maintain to his face that I am alive, and I do not fee why my word in fuch a cafe fhould not go as far as his.

There is yet another thing I will venture to fay, that I did never in the whole courfe of my life utter one half or even one tenth part of

the

the smart repartees and bon-mots he is
pleafed to impute to me: I don't know
what he means by laying fuch things at my
deer; I defy any one of my acquaintance to
fay I was a wit, which I always confidered as
another name for an ill-tempered fellow.   I
do acknowledge that I have lived upon
terms of acquaintance with my biographer,
and have paffed fome focial hours in his
company, but I never fufpected he was mi-
nuting down every foolifh thing, that efcaped my lips in the unguarded moments of
convivial gaiety; if I had, I would have
avoided him like the peftilence. It is hard
upon a man, let me tell you, Sir, very hard
indeed, to find his follies upon record, and
I could almoft wifh his words were true,
and that I were dead in earneft, rather than
alive to read fuch nonfenfe, and find myfelf
made the father of it.

Judge of my furprife, when paffing along
Vigo-lane upon a friendly call, as I intended it, to this very gentleman of whom
I complain, I took up a volume from a ftall
in a whitey-brown paper binding, and opening it at the title-page met my own face, ftaring me out of countenance full in the front :
I ftarted

I ftarted back with horror; nature never
gave me any reafon to be fond of my own
features; I never furvey my face but when
I fhave myfelf, and then I am afhamed
of it; I truft it is no true type of my
heart, for it is a forry fample of nature's
handy-work, to fay no worfe of it. What
the devil tempted him to ftick it there I
cannot guefs, any more than I can at his
publifhing a bundle of nonfenfical fayings
and doings, which I deteft and difavow.
As for his printing my laft will and tefta-
ment, and difpofing of my poor perfonals
at pleafure, I care little about it; if he had
taken only my money and fpared my life, I
would not have complained.

And now what is my redrefs? I apply
myfelf to you in my diftrefs, as an author
whofe book is in pretty general circulation,
and one, as I perceive, who affaults no man's
living fame and character; I defire therefore
you will take mine into your protection,
and if you can think of any thing to deter
the world in future from fuch flippancies,
you are welcome to make what ufe you
pleafe of this letter; for as I have always
ftrove to do what little fervice I could to

D 6   the

the living, when I was allowed to be one of their number, so now I am voted out of their company, I would gladly be of some use to the dead.

Your's whilst I lived,

H. POSTHUMOUS.

P. S. I am sorry I did not leave you something in my will, as I believe you deserve it as well, and want it more than some that are in it. If I live to die a second time, I will be sure to remember you.

As I am not versed in the law of libels, I know not what advice to give in Posthumous's case, whom I would by no means wish to see entangled in further difficulties; though I think he might fairly say to his biographer with a courtly poet of this century,

Oh! libel me with all things but thy praise!

The practice which some of our public news-writers are in, of treating their readers with a farrago of puerile anecdotes and scraps of characters, has probably led the way to a very foolish fashion, which is gaining ground amongst us: No sooner does a great

man

man die, than the fmall wits creep into his coffin, like the fwarm of bees in the carcafe of Sampfon's lion, to make honey from his corpfe. It is high time that the good fenfe of the nation fhould correct this impertinence.

I have availed myfelf of Pofthumous's permiffion to publifh his letter, and I fhall without fcruple fubjoin to it one of a very different fort, which I have received from a correfpondent, whofe name I do not mean to expofe; it is with fome reluctance I introduce it into this work, becaufe it brings a certain perfon on the ftage, whom I have no defire to exhibit oftener than I can help; but as I think it will be a confolation to Pofthumous to fhew him others in the fame hazard with himfelf, I hope my readers will let it pafs with this apology.

To the OBSERVER.

SIR,

I am a man, who fay a great many good things myfelf, and hear many good things faid by others; for I frequent clubs and coffee-rooms in all parts of the town,

attend

attend the pleadings in Weftminfter Hall, am remarkably fond of the company of men of genius, and never mifs a dinner at the Manfion Houfe upon my Lord Mayor's day.

I am in the habit of committing to paper every thing of this fort, whether it is of my own faying, or any other perfon's, when I am convinced I myfelf fhould have faid it, if he had not : Thefe I call my confcientious witticifms, and give them a leaf in my common-place book to themfelves.

I have the pleafure to tell you, that my collection is now become not only confiderable in bulk, but, (that I may fpeak humbly of it's merit) I will alfo fay, that it is to the full as good, and far more creditable to any gentleman's character, than the books which have been publifhed about a certain great wit lately deceafed, whofe memory has been fo completely diffected by the operators in Stationers Hall.

- Though I have as much refpect for pofterity as any man can entertain for perfons he is not acquainted with, ftill I cannot underftand how a poft-obit of this fort can profit me in my life, unlefs I could make it over

to

to some purchaser upon beneficial conditions.   Now, as there are people in the
world, who have done many famous actions,
without having once uttered a real good
thing, as it is called, I should think my collection might be an acceptable purchase to
a gentleman of this description, and such an
one should have it a bargain, as I would be
very glad to give a finishing to his character, which I can best compare to a coat of
Adams's plaister on a well-built house.

For my own part, being neither more nor
less than a haberdasher of small wares, and
having scarcely rambled beyond the boun-
daries of the bills of mortality, since I was
out of my apprenticeship, I have not the
presumption to think the anecdotes of my
own life important enough for posthumous
publication; neither do I suppose my writings, (though pretty numerous, as my books
will testify, and many great names standing
amongst them, which it is probable I shall
never cross out,) will be thought so interest-
ing to the public, as to come into compe-
tition with the lively memoirs of a *Bellamy*
and a *Baddeley*, who furnish so many agreeable records of many noble families, and are

the

the folace of more than half the toilets in
town and country.

But to come more clofely to the chief
purport of this letter—It was about a fort-
night ago, that I croffed upon you in the
Poultry near the fhop-door of your worthy
bookfeller : I could not help giving a glance
at your looks, and methought there was a
morbid fallownefs in your complexion, and
a fickly langour in your eye, that indicated
fpeedy diffolution : I watched you for fome
time, and as you turned into the fhop remarked the total want of energy in your ftep.
I know whom I am faying this to, and therefore am not afraid of ftartling you by my
obfervations, but if you actually perceive
thofe threatening fymptoms, which I took
notice of, it may probably be your wifh to
lay in fome ftore for a journey you are foon
to take. You have always been a friend and
cuftomer to me, and there is nobody I fhall
more readily ferve than yourfelf : I have
long noticed with regret the very little favour you receive from your contemporaries,
and fhall gladly contribute to your kinder
reception from pofterity ; now I flatter myfelf, if you adopt my collection, you will at
leaft

leaft be celebrated for your fayings, whatever may become of your writings.

As for your private hiftory, if I may guefs from certain events, which have been reported to me, you may, with a little allowable embellifhment, make up a decent life of it. It was with great pleafure I heard t'other day, that you was ftabbed by a monk in Portugal, broke your limbs in Spain, and was poifoned with a fallad at Paris; thefe, with your adventures at fea, your fufferings at Bayonne, and the treatment you received from your employers on your return, will be amufing anecdotes, and as it is generally fuppofed you have not amaffed any very great fortune by the plunder of the public, your narrative will be read without raifing any envy in the reader, which will be fo much in your favour. Still your chief dependance muft reft upon the collection I fhall fupply you with, and when the world comes to underftand how many excellent things you faid, and how much more wit you had than any of your contemporaries gave you credit for, they will begin to think you had not fair play whilft you was alive, and who knows but they may take it in mind to raife a mo-

nument

nument to you by fubfcription amongft other merry fellows of your day?

I am your's,

H. B.

I defire my correfpondent will accept this fhort but ferious anfwer: If I am fo near the end of life, as he fuppofes, it will behove me to wind it up in another manner from what he fuggefts: I therefore fhall not treat with my friend the haberdafher for his fmall wares.

No. XCIII.

'Αληθόμυθον χρὴ εἶναι, ὖ πολύλογον.

(DEMOCRATES.)

" *Remember only that your words be true,*
" *No matter then how many or how few.*"

To the OBSERVER.

I HAVE a habit of dealing in the marvellous, which I cannot overcome: Some people, who feem to take a pleafure in magnifying

nifying the little flaws to be found in all characters, call this by a name which no gentleman ought to ufe, or likes to hear: The fact is, I have fo much tender confideration for Truth in her ftate of nakednefs, that, till I have put her into decent cloathing, I cannot think of bringing her into company; and if her appearance is fometimes fo much altered by drefs, that her beft friends cannot find her out, am I to blame for that?

There is a matter-of-fact man of my acquaintance, who haunts me in all places, and is the very torment of my life; he fticks to me as the threfher does to the whale, and is the perfect night-mare of my imagination: This fellow never lets one of my ftories pafs without docking it like an attorney's bill before a mafter in chancery: He cut forty miles out of a journey of one hundred, which but for him I had performed in one day upon the fame horfe; in which I confefs I had ftretched a point for the pleafure of out-riding a fat fellow in company, who, by the malicious veracity of my aforefaid *Damper*, threw me at leaft ten miles diftance behind him.

This provoking animal cut up my fuccefs

cefs in fo many intrigues and adventures,
that I was determined to lay my plan out of
his reach, in a fpot which I had provided for
an evil day, and accordingly I led him a
dance into Corfica, where I was fure he
could not follow me : Here I had certainly
been, and knew my ground well enough to
prance over it at a very handfome rate : I
noticed a kind of fly leer in fome of the company, which was pointed towards a gentleman prefent, who was a ftranger to me, and
fo far from joining in the titter was very po-
litely attentive to what I was relating. I was
at this moment warm in the caufe of freedom, and had performed fuch prodigies of
valour in its defence, that, before my ftory
was well ended I had got upon fuch clofe
terms with General Paoli, that, had my
hearers been but half as credulous as they
ought to have been, they might have fet us
down for fworn friends and infeparables : But
here again, as ill luck would have it, my
evil genius tapt me on the fhoulder, and
remarking that I principally addreffed myfelf to the gentleman, whofe politenefs and
attention were fo flattering, faid to me with
a fmile, that had the malice of the devil in
it——

it—" Give me leave to introduce you to
" General Paoli here prefent."—Death and
confufion, what I felt! a ftroke of lightning
would have been charity compared to this.
—My perfecutor had not done with me.—"I
" am afraid you have forgot, your old friend
" and familiar, who no doubt will be over-
" joyed at recognizing a brother warrior,
" who has performed fuch noble fervices
" jointly with himfelf in the glorious ftrug-
" gle for the liberties of his beloved coun-
" try."—Can I paint the fhame I fuffered
at this moment? It is impoffible ; I can
only fay there is a generofity in true valour,
which fcorns to triumph over the fallen.—
" There were fo many brave men," (faid
that gallant perfon in a tone I fhall never
lofe the impreffion of) " of whofe fervices I
" fhall ever preferve a grateful memory, but
" whofe perfons have flipt from my recol-
" lection, that I have only to entreat your
" pardon for a forgetfulnefs, which I defire
" you to believe is not my fault, but my in-
" firmity,"—If a bottle had been vollied at
my head, I could not have been more in
need of a furgeon, than I was at this inftant:
I could never have fufpected Truth of play-

ing

ing me fuch a jade's trick; I always confidered her as a good-natured fimple creature
without gall or bitternefs, and was in the
habit of treating her accordingly; but this
was fuch a fpecimen of her malice, that
I fled out of her company as haftily as I
could.

The very next morning I took my paffage
in the ftage-coach for my native town in
the north of England, heartily out of humour with my trip to Corfica; but even
here I could not fhake off old habits, fo far
as to refift the temptation of getting into a
poft-chaife for the laft ftage, by which
manœuvre I took the credit of having travelled like a gentleman, and became intitled
to rail againft the poft-tax and the expences
of the road.

I was now voted into a club of the chief
inhabitants of the place, and as I had no
reafon to believe the ftory of my late difcom-
fiture had reached them, I foon recovered
my fpirits, and with them the amplifying
powers of my invention. My ftories for a
confiderable time were fwallowed fo glibly,
and feemed to fit fo eafy on the ftomachs of
thefe natural, unfophifticated people, that I

was

was encouraged to encreafe the dofe to fuch a degree, as feemed at length to produce fomething like a naufea with thofe I adminiftered it to: efpecially with a certain precife perfonage of the fect of Quakers, one *Simon Stiff*, a wealthy trader, and much refpected for his probity and fair-dealing. *Simon* had a way of afking me at the end of a ftory—*But is it true?*—which fometimes difconcerted me, and confiderably leffened the applaufes that the reft of the club had been accuftomed to beftow upon my narratives.

One evening, when I had been defcribing an enormous fhark, by which I had been attacked in one of my Weft-India voyages, *Simon Stiff*, lifting up both his hands in an attitude of aftonifhment, cried out—" Ve-" rily friend *Cracker*, thou draweft a long " bow." With an angry look I demanded the meaning of that expreffion.—" I mean," replied *Simon*, " thou fpeakeft the thing " which is not." " That is as much as to " fay I tell a lie."—" Even fo, friend, thou " haft hit it," faid *Simon* without altering his voice, or regarding the tone of rage I had thrown mine into: The fteady ferenity of his

his countenance put me down, and I ſuffered
him to proceed without interruption—
" Thou haſt told us many things, friend
" *Cracker*, that are perfectly incredible;
" were I to attempt impoſing upon my cuſ-
" tomers in the way of traffic, as thou doſt
" upon thy company in the way of talk,
" the world would juſtly ſet me down for a
" diſhoneſt man.   Believe me, thou mayeſt
" be a very good companion without ſwerv-
" ing from the truth, nay, thou canſt no
" otherwiſe be a good one than by adhering
" to it; for if thou art in the practice of ut-
" tering falſehoods, we ſhall be in the prac-
" tice of diſbelieving thee, even when thou
" ſpeakeſt the truth, and ſo there will be an
" end of all confidence in ſociety, and thy
" word will paſs for nothing.   I have ob-
" ſerved it is thy vanity that betrays thee
" into falſehood; I ſhould have hoped thou
" wou'dſt not have forgotten how thy falſe-
" hood betrayed thee into ſhame, and how
" we received and welcomed thee into our
" ſociety, when thy friends in the metropo-
" lis had hooted thee out of their's.   Think
" not thou canſt eſtabliſh a credit with us by
" the fictions of imagination; plain truths
                              " ſuit

" fuit men of plain underftandings. Had
" thy fhark been as big again as thou wou'dft
" have us believe it was, what wou'dft thou
" have gained by it? Nothing but the
" merit of having feen a monfter; and what
" is that compared to the rifque of being
" thought a monfter-maker? If thou waft
" fnatched from the jaws of the animal by
" the hand of God, give God the praife: If
" thine own courage and addrefs contribut-
" ed to fave thee, give Him ftill the praife,
" who infpired thee with thofe means of
" furthering his providence in thy refcue':
" Where is the ground for boafting in all
" this? Sometimes thou wou'dft perfuade
" us thou art a man of confequence, in the
" favour of princes, and in the fecrets of
" minifters: If we are to believe all this,
" thou doft but libel thofe minifters for let-
" ting fuch a babbler into their councils, and
" if thou thinkeft to gain a confequence
" with us thereby, thou art grievoufly de-
" ceived, friend *Cracker*, for we do not want
" to know what thou oughteft not to tell,
" and we defpife the fervant who betrayeth
" his mafter's truft. As for wonders, what
" fignifieth telling us of them? The time

" is full of wonders; the revolution of em-
" pires, the fall of defpotifm, and the eman-
" cipation of mankind, are objects, whofe
" fuperior magnitude makes thy fhark
" fhrink into an atom.   Had the monfter
" gorg'd thee at a mouthful, how many
" thoufands, nay tens of thoufands, have
" the voracious jaws of death devoured in a
" fucceffion of campaigns, which have made
" creation melt? Didft thou efcape the
" monfter? what then; how can we have
" leifure to reflect upon thy fingle deliver-
" ance, when we call to mind the numbers
" of defpairing captives, who have been
" liberated from the dungeons of tyranny?
" In a word, friend *Cracker*, if it is through
" a love for the marvellous thou makeft fo
" free with the facred name of truth, thou
" doft but abufe our patience and thine own
" time in hunting after fharks and monfters
" of the deep; and if thou haft any other
" motive for fiction than the above, it muft
" be a motive lefs innocent than what I have
" fuppofed, and in that cafe we hold thee
" dangerous to fociety and a difgrace to hu-
" man nature."

Here he concluded, and though the length
and

and deliberate folemnity of his harangue had given me time enough, yet I had not fo availed myfelf of it as to collect my thoughts, and prepare myfelf for any kind of defence: How to deal with this formal old fellow I knew not ; to cudgel him was a fervice of more danger than I faw fit to engage in, for he was of athletic limbs and ftature ; to challenge him to a gentleman's fatisfaction, being a Quaker, would have fubjected me to univerfal ridicule : I rofe from my chair, took my hat from the peg, and abruptly quitted the room : Next morning I fent to cut my name out of the club, but behold! they had faved me that ceremony over-night, and I had once more a new fet of acquaintance to go in fearch of.

In this folitary interim I ftrove to lighten the burthen of time by ftarting a correfpondence with one of our public prints, and fo long as I fupplied it with anecdotes from the country, I may fay without vanity there was neither fire nor flood, murder, rape nor robbery wanting to embellifh it : I broke two or three necks at a horfe-race without any detriment to the community, and for the amufement of my readers drove over blind

beggars,

beggars, drowned drunken farmers, and
toffed women with child by mad bullocks,
without adding one item to the bills of mortality; I made matches without number
which the regifter never recorded; I was at
the fame time a correfpondent at Bruffels, a
refident in Spain, and a traveller at Conftan-
:tinople, who gave fecret information of all
proceedings in thofe feveral places, and by
the myfterious ftile in which I enveloped
my difpatches, nobody could fix a falfehood
on my intelligence, till I imprudently fought
a battle on the banks of the Danube, after
the armies were gone into winter quarters,
which did the Turk no mifchief, and effectually blafted me with the compiler, and
him with the public.

I am now out of bufinefs, and, if you
want any thing in my way to enliven your
Obfervers, (which give me leave to remark
are fometimes rather of the dulleft) I fhall
be proud to ferve you, being

Your very humble fervant,
at command,

KIT CRACKER.

N. B. I

N. B. I do not want any thing in *Kit Cracker*'s way ; but though I decline the offer of his affiftance, I willingly avail myfelf of the moral of his example.

No. XCIV.

Λυπᾶντα τὸν πλησίον, ὁ ῥάδιον ἀυτὸν ἄλυπον ἰῖναι.

DEMOPHILI SENTENTIA.

" He, who another's peace annoys,
" By the fame act his own deftroys."

To the OBSERVER.

As I have lived long enough to repent of a fatal propenfity, that has led me to commit many offences, not the lefs irkfome to my prefent feelings for the fecrecy with which I contrived to execute them, and as thefe can now be no otherwife atoned for than by a frank confeffion, I have refolved upon this mode of addreffing myfelf to you. Few people chufe to difplay their own characters to the world in fuch colours as I fhall give to mine, but as I have mangled fo

E 3 many

many reputations in my time without
mercy, I fhould be the meaneft of mankind
if I fpared my own; and being now about
to fpeak of a perfon whom no man loves,
I may give vent to an acrimony at which
no man can take offence. If I have been
troublefome to others, I am no lefs uncom-
fortable to myfelf, and amidft vexations
without number, the greateft of all is, that
there is not one which does not originate
from myfelf.

I entered upon life with many advantages
natural and acquired; I am indebted to my
parents for a liberal education, and to nature for no contemptible fhare of talents :
my propenfities were not fuch as betrayed
me into diffipation and extravagance : my
mind was habitually of a ftudious caft; I
had a paffion for books, and began to collect them at an early period of my life : to
them I devoted the greateft portion of my
time, and had my vanity been of a fort to
be contented with the literary credit I had
now acquired, I had been happy; but I
was ambitious of convincing the world, I
was not the idle owner of weapons which
I did not know the ufe of; I feized every

fafe

safe opportunity of making my pretensions respected by such dabblers in the belles lettres who paid court to me, and as I was ever cautious of stepping an inch beyond my tether on these occasions, 1 soon found myself credited for more learning than my real stock amounted to.   I received all visitors in my library, affected a studious air, and took care to furnish my table with volumes of a select sort : upon these I was prepared to descant, if by chance a curious friend took up any one of them, and as there is little fame to be got by treading in the beaten track of popular opinion, I sometimes took the liberty to be eccentric and paradoxical in my criticisms and cavils, which gained me great respect from the ignorant, (for upon such only I took care to practise this chicanery) so that in a short time I became a sovereign dictator within a certain set, who looked up to me for second-hand opinions in all matters of literary taste, and saw myself inaugurated by my flatterers censor of all new publications.

My trumpeters had now made such a noise in the world, that I began to be in great request, and men of real literature laid

out.

out for my acquaintance; but here I acted
with a coldnefs, that was in me conftitu-
tional as well as prudential: I was refolved not to rifk my laurels, and throw
away the fruits of a triumph fo cheaply
purchafed: folicitations, that would have
flattered others, only alarmed me; fuch
was not the fociety I delighted in; againft
fuch attacks I entrenched myfelf with the
moft jealous caution: If however by accident I was drawn out of my faftneffes, and
trapped unawares into an ambufcade of
wicked wits, I armed myfelf to meet them
with a triple tier of fmiles; I primed my
lips with fuch a ready charge of flattery,
that when I had once engaged them in the
pleafing contemplation of their own merits,
they were feldom difpofed to fcrutinize into
mine, and thus in general I contrived to
efcape undetected: Though it was no eafy
matter to extort an opinion from me in fuch
companies, yet fometimes I was unavoid-
ably entangled in converfation, and then I
was forced to have recourfe to all my addrefs; happily my features were habituated
to a fmile of the moft convertible fort, for
it would anfwer the purpofes of affected
humility

humility as well as thofe of actual contempt, to which in truth it was more congenial: my opinion, therefore, upon any point of controverfy flattered both parties and befriended neither; it was calculated to imprefs the company with an idea that I knew much more than I profeft to know; it was in fhort fo infinuating, fo fubmitted, fo hefitating, that a man muft have had the heart of Nero to have profecuted a being fo abfolutely inoffenfive: but thefe facrifices coft me dear, for they were foreign to my nature, and, as I hated my fuperiors, I avoided their fociety.

Having fufficiently diftinguifhed myfelf as a critic, I now began to meditate fome fecret attempts as an author; but in thefe the fame caution attended me, and my performances did not rife above a little fonnet, or a parody, which I circulated through a few hands without a name, prepared to difavow it, if it was not applauded to my wifhes: I alfo wrote occafional effays and paragraphs for the public prints, by way of trying my talents in various kinds of ftile; by thefe experiments I acquired a certain facility of imitating other people's manner

and

and difguifing my own, and fo far my point was gained ; but as for the fecret fatisfaction I half promifed myfelf in hearing my productions applauded, of that I was altogether difappointed; for though I tried both praife and difpraife for the purpofe of bringing them into notice, I never had the pleafure to be contradicted by any man in the latter cafe, or feconded by a living foul in the former : I had circulated a little poem, which coft me fome pains, and as I had been flattered with the applaufe it gained from feveral of its readers, I put it one evening in my pocket, and went to the houfe of a certain perfon, who was much reforted to by men of genius : an opportunity luckily offered for producing my manufcript, which I was prepared to avow as foon as the company prefent had given fentence in its favour : it was put into the hands of a dramatic author of fome celebrity, who read it aloud, and in a manner as I thought that clearly anticipated his difguft : as foon therefore as he had finifhed it, and demanded of me if I knew the author, I had no hefitation to declare that I did not. —Then I prefume, rejoined he, it is no offence to fay I think it the mereft trafh I.

ever

ever read—None in life, I replied, and from that moment held him in everlasting hatred.

Disgusted with the world, I now began to dip my pen in gall, and as soon as I had singled out a proper object for my spleen, I looked round him for his weak side, where I could place a blow to best effect, and wound him undiscovered: the author above-mentioned had a full share of my attention; he was an irritable man, and I have seen him agonized with the pain, which my very shafts had given him, whilst I was foremost to arraign the scurrility of the age, and encourage him to disregard it : the practice I had been in of masking my stile facilitated my attacks upon every body, who either moved my envy or provoked my spleen.

The meanest of all passions had now taken entire possession of my heart, and I surrendered myself to it without a struggle : still there was a consciousness about me, that sunk me in my own esteem, and when I met the eye of a man whom I had secretly defamed, I felt abashed ; society became painful to me; and I shrunk into retirement, for my self-esteem was lost : though I had gratified my

E 6   malice,

malice, I had deſtroyed my comfort; I now contemplated myſelf a ſolitary being, at the very moment when I had every requiſite of fortune, health and endowments, to have recommended me to the world, and to thoſe tender ties and engagements which are natural to man, and conſtitute his beſt enjoyments.

The ſolitude I reſorted to, made me every day more moroſe, and ſupplied me with reflections that rendered me intoler-able to myſelf and unfit for ſociety. I had reaſon to apprehend, in ſpite of all my caution, that I was now narrowly watched, and that ſtrong ſuſpicions were taken up againſt me; when as I was feaſting my jaun-diced eye one morning with a certain newſ-paper, which I was in the habit of employing as the vehicle of my venom, I was ſtartled at diſcovering myſelf conſpicuouſly pointed out in an angry column as a cowardly defamer, and menaced with perſonal chaſtiſement, as ſoon as ever proofs could be obtained againſt me: and this threatening denunciation evi-dently came from the very author, who had unknowingly given me ſuch umbrage when he recited my poem.

The

The fight of this refentful paragraph was like an arrow to my brain: habituated to fkirmifh only behind entrenchments, I was ill-prepared to turn into the open field, and had never put the queftion to my heart, how it was provided for the emergency: In early life I had not any reafon to fufpect my courage, nay it was rather forward to meet occafions in thofe days of innocence; but the meannefs I had lately funk into, had fapped every manly principle of my nature, and I now difcovered to my forrow, that in taking up the lurking malice of an affaffin, I had loft the gallant fpirit of a gentleman.

There was ftill one alleviation to my terrors: it fo chanced that I was not the author of the particular libel which my accufer had imputed to me: and though I had been father of a thoufand others, I felt myfelf fupported by truth in almoft the only charge, againft which I could have fairly appealed to it. It feemed to me therefore advifeable to lofe no time in difculpating myfelf from the accufation, yet to feek an interview with this irafcible man was a fervice of fome danger: chance threw the
opportunity

opportunity in my way, which I had probably elfe wanted fpirit to invite; I accofted him with all imaginable civility, and made the ftrongeft affeverations of my innocence: whether I did this with a fervility that might aggravate his fufpicion, or that he had others impreffed upon him befides thofe I was labouring to remove, fo it was, that he treated all I faid with the moft contemptuous incredulity, and elevated his voice to a tone that petrified me with fear, bade me avoid his fight, threatening me both by words and actions in a manner too humiliating to relate.

" Alas! can words exprefs my feelings? Is there a being more wretched than myfelf? to be friendlefs, an exile from fociety, and at enmity with myfelf, is a fituation deplorable in the extreme: let what I have now written be made public; if I could believe my fhame would be turned to others' profit, it might perhaps become lefs painful to myfelf; if men want other motives to divert them from defamation, than what their own hearts fupply, let them turn to my example, and if they will not be reafoned,

let

let them be frightened out of their propensity.

   I am, Sir, &c.

    WALTER WORMWOOD.

The cafe of this correfpondent is a melancholy one, and I have admitted his letter, becaufe I do not doubt the prefent good motives of the writer; but I fhall not eafily yield a place in thefe effays to characters fo difgufting, and reprefentations fo derogatory to human nature. The hiftorians of the day, who profefs to give us intelligence of what is paffing in the world, ought not to be condemned, if they fometimes make a a little free with our foibles and our follies; but downright libels are grown too dangerous, and fcurrility is become too dull to find a market; the pillory is a great reformer. The detail of a court drawing-room, though not very edifying, is perfectly inoffenfive; a lady cannot greatly complain of the liberty of the prefs, if it is contented with the humble tafk of celebrating the workmanfhip of her mantua-maker: as for fuch inveterate malice, as my correfpondent *Wormwood* defcribes, I flatter myfelf it is

        very

very rarely to be found: I can only fay, that though I have often heard of it in converfation, and read of it in books, I do not meet in human nature originals fo ftrongly featured as their paintings: amongft a fmall collection of fonnets in manufcript, defcriptive of the human paffions, which has fallen into my hands, the following lines upon *Envy*, as coinciding with my fubject, fhall conclude this paper.

E N V Y.

" Oh! never let me fee that fhape again,
" Exile me rather to fome favage den,
    " Far from the focial haunts of men!
" Horible phantom, pale it was as death,
" Confumption fed upon its meager cheek,
" And ever as the fiend effay'd to fpeak,
" Dreadfully fteam'd it's peftilential breath.
    " Fang'd like the wolf it was, and all as gaunt,
" And ftill it prowl'd around us and around,
    " Rolling its fquinting eyes afkaunt,
" Wherever human happinefs was found.
    " Furious thereat, the felf-tormenting fprite
" Drew forth an afp, and (terrible to fight)
" To its left pap the envenom'd reptile preft,
" Which gnaw'd and worm'd into its tortur'd breaft.

    " The defperate fuicide with pain
    " Writh'd to and fro, and yell'd amain;
                        " And

" And then with hollow, dying cadence cries—
" It is not of this afp that *Envy* dies;
" 'Tis not this reptile's tooth that gives the fmart;
" 'Tis others happinefs, that gnaws my heart."

No. XCV.

Facilitas Anima ad partem ftultitiæ rapit.

(P. SYRUS.)

To the OBSERVER.

SIR,

THE antient family of the *Saplings*, whereof your humble fervant is the unworthy reprefentative, has been for many generations diftinguifhed for a certain pliability of temper, which with fome people paffes for good humour, and by others is called weaknefs; but however the world may differ in defcribing it, there feems à general agreement in the manner of making ufe of it.

Our family eftate, though far from contemptible, is confiderably reduced from its antient fplendor, not only by an unlucky tumble

tumble that my grandfather Sir Paul got in
the famous Miffiffippi fcheme, but alfo various loffes, bad debts, and incautious fecuri-
ties, which have fallen heavy upon the purfes
of my predeceffors at different times ; but as
every man muft pay for his good character,
I dare fay they did not repent of their pur-
chafe, and for my part it is a reflection that
never gives me any difturbance. This aforefaid grandfather of mine, was fuppofed to have
furnifhed *Congreve* with the hint for his character of *Sir Paul Pliant*, at leaft it hath
been fo whifpered to me very frequently by
my aunt Jemima, who was a great collector
of family anecdotes ; and, to fpeak the
truth, I am not totally without fufpicion,
that a certain ingenious author, lately deceafed, had an eye towards my infignificant
felf in the dramatic pourtrait of his *Good
natured Man*.

Though I fcorn the notion of fetting myfelf off to the public and you by panegyrics
of my own penning, (as the manner of fome
is) yet I may truly fay without boafting,
that I had the character at fchool of being
the very beft *fag* that ever came into it ; and
this I believe every gentleman, who was my
contemporary

contemporary at *Weſtminſter*, will do me the juſtice to acknowledge : it was a reputation I confeſs that I did not earn for nothing, for whilſt I worked the clothes off my back, and the ſkin off my bones in ſcouting upon every body's errands, I was pummeled to a mummy by the boys, *ſhewed up* by the uſhers, flead alive by the maſters, and reported for an incorrigible dunce at my book ; a report which, under correction, I muſt think had ſome degree of injuſtice in it, as it was impoſſible for me to learn a book I was never allowed to open : In this period of my education I took little food and leſs ſleep, ſo that whilſt I ſhot up in ſtature after the manner of my progenitors, who were a tall race of men, I grew as gaunt as a greyhound ; but having abundantly more ſpirit than ſtrength, and being *voted* by the great boys to be what is called *true game*, I was ſingled out as a kind of trial-cock, and pitted againſt every new comer to make proof of his bottom in fair fighting, though I may ſafely ſay I never turned out upon a quarrel of my own making in all my life. Notwithſtanding all theſe honours, which I obtained from my colleagues, I will not

attempt

attempt to difguife from you that I left·
the fchool in difgrace, being expelled by
the mafter, when head · of my boarding
houfe, for not fupporting my authority over
the petty boys belonging to it, who, I muft
confefs, were juft then not in the moft or-
derly and correct ftate of difcipline.

My father, whofe maxim it was never to
let trifles vex him, received me with all the
good humour in life, and admitted me of
the univerfity of Oxford : here I was overjoyed to find, that the affair of the expulfion
was fo far from having prejudiced my contemporaries againft me, that I was reforted
to by numbers whofe time hung upon their
hands, and my rooms became the rendezvous of all the loungers in the college : few
or no fchemes were fet on foot without me,
and if a loofe guinea or two was wanted
for the purpofe, every body knew where to
have it : I was allowed a horfe for my
health's fake, which was rather delicate, but
I cannot fay my health was much the better for him, as I never mounted his back
above once or twice, whilft my friends kept
him in exercife morning and evening, as
long as he lafted, which indeed was only till
the

the hunting feafon fet in, when the currier
had his hide, and his flefh went to the kennel.   I muft own I did not excel in any of
my academical exercifes, fave that of cir-
cumambulating the colleges and public
buildings with ftrangers, who came to gaze
about them for curiofity's fake; in this
branch of learning I gained fuch general reputation, as to be honoured with the title of
Keeper of the Lions : neither will I difguife
the frequent *jobations* I incurred for negleft
of college duties, and particularly for non-
attendance at chapel, but in this I fhould
not perhaps have been thought fo repre-
henfible, had it been known that my fur-
plice never failed to be there, though I had
rarely the credit of bearing it company.

My mother died of a cold fhe caught by
attending fome young ladies on a water-
party before I had been a month in the
world ; and my father never married again,
having promifed her on her death-bed not
to bring a ftep-dame into his family whilft
I furvived : I had the misfortune to lofe
him when I was in my twenty-fecond year;
he got his death at a country canvafs for
Sir Harry Ofier, a very obliging gentleman,

and

and nearly related to our family: I attended my father's corpfe to the grave, on which
melancholy occafion fuch were the lamenta-
tions and bewailings of all the fervants in
the houfe, that I thought it but a proper
return for their affection to his memory, to
prove myfelf as kind a mafter by continu-
ing them in their feveral employs: this
however was not altogether what they
meant, as I was foon convinced every one
amongft them had a remonftrance to make,
and a new demand to prefer: the butler
would have better perquifites, the footman
wanted to be out of livery, the fcullion demanded tea-money, and the cook murmured about kitchen-ftuff.

Though I was now a fingle being in the
world, my friends and neighbours kindly
took care I fhould not be a folitary one! I
was young indeed, and of fmall experience
in the world, but I had plenty of counfel-
lors; fome advifed me to buy horfes they
wanted to fell, others to fell horfes they
wanted to buy: a lady of great tafte fell in
love with two or three of my beft cows for
their colour; they were upon her lawn the
next day: a gentleman of extraordinary

vertue

vertue difcovered a picture or two in my collection, that exactly fitted his pannels : an
eminent improver, whom every body declared to be the firft genius of the age for
laying out grounds, had taken meafures for
tranfporting my garden a mile out of my
fight, and floating my richeft meadow
grounds with a lake of muddy water : as
for my manfion and its appendages, I am
perfuaded I could never have kept them in
their places, had it not been that the feveral projectors, who all united in pulling
them down, could never rightly agree in
what particular fpot to build them up
again : one kind friend complimented me
with the firft refufal of a miftrefs, whom for
reafons of œconomy he was obliged to part
from ; and a neighbouring gentlewoman,
whofe daughter had perhaps ftuck on hand
a little longer than was convenient, more
than hinted to me that Mifs had every re-
quifite in life to make the married ftate perfectly happy.

In juftice however to my own difcretion, let me fay, that I was not haftily furprized into a ferious meafure by this
latter overture, nor did I afk the young
lady's hand in marriage, till I was verily perfuaded,

'fuaded, ·by her exceffive fondnefs,' that
there were no other means to fave her life.
Now whether it was the violence of her
paffion before our marriage, that gave fome
:fhock to her intellects, or from what other
caufe it might proceed, I know not, certain
however it is, that after marriage fhe became fubject to very odd whims and ca-
prices; and though I made it a point of
humanity never to thwart her in thefe humours, yet I was feldom fortunate enough
to pleafe her; fo that, had I not been fure
to demonftration that love for me was the
caufe and origin of them all, I might have
been fo deceived by appearances as to have
imputed them to averfion. She was in the
habit of deciding upon almoft every action in
her life by the interpretation of her dreams, in
which I cannot doubt her great fkill, though
I could not always comprehend the principles on which fhe applied it; fhe never
failed, as foon as winter fet in, to dream of
going to London, and our journey as certainly fucceeded. I remember upon our arrival there the firft year after our marriage,
fhe dreamt of a new coach, and at the fame
time put the fervants in new liveries, the

colours

colours and pattern of which were circum-
ftantially revealed to her in fleep: fometimes, (dear creature !) fhe dreamt of win-
ning large fums at cards, but I am apt to
think thofe dreams were of the fort, which
fhould have been interpreted by their con-
traries : fhe was not a little fond of running
after conjurors and deaf and dumb fortune-
tellers, who dealt in figures and caft nativi-
ties ; and when we were in the country my
barns and outhoufes were haunted with
gypfies and vagabonds, who made fad ha-
voc with our pigs and poultry: of ghofts
and evil fpirits fhe had fuch terror, that I
was fain to keep a chaplain in my houfe to
exorcife the chambers, and when bufinefs
called me from home, the good man con-
defcended fo far to her fears, as to fleep in
a little clofet within her call in cafe fhe was
troubled in the night; and I muft fay this
for my friend, that if there is any truft to
be put in flefh and blood, he was a match for
the beft fpirit that ever walked: fhe had all
the fenfibility in life towards omens and prog-
noftics, and though I guarded every motion
and action that might give any poffible alarm
to her, yet my unhappy awkwardneffes were

always boding ill luck, and I had the grief of heart to hear her declare in her laft moments, that a capital overfight I had been guilty of in handing to her a candle with an enormous winding-fheet appending to it, was the immediate occafion of her death and my irreparable misfortune.

My fecond wife I married in mere charity and compaffion, becaufe a young fellow, whom fhe was engaged to, had played her a bafe trick by fcandaloufly breaking off the match, when the wedding clothes were bought, the day appointed for the wedding, and myfelf invited to it. Such tranfactions ever appeared fhocking to me, and therefore to make up her lofs to her as well as I was able, I put myfelf to extraordinary charges for providing her with every thing handfome upon our marriage: fhe was a fine woman, loved fhew, and was particularly fond of difplaying herfelf in public places, where fhe had an opportunity of meeting and mortifying the young man, who had behaved fo ill to her: fhe took this revenge againft him fo often, that one day to my great furprize I difcovered that fhe had eloped from me and fairly gone off with him.

him. There was fomething fo unhand-
fome, as I thought, in this proceeding, that
I fhould probably have taken legal meafures
for redrefs, as in like cafes other husbands
have done, had I not been diverted from
my purpofe by a very civil note from the
gentleman himfelf, wherein he fays—" That
" being a younger fon of little or no for-
" tune, he hopes I am too much of a gen-
" tleman to think of reforting to the vexa-
" tious meafures of the law for revenging
" myfelf upon him; and, as a proof of his
" readinefs to make me all the reparation
" in his power in an honourable way; he
" begs leave to inform me, that he fhall
" moft refpectfully attend upon me with
" either fword or piftols, or with both,
" whenever I fhall be pleafed to lay my
" commands upon him for a meeting, and
" appoint the hour and place."

After fuch atonement on the part of the
offender, I could no longer harbour any
thoughts of a divorce, efpecially as my younger brother the parfon has heirs to continue
the family, and feems to think fo entirely with
me in the bufinefs, that I have determined
to drop it altogether, and give the parties no

further

further moleftation; for, as my brother very properly obferves, it is the.part of a chriftian to forget and to forgive; and in truth I fee no reafon why I fhould difturb them in their enjoyments, or return evil for good to an obliging gentleman, who has taken a tafk of trouble off my hands, and fet me at my eafe for the reft of my days; in which tranquil and contented ftate of mind, as becomes a' man, whofe inheritance is philanthropy, and whofe mother's milk hath been the milk of human kindnefs, I remain in all brotherly charity and good will,

Your's and the world's friend,
SIMON SAPLING.

No. XCVI.

Quis fcit an adjiciant hodiernæ craftina fummæ.
Tempora Dii Superi ?   (HORAT.)

TO-MORROW is the day, which procrafti-nation always promifes to employ and never overtakes: My correfpondent *Tom Tortoife*, whofe letter I fhall now lay before

the

the public, feems to have made thefe promifes and broken them as often as moft
men.

To the OBSERVER.

I have been refolving to write to thee
every morning for thefe two months, but
fomething or other has always come athwart
my refolution to put it by. In the firft place
I fhould have told thee that aunt Gertrude
was taken grievoufly fick, and had a mighty
defire to fee thee upon affairs of confequence, but as I was in daily hopes fhe
would mend and be able to write to thee
herfelf, (for every body you know underftands their own bufinefs beft) I thought I
would wait till 'fhe got well enough to tell
her own ftory; but alas ! fhe dwindled and
dwindled away till fhe died; fo, if fhe had
any fecrets they are buried with her, and
there's an end of that matter.

Another thing I would fain have written
to thee about, was to enquire into the character of a fellow, one John Jenkyns, who
had ferved a friend of thine, Sir Theodore
Thimble, as his houfe-fteward, and offered

himfelf

himfelf to me in the fame capacity : But this was only my own affair do you fee, fo I put it by from day to day, and in the mean time took the rafcal upon his word without a character : But if he ever had one, he would have loft it in my fervice, for he plundered me without mercy, and at laft made off with a pretty round fum of money, which I have never been able to get any wind of, probably becaufe I never took the trouble to make any enquiry.

I now fit down to let you know fon Tom is come from Oxford, and a ftrapping fine fellow he is grown of his age : He has a mighty longing to fet out upon his travels to foreign parts, which you muft know feems to me a very foolifh conceit in a young lad, who has only kept his firft term and not completed his nineteenth year ; fo I oppofed his whim manfully, which I think you will approve of, for I recollected the opinion you gave upon this fubject when laft here, and quoted it againft him : To do him juftice, he fairly offered to be ruled by your advice, and willed me to write to you on the matter ; but one thing or other always ftood in the way, and in the mean time came Lord

Ramble

Ramble in his way to Dover, and being a great crony of Tom's and very eager for his company, and no letter coming from you (which indeed I acquit you of, not having written to you on the fubject) away the youngfters went together, and probably before this are upon French ground. Pray tell me what you think of this trip, which appears to me but a wild-goofe kind of chace, and if I live till to-morrow I intend to write Tom a piece of my mind to that purpofe, and give him a few wholefome hints, which I had put together for our parting, but had not time juft then to communicate to him.

I intend very fhortly to brufh up your quarters in town, as my folicitor writes me word every thing is at a ftand for want of my appearance: What dilatory doings muft we experience, who have to do with the law! putting off from month to month and year to year: I wonder men of bufinefs are not afhamed of themfelves: as for me, I fhould have been up and amongft them long enough ago, if it had not been for one thing or another that hampered me about my journey: Horfes are for ever

falling

falling lame, and farriers are such lazy raf-
cals, that before one can be cured, another
cries out; and now I am in daily expectation of my favourite brood-mare dropping
a foal, which I am in great hopes will prove
a colt, and therefore I cannot be abfent at
the time, for a mafter's eye you know is
every thing in thofe cafes : Befides I fhould
be forry to come up in this dripping feafon,
and as the parfon has begun praying for fair
weather, I hope it will fet in ere long in
good earneft, and that it will pleafe God to
make it pleafant travelling.

You will be pleafed to hear that I mean
foon to make a job of draining the marfh
in front of my houfe: Every body allows
that as foon as there is a channel cut to the
river, it will be as dry as a bowling-green,
and as fine meadow land as any on my
eftate: It will alfo add confiderably to the
health as well as beauty of our fituation,
for at prefent 'tis a grievous eye-fore, and
fills us with fogs and foul air at fuch a rate,
that I have had my whole family down with
the ague all this fpring: Here is a fellow
ready to undertake the job at a very eafy
expence, and will complete it in a week, fo
that

that it will foon be cone when once begun; therefore you fee I need not hurry myfelf for fetting about it, but wait till leifure and opportunity fuit.

I am forry I can fend you no better news of your old friend the vicar; he is fadly out of forts: You muft know the incumbent of *Slow-in-the-Wilds* died fome time ago, and as the living lies fo handy to my own parifh I had always intended it for our friend, and had promifed him again and again: When behold! time flipt away unperceived, and in came my lord bifhop of the diocefe with a parfon of his own, ready cut and dried, and claimed it as a lapfed living, when it has been mine and my anceftors any time thefe five hundred years for aught I know: If thefe are not nimble doings I know not what are: Egad! a man need have all his eyes about him, that has to do with thefe bifhops. If I had been aware of fuch a trick being played me, I would have hoifted the honeft vicar into the pulpit, before the old parfon who is dead and gone had been nailed in his coffin; for no man loves lefs to be taken napping (as they call it) than I do; and as for the poor vicar 'tis

furprifing

furprifing to fee how he takes to heart the
difappointment; whereas I tell him he has
nothing for it but to outlive the young fellow who has jumped into his fhoes, and
then let us fee if any bifhop fhall jockey us
with the like jade's trick for the future.

I have now only to requeft you will fend
me down a new almanack, for the year wears
out apace, and I am terribly puzzled for
want of knowing how it goes, and I love
to be regular. If there is any thing I can
do for you in thefe parts, pray employ me,
for I flatter myfelf you believe no man
living would go further, or more readily
fly to do you fervice than your's to command, ,

THOMAS TORTOISE.

Alas! though the wife men in all ages
have been calling out as it were with one
voice for us *to know ourfelves*, it is a voice
that has not yet reached the ears or underftanding of my correfpondent Tom Tortoife.
Somebody or other hath left us another
good maxim, *never to put off till to-morrow
what we can do to-day*.—Whether he was
indeed a wife man, who firft broached this
maxim,

maxim, I'll not take on myfelf to pronounce, but I am apt to think he would be no fool who obferved it.

If all the refolutions, promifes and engagements of To-day, that lie over for To-morrow,. were to be fummed up and pofted by items, what a cumbrous load of procraftinations would be transferred in the midnight crifis of a moment! Something perhaps like the following might be the outline of the deed, by which To-day might will and devife the forefaid contingencies to its heir and fucceffor.

" Confcious that my exiftence is draw-
" ing to its clofe, I hereby devife and make
" over to my natural heir and fucceffor, all
" my right and title in thofe many vows,
" promifes and obligations, which have
" been fo liberally made to me by fundry
" perfons in my lifetime, but which ftill re-
" mained unfulfilled on their part, and ftand
" out againft them : But at the fame time
" that I am heartily defirous all engage-
" ments, fair and lawful in their nature, may
" be punctually complied with, I do moft
" willingly cancel all fuch as are of a con-
" trary defcription ; hereby releafing and

F 6 " difcharging

" discharging all manner of persons, who
" have bound themselves to me under rash
" and inconsiderate resolutions, from the
" performance of which evil might ensue to
" themselves, and wrong or violence be done
" society.

" In the first place I desire my said heir
" and successor will call in all those debts
" of conscience, which have been incurred
" by, and are due from, certain defaulters,
" who stand pledged to repentance and
" atonement, of all which immediate pay-
" ment ought in justice and discretion to be
" rigorously exacted from the several par-
" ties, forasmuch as every hour, by which
" they outrun their debt, weakens their se-
" curity.

" It is my further will and desire, that all
" those free livers and profest voluptuaries,
" who have wasted the hours of my existence
" in riot and debauchery, may be made to
" pay down their lawful quota of sick sto-
" machs and aching heads, to be levied upon
" them severally by poll at the discretion of
" my heir and successor.

" Whereas I am apprized of many dark
" dealings and malicious designs now in
" actual

" actual execution, to the great annoyance
" of fociety and good-fellowfhip, I earneftly
" recommend the detection of all fuch evil-
" minded perfons with To-morrow's light,
" heartily hoping they will meet their due
" fhame, punifhment and difappointment :
" And I fincerely wifh that every honeft
" man, who hath this night gone to reft with
" a good reputation, may not be deprived
" of To-morrow's repofe by any bafe ef-
" forts, which Slander, who works in the
" dark, may conjure up to take it from
" him.

" It is with fingular fatisfaction I have
" been made privy to fundry kind and cha-
" ritable benevolences, that have been pri-
" vately beftowed upon the indigent and
" diftreft, without any oftentation or parade
" on the part of the givers, and I do there-
" upon ftrictly enjoin and require a fair and
" impartial account to be taken of the fame
" by my lawful heir and fucceffor, (be the
" amount what it may) that intereft for the
" fame may be put into immediate courfe of
" payment ; whereby the parties fo intitled
" may enjoy, as in juftice they ought to do,
" all thofe comforts, bleffings and rewards,
" which

" which talents fo employed are calculated
" to produce.

" All promifes made by men of power to
" their dependants, and all verbal engage-
" ments to tradefmen on the fcore of bills,
" that lie over for To-morrow, I hereby
" cancel and acquit ; well affured they were
" not meant by thofe who made them, nor
" expected by any who received them, then
" to be made good and fulfilled.

" To all gamefters, rakes and revellers,
" who fhall be found out of bed at my de-
" ceafe, I bequeath rotten conftitutions,
" reftlefs thoughts and fqualid complexions ;
" but to all fuch regular and induftrious
" people, who rife with the fun and care-
" fully refume their honeft occupations, I
" give the greateft of all human bleffings—
" health of body, peace of mind and length
" of days.

" Given under my hand, &c. &c.

" To-Day."

No. XCVII.

To the OBSERVER.

SIR,

THERE is an old gentleman of my acquaintance who annoys me exceedingly with his predictions: I have reafon to believe he bears me good will in the main, and does not know to what a degree he actually difturbs my peace of mind, I would therefore fain put up with his humour if I could; but when he is for ever ringing his knell in my ears, he fometimes provokes me to retort upon him, oftentimes to laugh at him, and never fails to put me out of patience or out of fpirits.

I have read your account of the *Dampers* with great fellow-feeling, and perceive that my old gentleman is very deep in that philofophy; but as I unfortunately have very little philofophy of any fort to fet againft it, I find myfelf frequently at his mercy and without defence.

I do not think this proceeds fo much from
any

any radical vice in his nature, as from a foolish vanity to seem wiser than his neighbours, and to put himself off for a man who knows the world: The fact is he is an old bachelor, lives in absolute retirement, and has scarcely stept out of the precincts of his own village three times in his life; yet he is ever telling me of his experience and his observations: If I was to put implicit faith in what he says, common honesty in mankind would be a miracle, and happiness a disappointment; as for hope, that moonshine diet as he calls it, which is so plentifully served up in the fanciful repasts of the poets, and which is too often the only standing dish at their tables, I should never get a taste of it; and yet if ruining a merchant's credit is tantamount to robbing him of his property, I must think the *Damper*, who blasts my hope, is in fact little better than a thief.

I have a natural prejudice for certain people at first sight, where a countenance impresses me in its favour, for I am apt to fancy that honesty sets a mark upon its owners; there is not a weakness incident to human nature, for which he could hold my

under-

understanding in more sovereign contempt : If I was to be advised by him, I should not trust my wife out of my sight, for it is a maxim with him, that no love-matches can be happy ; mine was of that sort and I am happy ; still I am out of credit with my *Damper*. I was bound for a relation in public trust some years ago ; there I confess his augury sometimes staggered me, and he urged me with proverbs out of holy writ, which I was rather puzzled to parry ; my friend however has done well in the world, discharged his obligation, and repaid it with grateful returns ; still I am out of credit with my *Damper*. I invested a small sum in a venture to the East Indies ; he descanted upon the risque of the sea ; I insured upon the ship, he denounced bankruptcy against the underwriter, the ship came home, and I doubled the capital of my investment ; still I am out of credit with my *Damper*, and he shakes his head at my folly.

I can plainly perceive that his predictions oftentimes are as troublesome to himself as to me ; he loses many a fine morning's walk by foreseeing a change of weather ; he never

goes

goes to church becaufe he has had a fuit with the parfon; and part of his eftate remains untenanted, becaufe a farmer fome time ago broke in his debt.

Though I am no philofopher, I am not fuch a fimpleton, as not to know how little we ought to depend upon worldly events in general; yet it appears to me that what a man has already enjoyed, he can no longer be faid to depend upon : If therefore I have had real pleafure in any innocent and agreeable expectation, difappointment can at worft do no more than remove the meat after I have made my meal.

Though I do not know how to define hope as a metaphyfician, I am inclined to fpeak of it with refpect, becaufe I find it has been a good friend to me in my life; it has given me a thoufand things, which malice and misfortune would have ravifhed from me, if I had not fairly worn them out before they could lay their fingers upon them: *Spe pafcit inani*—fays the poet, and contradicts himfelf in the fame breath : for my part, if it was not for the fear of appearing paradoxical, I fhould fay upon experience that hope, though called a fhadow,

is,

is, together with that other phantom death, the sole reality beneath the sun; the unfaithfulness of friends, from whom I had the claim of gratitude, can never rob me of those pleasures I enjoyed, when I served them, loved them, and confided in them; and, in spite of all my friend the *Damper* can say to the contrary, it is not on my own account I am sorry to have thought better of mankind than they deserve.

I am, Sir, &c.

BENEVOLUS.

To the OBSERVER.

SIR,

I HAVE the honour to belong to a club of gentlemen of public spirit and talents, who make it a rule to meet every Sunday evening, in a house of entertainment behind St. Clement's, for the regulation of literature in this metropolis. Our fraternity consists of two distinct orders, *The Dampers* and *The Puffers*; and each of these are again classed into certain inferior subdivisions. We take notice that both these descriptions of persons have in turn been the objects of your

feeble

feeble raillery; but I muſt fairly tell you,
we neither think worſe of ourſelves nor any
better of you for thoſe attempts.   We con-
ſider the republic of letters under obligations
to us for its very exiſtence, for how could
it be a republic, unleſs its members were
kept upon an equality with each other ?
Now this is the very thing which our inſti-
tution profeſſes to do.

We have an ingenious member of our ſociety, who has invented a machine for this
purpoſe, which anſwers to admiration : He
calls it—*The Thermometer of Merit :* This
machine he has ſet in a frame, and laid down
a very accurate ſcale of gradations by the
ſide of it : One glance of the eye gives every
author's altitude to a minute.   The middle
degree on this ſcale, and which anſwers to
temperate on a common thermometer, is
that ſtandard, or common level of merit, to
which all contemporaries in the ſame free
community ought to be confined ; but as
there will always be ſome eccentric beings
in nature, who will either ſtart above ſtandard heighth, or drop below it ; it is our
duty by the operation of the daily *preſs*
either to ſcrew them down, or to ſcrew
them

them up, as the cafe requires; and this
brings me to explain the ufes of the two
grand departments of our fraternity : Authors above par fall to the province of the
Dampers, all below par appertain to the
Puffers. The daily prefs being common to
all men, and both the one clafs and the
other having open accefs thereto, we can
work either by *forcers* or *repellers,* as we fee
fit ; and I can fafely affure you our procefs
feldom fails in either cafe, when we apply it
timely, and efpecially to young poets in
their *veal-bones,* as the faying is : With this
view we are always upon terms with the
conductors of the faid prefs, who are fully
fenfible of the benefits of our inftitution,
and live with us in the mutual inter-
change of friendly offices, like Shakefpeare's
Zephyrs———

 " Stealing and giving odours.———

As we act upon none but principles of
general juftice, and hold it right that parts
fhould be made fubfervient to the whole,
our fcheme of equalization requires, that
accordingly as any individual rifes on the
fcale, our depreffing powers fhould counter-
act

act and balance his afcending powers : This procefs, as I faid before, belongs to the *Dampers'* office, and is by them termed *preffing* an author, or more literally committing him to the *prefs*. This is laid on more or lefs forcibly, according to his degree of afcenfion ; in moft cafes a few turns fqueeze him down to his proper bearing, but this is always done with reafonable allowance for the natural re-action of elaftic bodies, fo that it is neceffary to bring him fome degrees below ftandard, left he fhould mount above it when the *prefs* is taken off: If by chance his afcending powers run him up to *fultry* or *fever-heat*, the *Dampers* muft proportion their difcipline accordingly ; in like manner the *Puffers* have to blow an author up by mere ftrength of lungs, when he is heavy in ballaft, and his finking powers fall below the *freezing-point*, as fometimes happens even to our beft friends : In that cafe the *Puffers* have *burfts of applaufe* and *peals of laughter* in petto, which, though they never reach vulgar ears, ferve his purpofe effectually—But thefe are fecrets, which we never reveal but to the *Initiated*, and I fhall conclude by affuring you I am your's as you deferve.

PRO BONO PUBLICO.

No. XCVIII.

A WRITER of miscellaneous essays is open to the correspondence of persons of all descriptions, and though I think fit to admit the following letter into my collection, I hope my readers will not suppose I wish to introduce the writer of it into their company, or even into my own.

To the OBSERVER.

SIR,

As we hear a great deal of the affluence of this flourishing country, and the vast quantity of *sleeping cash*, as it is called, lockt up in vaults and strong boxes, we conceive it would be a good deed to waken some of it, and put it into use and circulation: we have therefore associated ourselves into a patriotic fraternity of circulators, commonly called pick-pockets: But with sorrow we let you know, that notwithstanding our best endeavours to put forward the purposes of our institution, and the great charges of providing

2   ourselves

ourſelves with inſtruments and tools of all
ſorts for the better furtherance of our buſineſs, we have yet hooked up little except dirty
handkerchiefs, leathern ſnuff-boxes, empty
purſes and bath-metal watches from the
pockets of the public; articles theſe, let me
ſay, that would hardly be received at the
depôt of the patriotic contributors at Paris.
Are theſe the ſymptoms of a great and
wealthy nation ? we bluſh for our country,
whilſt we are compelled by truth and can-
dour to reply—They are not.

As we have a number of pretty articles
on hand, which will not paſs in our trade,
nothing deters us from putting them up to
public cant but the tax our unworthy parliament has laid upon auctions.   I ſend you
two or three papers, which a brother artiſt
angled out of the pocket of a pennileſs gentleman the other night at the playhouſe
door: the one a letter ſigned *Urania*, the
other *Gorgon:* they can be no uſe to us, as
we have nothing to do with *Urania*'s virtue,
nor ſtand in need of *Gorgon* to paint ſcenes,
which we can act better than he deſcribes;
neither do we want his effigy of a man under
the

the gallows to remind us of what we muft all come to.

Your's,

CROOK-FINGERED JACK.

The letter from *Urania* breathes the full fpirit of that amiable ambition, which at prefent feems generally to infpire our heroines of the ftage to accept of none but fhining charaċters, and never to prefent themfelves to the public but as illuftrious models of purity and grace. If virtue be thus captivating by refemblance only, how beautiful muft it be in the reality! I cannot however help pitying the unknown poet, whofe hopes were dafht with the following rebuke:

SIR,

I have run my eye over your tragedy, and am beyond meafure furprized you could think of allotting a part to me, which is fo totally unamiable. Sir, I neither can, nor will, appear in any public charaċter, which is at variance with my private one; and, though I have no objeċtion to your fcene of felf-murder, and flatter myfelf I could do it justice, yet my mind revolts from spilling any blood but my own.

I confess there are many fine passages and some very striking situations, that would fall to my lot in your drama, but permit me to tell you, Sir, that until you can clear up the legitimacy of the child, you have been pleased therein to lay at my door, and will find a father for it, whom I may not blush to own for a husband, you must never hope for the assistance of your humble servant,

URANIA.

The other letter is addressed to the same unfortunate poet from an artist, who seems to have studied nature in her deformities only.

Dear Dismal,

I wait with impatience to hear of the success of your tragedy, and in the mean time have worked off a frontispiece for it, that you, who have a passion for the terrific, will be perfectly charmed with.

I am scandalized when I hear people say that the fine arts are protected in this country; nothing can be further from the truth,

as

as I am one amongſt many to witneſs. Painting I preſume will not be diſputed to be one of the fine arts, and I may ſay without vanity I have ſome pretenſions to rank with the beſt of my brethren in that profeſſion.

My firſt ſtudies were carried on in the capital of a certain county, where I was born; and being determined to chuſe a ſtriking ſubjeſt for my *debut* in the branch of portrait-painting, I perſuaded my grandmother to ſit to me, and I am bold to ſay there was great merit in my piſture, conſidering it as a maiden produſtion: particularly in the execution of a hair-mole upon her chin, and a wart under her eye, which I touched to ſuch a nicety, as to make every body ſtart who caſt their eyes upon the canvaſs.

There was a little dwarfiſh lad in the pariſh, who beſides the deformity of his perſon, had a remarkable hare-lip, which expoſed to view a broken row of diſcoloured teeth, and was indeed a very brilliant ſubjeſt for a painter of effeſt: I gave a full-length of him, that was executed ſo to the life, as to turn the ftomach of every body, who looked upon it.

At this time there came into our town a travelling fhow-man, who amongft other curiofities of the favage kind brought with him a man-ape, or Ourong-outong : and this perfon, having feen and admired my portrait of the little hump-backed dwarf, employed me to take the figure of his celebrated favage for the purpofe of difplaying it on the outfide of his booth. Such an occafion of introducing my art into notice, fpurred my genius to extraordinary exertions, and though I muft premife that the favage was not the beft fitter in the world, yet I flatter myfelf I acquitted myfelf to the fatisfaction of his keeper and did juftice to the ferocity of my fubject : I caught him in one of his moft ftriking attitudes, ftanding erect with a huge club in his paw : I put every mufcle into play, and threw fuch a terrific dignity into his features, as would not have difgraced the character of a *Nero* or *Caligula*. I was happy to obferve the general notice, which was taken of my performance by all the country folks, who reforted

forted to the fhow, and I believe my employer had no caufe to repent of having fet me upon the work. .

The figure of this animal with the club in his paw fuggefted a hint to a publican in the place of treating his ale-houfe with a new fign, and as he had been in the fervice of a noble family, who from antient time have borne the *Bear* and *ragged ftaff* for their creft, he gave me a commiffion to provide him with a fign to that effect: Though I fpared no pains to get a real bear to fit to me for his portrait, my endeavours proved abortive, and I was forced to refort to fuch common prints of that animal as I could obtain, and trufted to my imagination for fupplying what elfe might be wanted for the piece: As I worked upon this capital defign in the room where my grandmother's portrait was before my eyes, it occurred to me to introduce the fame hairmole into the whifkers of Bruin, which I had fo fuccefsfully copied from her chin, and certainly the thought was a happy one, for it had a picturefque effect ; but in doing this I was naturally enough, though undefignedly, betrayed into giving fuch a gene-

ral

ral refemblance to the good dame in the reft
of Bruin's features, that when it came to be
exhibited on the fign-poft all the people
cried out upon the likenefs, and a malicious
rumour ran through the town, that I had
painted my grandmother inftead of the
bear; which loft me the favour of that in-
dulgent relation, though Heaven knows I
was as innocent of the intention as the
child unborn.

The difguft my grandmother conceived
againft her likenefs with the ragged ftaff,
gave me incredible uneafinefs, and as fhe
was a good cuftomer to the landlord and
much refpected in the place, he was induced
to return the bear upon my hands. I am
now thinking to what ufe I can turn him,
and as it occurs to me, that by throwing a
little more authority into his features, and
gilding his chain, he might very poffibly hit
the likenefs of fome lord mayor of London
in his fur-gown and gold chain, and make a
refpectable figure in fome city hall, I am
willing to difpofe of him to any fuch at an
eafy price.

As I have alfo preferved a fketch of my
famous Ourong-Outong, a thought has

ftruck

ftruck me that with a few finifhing touches he might eafily be converted into a *Caliban* for the *Tempeft*, and, when that is done, I fhall not totally defpair of his obtaining a niche in the Shakfpeare gallery.

It has been common with the great maf-ters, *Rubens*, *Vandyke*, Sir *Jofhua Reynolds* and others, when they paint a warrior, or other great perfonage, on horfeback, to throw a dwarf, or fome fuch contrafted figure, into the back ground : Should any artift be in want of fuch a thing, I can very readily fupply him with my hare-lipped boy; if otherwife, I am not totally without hopes that he may fuit fome Spanifh grandee, when any fuch fhall vifit this country upon his travels, or in the character of ambaffador from that illuftrious court.

Before I conclude I fhall beg leave to ob-ferve, that I have a complete fet of ready-made devils, that would do honour to Saint Antony, or any other perfon, who may be in want of fuch accompaniments to fet off the felf-denying virtues of his character : I have alfo a fine parcel of murdered innocents, which I mean to have filled up with the ftory of Herod; but if any gentleman thinks fit to

G 4   lay

lay the scene in Ghent, and make a modern
compofition of it, I am bold to fay my pretty
babes will not difgrace the pathos of the
fubject, nor violate the *Coftuma*.   I took
a notable fketch of a man hanging, and
feized him juft in the dying twitches, before
the laft ftretch gave a ftiffnefs and rigidity
unfavourable to the human figure; this I
would willingly accommodate to the wifhes
of any lady, who is defirous of preferving a
portrait of her lover, friend or hufband in
that interefting attitude.

Thefe, *cum multis aliis*, are part of my
ftock on hand, and I hope, upon my arrival at my lodgings in Blood-bowl-alley to
exhibit them with much credit to myfelf,
and to the entire fatisfaction of fuch of my
neighbours in that quarter, as may incline
to patronize the fine arts, and reftore the
credit of this drooping country.

Your's,

GORGON.

No. XCIX.

Cuncti adsint, meritæque expectent præmia palmæ !

A CURIOUS Greek fragment has been lately difcovered by an ingenious traveller at Conftantinople, which is fuppofed to have been faved out of the famous Alexandrian library, when fet on fire by command of the Caliph. There is nothing but conjecture to guide us to the author: Some learned men, who have examined it, give it to *Paufanias*, others to *Ælian*; fome contend for *Suidas*, others for *Libanius*; but moft agree in afcribing it to fome one of the Greek fophifts, fo that it is not to be difguifed that juft doubts are to be entertained of its veracity in point of fact. There may be much ingenuity in thefe difcuffions, but we are not to expect conviction; therefore I fhall pafs to the fubject-matter, and not concern myfelf with any previous argumentation on a queftion, that is never likely to be fettled.

G 5   " This

" This fragment fays, that fome time after the death of the great dramatic poet
Æfchylus, there was a certain citizen of
Athens named *Philoteuchus*, who by his in-
duftry and fair character in trade had acquired a plentiful fortune, and came in time
to be actually chofen one of the Areopa-
gites : This man in an advanced period of
his life engaged in a very fplendid undertaking for collecting a feries of pictures to
be compofed from fcenes in the tragedies of
the great poet above-mentioned, and to be
executed by the Athenian artifts, who were
then both numerous and eminent.

" The old Areopagite, with a fpirit that
would have done honour to *Pififtratus* or
Pericles, conftructed a fpacious lyceum for
the reception of thefe pictures, which he
laid open to the refort both of citizens and
ftrangers, and the fuccefs of the work reflected equal credit upon the undertaker and
the artifts, whom he employed.

The chain of the narration is here broken
by a lofs of a part of the fragment, which
however is fortunately refumed in that place,
where the writer gives fome account of the
mafters, who painted for this collection, and
of

of the scenes they made choice of for their several pictures.

" He tells us that *Apelles* was then living and in the vigour of his genius, though advanced in years; he describes the scene chosen for his composition minutely, and it appears to have been taken from that suite of dramas, which we know *Æschylus* composed from the story of the *Atridæ*, and of which we have still such valuable remains. He represents *Ægisthus*, after the murder of *Agamemnon* by the instigation of *Clytemnestra*, in the act of consulting certain Sybils, who by their magical spells and incantations have raised the ghost of *Agamemnon*, which is attended by a train of phantoms, emblematic of eight successive kings of Argos, his immediate descendants : The spectre is made *pointing* to his posterity, and at the same time looking on his murderer with a smile, in which *Apelles* contrived to give the several expressions of contempt, exultation and revenge, with such a character of ghastly pain and horror, as to make the beholders shrink.   Amongst these Sybils he introduces the person of *Cassandra* the prophetess, whom *Agamemnon* brought captive from the deftruction of Troy. The light, he fays, proceeds only from a flaming cauldron, in which the Sybils have been making their libations to the infernal deities or furies, and he fpeaks of the reflected, ruddy tints, which by this management of the artift were caft upon the figures, as producing a wonderful effect, and giving an amazing horror and magnificence to the group. Upon the whole he ftates it as the moft capital performance of the mafter, and that he got fuch univerfal honour thereby, that he was afterwards employed to paint for the Perfian monarch, and had a commiffion even from the queen of Scythia, a country then emerging from barbarity.

" *Parrhafius*, though born in the colony of Miletus on the coaft of Afia, was an adopted citizen of Athens, and in great credit there for his celebrated picture on the death of *Epaminondas :* He contributed to this collection by a very capital compofition taken from a tragedy, which was the third in a feries of dramas, founded by *Æfchylus* on the well-known ftory of *Oedipus*, all which are loft. The miferable monarch, whofe misfortunes had overturned his reafon, is
here

here depicted taking shelter under a wretched hovel in the midst of a tremendous
storm, where the elements seem conspiring
against a helpless being in the last stage of
human misery.   The painter has thrown a
very touching character of insanity into his
features, which plainly indicates that his loss
of reason has arisen from the tender rather
than the inflammatory passions; for there is
a majestic sensibility mixed with the wildness
of his distraction, which still preserves the
traces of the once benevolent monarch.   In
this desolate scene he has a few forlorn companions in his distress, which form a very
peculiar group of personages; for they con-
sist of a venerable old man in a very piteous
condition, whose eyes have been torn from
their sockets, together with a naked maniac,
who is starting from the hovel, where he had
housed himself during the tempest: The
effect of this figure is described with rapture, for he is drawn in the prime of youth,
beautiful and of a most noble air; his naked
limbs display the finest proportions of the
human figure, and the muscular exertion
of the sudden action he is thrown into furnish ample scope to the anatomical science

of

of the artiſt. The fable feigns him to be the
ſon of the blind old man above defcribed,
and the fragment relates that his phrenfy
being not real but affumed, *Parrhafius* availed himſelf of that circumſtance, and touched the character of his madneſs with fo nice
and delicate a difcrimination from that of
Oedipus, that an attentive obferver might
have difcovered it to be counterfeited even
without the clue of the ftory. There are
two other attendant characters in the group :
One of thefe is a rough, hardy veteran, who
feems to brave the ftorm with a certain air
of contemptuous petulance in his countenance, that befpeaks a mind fuperior to fortune, and indignant under the vifitation even
of the gods themfelves. The other is a character, that feems to have been a kind of imaginary creature of the poet, and is a buffoon
or jefter upon the model of Homer's Ther-
fites, and was employed by *Æfchylus* in his
drama upon the old burlefque fyftem of the
Satyrs, as an occafional chorus or parody
upon the feverer and more tragic characters
of the piece.

" The next picture in our author's cata-
logue was by the hand of *Timanthes :* This
modeſt

modeſt painter, though reſiding in the capital of *Attica*, lived in ſuch retirement from
ſociety, and was ſo abſolutly devoted to his
art, that even his perſon was ſcarce known
to his competitors. Envy never drew a
word from his lips to the diſparagement of a
contemporary, and emulation could hardly
provoke his diffidence into a conteſt for
fame, which ſo many bolder rivals were prepared to diſpute.

" *Æſchylus*, it is well known, wrote three
plays on the fable of *Prometheus*; the ſecond
in this ſeries is the *Prometheus chained*, which
happily ſurvives; the laſt was *Prometheus
delivered*, and from the opening ſcene of
this drama *Timanthes* formed his picture.
Prometheus is here diſcovered on the ſea-ſhore
upon an iſland inhabited only by himſelf
and his daughter, a young virgin of exquiſite beauty, who is ſuppoſed to have ſeen
none other of the human ſpecies but her
father, beſides certain imaginary beings,
whom *Prometheus* had either created by his
ſtolen fire, or whom he employed in the capacity of familiars for the pupoſes of his
enchantments, for the poet very juſtifiably
ſuppoſes him endowed with ſupernatural
powers,

powers, and by that vehicle brings to pafs all the beautiful and furprifing incidents of his drama. One of thefe aërial fpirits had by his command conjured up a moft dreadful tempeft, in which a noble fhip is reprefented as finking in the midft of the breakers on this enchanted fhore. The daughter of *Prometheus* is feen in a fupplicating attitude imploring her father to *allay* the ftorm, and fave the finking mariners from deftrudtion. In the back ground of the pidture is a cavern, and at the entrance of it a misfhapen favage being, whofe evil nature is depidted in the deformity of his perfon and features, and who was employed by *Prometheus* in all fervile offices, neceffary for his accommodation in this folitude. The aërial fpirit is in the clouds, which he is driving before him at the *beheft* of his great mafter. In this compofition therefore, although not replete with charadters, there is yet fuch diverfity of ftile and fubjedt, that we have all, which the majefty and beauty of real nature can furnifh, with beings out of the regions of nature, as ftrongly contrafted in form and charadter, as fancy can devife: The fcenery alfo is of the fublimeft caft, and

and whilst all Greece refounded with applaufes upon the exhibition of this picture, *Timanthes* alone was filent, and ftartled at the very echo of his own fame, fhrunk back again to his retirement."

As this fragment is now in the hands of an ingenious tranflator, I forbear for the prefent to intrude upon his work by any further anticipation of it, confcious withal as I am that the public curiofity will fhortly be gratified with a much more full and fatisfactory delineation of this interefting narrative, than I am able to give.

No. C.

Magnum iter ad doctas proficifci cogor Athenas.
(PROPERT.)

I WAS agreeably furprized the other day with an unexpected vifit from a country friend, who once made a confiderable figure in the fafhionable world, and, with an elegant tafte for the fine arts, is poffeft of many valuable paintings and fculptures of his own collecting

collecting in Italy: He told me, that after
fix years abfence from town, he had made
a journey purpofely to regale his curiofity for
a few days with the fpectacles of this great
capital, and defired I would accompany him
on his morning's tour to fome of the eminent artifts, and afterwards conduct him to
. the theatre, where he had fecured himfelf
a feat for the reprefentation of Mr. South-
ern's tragedy of *The Fatal Marriage.*
Though I had juft been honoured with a
card from Vaneffa, purporting that fhe
would hold *The Feaft of Reafon* that evening
at her houfe, where my company was expected, I did not hefitate to accept the in-
vitation of my country friend, and excufe
myfelf from that of Vaneffa, though I muft
confefs my curiofity was fomewhat roufed
by the novelty of the entertainment to which
I was bidden.   Our day paffed fo entirely
to the fatisfaction of my candid companion,
that, when we parted at night, he fhook me by .
the hand, and with a fmile of complacency,
declared, that a day fo fpent would not difgrace the diary of Pericles.

When I had returned to my apartment,
this allufion of my friend to the age of Pericles,

ricles, with the recollection of what had paffed in the day, threw me into a reverie, in the courfe of which I fell afleep, whilft my mind with more diftinctnefs than is ufual in dreaming, purfued its waking train of thought after the following manner:

"I found myfelf in a ftately portico, which being on an eminence, gave me the profpect of a city, inclofing a prodigious circuit, with groves, gardens, and fields, feemingly fet apart for martial exercifes and fports; the houfes were not cluftered into ftreets and alleys like our great trading towns, but were placed apart and feparated without any regular order, as if each man had therein confulted his own particular tafte and enjoyments. I thought I never faw fo delightful a place, nor a people who lived fo much at their eafe: I felt a frefhnefs and falubrity in the climate, that feemed to clear the brain, and give a fpring to the fpirits and whole animal frame: The fun was bright and glowing, but the lightnefs of the atmofphere and a refrefhing breeze qualified the heat in the moft delicious manner. As I looked about me with wonder and delight, I obferved a great many edifices of the pureft pureſt architecture, that ſeemed calculated for public purpoſes; and wherever my eye went, it was encountered by a variety of ſtatues in braſs or marble; immediately at the foot of the ſteps, leading to the portico, in which I ſtood, I obſerved a figure in braſs of exquiſite workmanſhip, which by its attributes I believed deſigned to repreſent the heathen deity Mercurius. In the center of the city there was an edifice incloſed within walls, which I took to be the citadel; a rapid ſtream of clear water meandered about the place, and was trained through groves and gardens in the moſt picturefque and pleaſing manner, while the proſpect at diſtance was bounded by the ſea.

" As I ſtood wrapt in contemplation of this new and brilliant ſcenery, methought I was accoſted by a middle-aged man in a looſe garment of fine purple, who wore his hair after the manner of our ladies, braided and coiled round upon the crown of his head with great care and delicacy to a conſiderable heighth; and (which I thought remarkable) he had faſtened the braids in ſeveral places with golden pins, on which were ſeveral figures of ſmall graſhoppers of

the

the fame metal; behind him walked a fer-
vant-youth, or flave, carrying a light wicker
chair for his mafter to repofe in, a cuftom
that feemed to me to argue great effemi-
nacy; and looking about me I found it was
pretty univerfal, many of the bettermoft
fort of citizens being feated in the ftreets,
converfing at their eafe, though there was
certainly nothing in the climate, that made
fuch an indulgence neceffary.

"As I was eyeing this gentleman with a
furprize, that I muft own had fome fmall tinc-
ture of contempt in it, he turned himfelf to
me, and in the moft complaifant manner
imaginable accofted me in my own language,
telling me, he perceived I was a ftranger in
Athens, and if I was curious to fee what was
remarkable in the place, he was ready to dedicate the day to my fervice. To this courteous addrefs I returned the beft anfwer I
was able, adding that every thing was new
to me and many things appeared admirable.
You will fay fo, replied he, before the day
is paft, and yet I cannot fhew you in the
fpace of a day the hundredth part of what
this city contains worth a ftranger's obfervation: Of a certain Arts and Sciences are

now carried to their utmoſt pitch, and no future-age I think will ſucceed, in which the glory of the Athenian commonwealth, and the genius of its citizens ſhall be found ſuperior to their preſent luſtre.

· " The portico, in which you ſtand, conti-nued the Athenian, is what we call *Pœcile*, or the *painted Portico*; the brazen ſtatue at the foot of the ſteps was raiſed by the nine Archons in honour of *Mercurius Agoræus*, or the *Forenſal*; and dedicated by them to the tribes: That by its ſide is the ſtatue of Solon, the other at ſome diſtance is the law-giver Lycurgus. The gate before you, on which you ſee thoſe warlike trophies, was ſo adorned in memory of the defeat of Pliſtar-chus, who was brother of the famous Caſ-ſander, and commanded his cavalry and auxi-liary troops in the action recorded. Theſe paintings behind you, with which the portico is furniſhed and from which it has its name, are all upon public ſubjects in commemora-tion of wiſe or valiant citizens: The pictures on your right hand are by the celebrated Polygnotus, theſe on your left by Micon, equal to his rival in art, but not in munifi-cence; for Polygnotus would accept no other

reward

reward for his works, than the fame infeparable from fuch eminent performances;
Micon on the contrary was paid by the ftate.
There are feveral others by the hands of our
great mafters, particularly that incomparable piece, which reprefents the field of
Marathon, a compofition by the great Panænus, brother of the ftatuary Phidias; but
this, as well as the others, will demand a
more particular defcription.

" Examine this compofition on your right;
it is the work of Polygnotus: you fee two
armies drawn up front to front and on the
point of engaging; thefe are the Athenians,
the adverfe troops are the Lacedemonians;
the fcene is Œnoe; fuch is the contrivance
of the artift, that you are fure victory is to
declare for the Athenians, though the battle
is not yet commenced.

" In the oppofite piece you fee the battle
of Thefeus with the Amazons; a capital
compofition by Micon; thefe warlike ladies are fighting on horfeback; with what
wonderful art has the mafter expreffed the
character of athletic beauty without deviat-
ing into vulgarity and groffnefs! If you recollect the Lyfiftrata of Ariftophanes you
will

will meet an elogium on this picture; it is thus the sister arts encourage and support each other.

" Now turn to Polygnotus's side and look at that magnificent piece of art : The painter has chosen for the subject of his composition the council of the Grecian chiefs upon the violence done to Cassandra by Ajax after the capture of Troy; you see the brutal character of the man strongly expressed in the hero of the piece; amongst that group of Trojan captives Cassandra is conspicuous; that figure which represents Laodice, is worth your notice, as being a portrait of Elpinice a celebrated courtesan: Scrupulous people have taken offence at it, but great painters will indulge themselves in these liberties, and are fond of painting after beautiful nature; of which I could give you innumerable examples.

" Now let us in the last place regale our eyes with this inestimable battle of Marathon by Panænus: What think you of it? Was it not a reward worthy of the heroes, who preserved their country on that glorious day? Which party is most honoured by the work, the master who wrought it, or the

valiant

valiant perfonages who are recorded by it?
It is a queftion difficult to decide. You
will obferve three different groups in this
fuperb compofition, defcribing three different periods of the action: Here you fee the
Athenians and their allies the Platæans juft
commencing the action.—There, further
removed in perfpective, the barbarians
are defeated; the flaughter is raging, and
the Medes are plunging defperately into the
marfhy lake to avoid their purfuers; examine the back ground, and you fee the
Phœnician gallies; the barbarians are making a bold attack, and the fea is covered
with wrecks: All mouths are open in applaufe of this picture, and it was but the
other day, that the great orator Demof-
thenes referred to it in a folemn harangue
upon Neæra, as did Efchines in his pleadings againft Ctefiphon. All our Captains
are taken from the life; that General who
is encouraging his troops is Miltiades; he
is the hero of the piece, and I can affure
you the refemblance is in all points exact:
This is the portrait of Callimachus the
Polemarck: There you fee the hero Echet-
lus, and this is the brave Epizelus; that

Athenian, who is valiantly fighting, is Cynœgirus himfelf, who loft both his hands in the action; there goes an extraordinary ftory with that dog which is by his fide, and has feized the dying barbarian by the throat; the faithful creature would not forfake his mafter; he was killed in the action, and is now defervedly immortalized in company with the illuftrious heroes, who are the fubject of the piece. Thofe fplendid warriors in the army of the Medes, who are ftanding in their chariots, and calling to their troops, are the generals Datis and Artaphanes. They are drawn in a proud and fwelling ftile, and feem of a larger fize and proportion than our Athenian champions; and the fact is, that this group was inferted by another mafter; they are by the hand of Micon, and perhaps do not exactly harmonize with the reft; the filly Athenians were piqued at their appearance, and in a fit of jealoufy punifhed Micon by a fine for having painted them too flatteringly; the painter fuffered in his pocket, but the people in my opinion were difgraced by the fentence: This circumftance has given occafion for many on the part of Micon to

conteft

conteft the honour of the painting with
Panænus, who in juftice muft be confidered
as principal author of the work; and in
courfe of time it may happen, that pofterity will be puzzled which mafter to afcribe
it to.

"There are many more pictures well
deferving your attentive notice, particularly
that by Pamphilus, which reprefents Alc-
mena with Heraclidæ afking aid of the
Athenians againft Euryftheus: and this infpired old figure by Polygnotus with a lyre
in his hand, which is the portrait of no lefs a
perfon than the great Sophocles;—but come,
let us be gone, for we have much befides to
fee; and I perceive Zeno coming this way
with his fcholars to hold his lectures in this
portico; and I for one muft confefs I am
no friend to the Stoics, or as we call them
the Zenonians.

No. CI.

Ad vetuſtiſſimam et ſapientiſſimam et diis cariſſi-
mam en communem amaſiam, hominumque ac
Deorum terram, Athenas mittebaris.

(Libanius in Oratione.)

" From the painted portico, in which my
laſt was dated, my Athenian conductor took me to the Ptolemaic Gymnaſium,
in which I obſerved ſeveral ſtatues of Mer-
cury in marble, and others of braſs, which
he explained to me to be of Ptolemy the
founder, Juba and Chryſippus the philoſo-
pher. There was one of Beroſus the aſtro-
loger with a tongue of pure gold, in com-
memoration of his divine predictions : On
one hand of me ſtood the doric temple of
Theſeus, enriched with ſome ineſtimable
paintings of Micon, particularly one upon
the ſubject of the fight of the Lapithæ and
Centaurs : on the other hand was the antient
temple of the Dioſcuri, in which I was
ſhewn many capital pictures by Polygnotus ;
it is here, ſays my conductor, we adminiſter

to

to the Athenian youth that folemn oath,. which binds them not to defert their ranks in action, but to perifh, when neceffity fo requires, in defence of their country; the form is rather long, fays he, but this is the fubftance of the oath. The Prytaneum, or Court-houfe, was now in view, where the magiftracy of the city affemble for the dif-patch of public bufinefs: Here I faw the venerable laws of Solon in a cheft of ftone, the ftatues of Pax and Vefta, and (which were more interefting to me) the figures of Miltiades and Themiftocles of exquifite workmanfhip in pure marble; in this place all thofe citizens, and the pofterity of thofe who have deferved well of the ftate, receive their public doles or allowance of bread in cakes compofed of meal, oil, and water; here alfo I faw the perpetual fire upon the altar of Vefta, and the celebrated image of the Bona Fortuna of the Athenians. In the adjoining temple of Lucina I was fhewn the famous ftatues of that deity clothed in drapery to the feet: My guide now carried me to the great temple of Olympian Jupi-ter, founded by the tyrant Pififtratus, and perfected by his fons and fucceffors. I ob-

H 3

ferved to my conductor, that I had feen no
temple in Athens, except this, with interior columns; he informed me that the
great fpan of the roof made it neceffary in
this inftance, but that it was contrary to
their rule of architecture and obtained in
no other: He further told me, that the city
had expended ten thoufand talents in this
edifice: The image of the god was cut in
ivory and gold; to every column was affixed
a brazen ftatue, reprefenting the colonial
cities of the Athenian empire. The difplay of ftatuary exceeded all defcription or
belief, nor was the painter's art wanting in
its fhare of the decoration; for wherever
pictures could be difpofed, and particularly
about the pedeftal of the ftatue of Jupiter, the moft capital paintings were to be
feen.

" My fight was now fo dazzled with the
difplay of brilliant images, and my mind fo
overpowered with the miracles of art, which
had paffed in review, that I befeeched my
guide to carry me either to fome of thofe
groves which were in my eye, where I could
meditate on what I had feen, or to fpectacles of any other fort according to his
choice

choice and difcretion, for otherwife I fhould apprehend, from the variety of objects, I fhould retain the memory of none.   He told me in reply, that this was his intention, obferving that the proportion I had feen was very fmall indeed to what the city contained; there was however one more ftatue, which he could not difpenfe with himfelf from fhewing me, being a model of beauty and perfection; and having fo faid methought he took me into a neighbouring garden, and in a grove of cyprefs and myrtle prefented to my view the moft exquifite piece of fculpture I had ever beheld.——This, fays he, is the Venus' called Celeftial, the workmanfhip of the immortal Alcamen.——After I had contemplated this divine original with aftonifhment and rapture, I was fatisfied within myfelf, that we are miftaken in fuppofing it has defcended to us, and I now acknowledge that our celeftial Venus is a copy far inferior to its inimitable prototype.   Having examined this ftatue for fome time, I turned to my conductor and faid:——Let us gratify our fenfes in fome other way; I have feen enough of art.

" It is impoffible to avoid it, replies he,

in

in this city, and fo faying led me into the
Lyceum; this Gymnafium, fays he, has
been lately inftituted by Pericles, and thefe
plantations of plane-trees are of his making;
fo are thefe aqueducts; the Lyceum was
originally dedicated to Paftoral Apollo;
and owes its foundation and beauty in the
firft inftance to the elegant Pififtratus, who
from the furprifing refemblance of their
perfons we now call the elder Pericles. The
place is delightful, and before you leave it
take notice of this ftatue of Apollo; the artift
has defcribed him in the attitude of refting
after his daily courfe; you fee he leans
againft a column; his right arm bent over
his head, and in his left he holds his
bow; it is a firft-rate piece of fculpture.
Leaving the Lyceum my conductor took
me by the way of the Tripods; here he
fhewed me the inimitable fatyr in brafs,
the boafted mafter-piece of Praxiteles, and
the Cupid and Bacchus of Thymilus; we
were now clofe by the theatre, in the portico of which I was fhewn the ftatue of
Efchylus, and two pedeftals for the ftatues
of Sophocles and Euripides, then under the
artifts hands, although both thofe poets were

now

now living: The doors of the theatre were not yet opened, and the temple of Venus being near at hand, methought we entered, and I beheld the beautiful Cupid crowned with roses, painted by Zeuxis; from hence I could see the works that Pericles had been carrying on upon the citadel, but this we did not enter.

" Methought I was now carried into the theatre amidst a prodigious crowd of people; the comedy of the night was intitled *The Clouds*, and the famous Ariftophanes was announced to be the author of it. It was expected that Socrates would be perfonally attacked, and a great party of that philofopher's enemies were affembled to fupport the poet. I was much furprized, when my companion pointed out to me that great philofopher in perfon, who had actually taken his feat in the theatre, and was fitting between Alcibiades and Antipho the fon of Pericles; by the fide of Alcibiades fate Euripides, and at Antipho's left hand fate Thucydides; I never beheld two more venerable old men than the poet and the hiftorian, nor fuch comely perfons as Alcibiades and Antipho: Socrates was exceedingly like

the

the bufts we have of him, his head was bald, his beard bufhy, and his ftature low; there was fomething very deterring in his countenance; his perfon was mean and his habit fqualid; his veft was of loofe drapery, thrown over his left fhoulder after the fafhion of a Spanifh Capa, and feemed to be of coarfe cloth, made of black wool undyed; he had a fhort ftaff in his hand of knotted wood with a round head, which he was continually rubbing in the palm of his hand, as he talked with Alcibiades, to whom he principally addreffed his difcourfe: Thucydides had lately returned from exile upon a general amnefty, and I obferved a melancholy in his countenance mixed with indignation; Euripides feemed employed in examining the countenances of the fpectators, whilft Antipho with great modefty paid a moft refpectful attention to the venerable philofopher on his right hand. Whilft I was engaged in obferving this refpectable groupe, my conductor whifpered the following words in my ear—*This is the fecond attack from the fame hands upon Socrates; that of laft year was defeated by Alcibiades; but if this night's comedy fucceeds, I predict that our philofopher*

is

*is undone : and in truth his school is much out
of credit ; for some of the worst characters of
the age have come out of his hands of late.*

" When the players came first on the stage
there was so great a murmur in the theatre,
that I could scarce hear them ; after a short
time however the silence became pretty general, and the plot of the play, such as it
was, began to open. I perceived that the
poet had devised the character of an old
clownish father, who being plunged in debt
by the extravagancies of a flanting wife
and a spendthrift son, who wasted his fortune
upon race-horses, was for ever puzzling his
brains to strike upon some expedient for
cheating his creditors. With this view he
goes to the house of Socrates to take coun-
sel of that philosopher, who gives him a
great many ridiculous instructions, seem-
ingly not at all to the purpose, and amongst
other extravagancies assures him that Jupiter has no concern in the government
of the world, but that all the functions of
providence are performed by *The Clouds*,
which upon his invocation appear and perform the part of a chorus throughout the
play : The philosopher is continually foiled

H 6   by

by the ruftic wit of the old father, who, after being put in Socrates's truckle-bed and
miferably ftung with vermin, has a meeting
with his creditors, and endeavours to parry
their demands with a parcel of pedantic
quibbles, which he has learnt of the philofopher, and which give occafion to fcenes
of admirable comic humour : My conductor informed me this incident was pointed
at Efchines, a favorite difciple of Socrates ;
a man, fays he, plunged in debts and a moft
notorious defrauder of his creditors.   In the
end the father brings his fon to be inftruct-
ed by Socrates; the fon, after a fhort lecture, comes forth a perfect Atheift, and gives
his father a fevere cudgelling on the ftage,
which irreverend act he undertakes to defend upon the principles of the new philofophy he had been learning.   This was the
fubftance of the play, in the courfe of which
there were many grofs allufions to the unnatural vice of which Socrates was accufed,
and many perfonal ftrokes againft Clifthenes,
Pericles, Euripides, and others, which told
ftrongly, and were much applauded by the
theatre.

    " It is not to be fuppofed, that all this
paffed

paffed without fome occafional difguft on the part of the fpectators, but it was evident there was a party in the theatre, which carried it through, notwithftanding the prefence of Socrates and the refpectable junto that attended him: For my part I fcarce ever took my eyes from him during the reprefentation, and I obferved two or three little actions, which feemed to give me fome infight into the temper of his mind, during the fevereft libel that was ever exhibited againft any man's perfon and principles.

" Before Socrates appears on the ftage, the old man raps violently at his door, and is reproved by one of his difciples, who comes out and complains of the difturbance; upon his being queftioned what the philofopher may be then employed upon, he anfwers that he is engaged in meafuring the leap of a flea, to decide how many of its own lengths it fprings at one hop; the difciple alfo informs him with great folemnity, that Socrates has difcovered that the hum of a gnat is not made by the mouth of the animal, but from behind: This raifed a laugh at the expence of the naturalifts and minute philofophers,

philofophers, and I obferved that Socrates himfelf fmiled at the conceit.

- " When the fchool was opened to the ftage, and all his fcholars were difcovered with their heads upon the floor and their pofteriors mounted in the air, and turned towards the audience, though the poet pretends to account for it, as if they were fearching for natural curiofities on the furface of the ground, the action was evidently intended to convey the groffeft allufion, and was fo received by the audience: When this fcene was produced, I remarked that Socrates fhook his head, and turned his eyes off the ftage; whilft Euripides, with fome indignation, threw the fleeve of his mantle over his face; this was obferved by the fpectators, and produced a confiderable tumult, in which the theatre feemed pretty fairly divided, fo that the actors ftood upright, and quitted the pofture they were difcovered in.

" When Socrates was firft produced ftanding on a bafket mounted into the clouds, the perfon of the actor and the mafk he wore, as well as the garment he was dreffed in, was the moft direct counterpart of the philofopher

fopher himfelf that could be devifed. But
when the actor, fpeaking in his character,
in direct terms proceeded to deny the divi-
nity of Jupiter, Socrates laid his hand upon
his heart, and caft his eyes up with aftonifhment; in the fame moment Alcibiades
ftarted from his feat, and in a loud voice
cried out—*Anthenians! is this fitting?* Upon
this a great tumult arofe, and very many of
the fpectators called upon Socrates to fpeak
for himfelf, and anfwer to the charge; when
the play could not proceed for the noife and
clamour of the people, all demanding Socrates to fpeak for himfelf, the philofopher
unwillingly ftept forward and faid—*You re-*
quire of me, O Athenians, to anfwer to the
charge; there is no charge; neither is this a
place to difcourfe in about the gods: Let the
actor proceed!—Silence immediately took
place, and Socrates's invocation to *The*
Clouds foon enfued; the paffage was fo
beautiful, the machinery of the clouds fo
finely introduced, and the chorus of
voices in the air fo exquifitely conceived,
that the whole theatre was in raptures, and
the poet from that moment had entire poffeffion of their minds, fo that the piece was
                                    carried

carried triumphantly to its period. In the heat of the applause my Athenian friend whispered me in the ear and said—*Depend upon it, Socrates will hear of this in another place; he is a lost man; and remember I tell you, that if all our philosophers and sophists were driven out of Attica, it would be happy for Athens."*—At these words I started and awaked from my dream.

No. CII.

Natio comœda est.

I F the present taste for private plays spreads as fast as most fashions do in this country, we may expect the rising generation will be, like the Greeks in my motto, one entire nation of actors and actresses. A father of a family may shortly reckon it amongst the blessings of a numerous progeny, that he is provided with a sufficient company for his domestic stage, and may cast a play to his own liking without going abroad for his theatrical amusements. Such a steady

a steady troop cannot fail of being under
better regulation than a set of strollers, or
than any set whatever, who make acting a
vocation : Where a manager has to deal with
none but players of his own begetting, every
play bids fair to have a strong cast, and in
the phrase of the stage to be well got up.
Happy author, who shall see his characters
thus grouped into a family-piece, firm as the
Theban band of friends, where all is zeal
and concord ; no bickerings nor jealousies
about stage-precedency; no ladies to fall sick
of the spleen, and toss up their parts in a
huff; no heart-burnings about flounced pet-
ticoats and silver trimmings, where the mother of the whole company stands ward-
robe-keeper and property-woman, whilst the
father takes post at the side scene in the capacity of prompter, with plenipotentiary
controul over PS's and OP's.

I will no longer speak of the difficulty of
writing a comedy or tragedy, because that is
now done by so many people without any
difficulty at all, that if there ever was any
mystery in it, that mystery is thoroughly
bottomed and laid open ; but the art of
acting was till very lately thought so rare
and

and wonderful an excellence, that people began to look upon a perfect actor as a phenomenon in the world, which they were not to expect above once in a century; but now that the trade is laid open, this prodigy is to be met at the turn of every street; the nobility and gentry, to their immortal honour, have broken up the monopoly and new-made players are now as plentiful as new-made peers.

Nec tamen Antiochus, necnerit mirabilis illic
Aut Stratocles aut cum molli Demetrius Hæmo.

Garrick and Powell would be now no wonder,
Nor Barry's silver note, nor Quin's heroic thunder.

Though the public professors of the art are so completely put down by the private practitioners of it, it is but justice to observe in mitigation of their defeat, that they meet the comparison under some disadvantages, which their rivals have not to contend with.

One of these is diffidence, which volunteers cannot be supposed to feel in the degree they do who are pressed into the service: I never yet saw a public actor come

upon

upon the ftage on the firft night of a new
play, who did not feem to be nearly, if not
quite, in as great a fhaking fit as his author;
but as there can be no luxury in a great
fright, I cannot believe that people of fafhion,
who act for their amufement only, would
fubject themfelves to it; they muft certainly have a proper confidence in their own
abilities, or they would never ftep out of a
drawing-room, where they are fure to figure,
upon a ftage where they run the rifque of
expofing themfelves; fome gentlemen perhaps, who have been *mutæ perfonæ* in the
fenate, may ftart at the firft found of their
own voices in a theatre, but graceful action,
juft elocution, perfect knowledge of their
author, elegant deportment, and every advantage that refined manners and courtly
addrefs can beftow, is exclufively their own:
In all fcenes of high life they are at home;
noble fentiments are natural to them; love-
parts they can play by inftinct, and as for all
the cafts of rakes, gamefters, and fine-gen-
tlemen, they can fill them to the life. Think
only what a violence it muft be to the
nerves of an humble unpretending actor, to
be obliged to play the gallant gay feducer,

and

and be the cuckold-maker of the comedy, when he has no other object at heart but to go quietly home, when the play is over, to his wife and children, and participate with them in the honeſt earnings of his vocation; can ſuch a man compete with the Lothario of high life?

And now I mention the cares of a family, I ſtrike upon another diſadvantage, which the public performer is ſubject to and the private exempt from: The Andromache of the ſtage may have an infant Hector at home, whom ſhe more tenderly feels for than the Hector of the ſcene; he may be ſick, he may be ſupperleſs; there may be none to nurſe him, when his mother is out of ſight, and the maternal intereſt in the divided heart of the actreſs may preponderate over the heroine's: This is a caſe not within the chances to happen to any lady-actreſs, who of courſe conſigns the taſk of education to other hands, and keeps her own at leiſure for more preſſing duties.

Public performers have their memories loaded and diſtracted with a variety of parts, and oftentimes are compelled to ſuch a repetition of the ſame part, as cannot fail to

quench

quench the fpirit of the reprefentation; they muft obey the call of duty, be the caft of the character what it may—

————*Cum Thaida fuftinet, aut cum*
Uxorem comœdus agit.

Subject to all the various cafts of life,
Now the loofe harlot, now the virtuous wife.

But, what is worfe than all, the veterans of the public ftage will fometimes be appointed to play the old and ugly, as I can inftance in the perfon of a moft admirable actrefs, whom I have often feen, and never without the tribute of applaufe, in the cafts of *Juliet's Nurfe*, *Aunt Deborah*, and other venerable damfels in the vale of years, when I am confident there is not a lady of independent rank in England of *Mrs. Pitt's* age, who would not rather ftruggle for *Mifs Jenny* or *Mifs Hoyden*, than ftoop to be the reprefentative of fuch old hags.

These, and the fubjection public performers are under to the caprice of the fpectators, and to the attacks of conceited and misjudging critics, are amongft the many difagreeable circumftances which the moft

eminent

eminent muſt expect, and the moſt fortunate cannot eſcape.

It would be hard indeed if performers of diſtinction, who uſe the ſtage only as an elegant and moral reſource, ſhould be ſub-ject to any of theſe unpleaſant conditions; and yet as a friend to the riſing fame of the domeſtic drama I muſt obſerve, that there are ſome precautions neceſſary, which it's patrons have not yet attended to. There are ſo many conſequences to be guarded againſt, as well as proviſions to be made for an eſtabliſhment of this ſort, that it be-hoves it's conductors to take their firſt ground with great judgment; and above all things to be very careful that an exhibition ſo ennobled by it's actors, may be caſt into ſuch a ſtile and character, as may keep it clear from any poſſible compariſon with ſpectacles, which it ſhould not condeſcend to imitate, and cannot hope to equal. This I believe has not been attempted, perhaps not even reflected upon, and yet, if I may ſpeak from information of ſpecimens which I have not been preſent at, there are many reforms needful both in it's external as well as internal arrangement.

By

By external I mean spectacle, comprehending theatre, stage, scenery, orchestra, and all things else which fall within the province of the *arbiter deliciarum :* These should be planned upon a model new, original and peculiar to themselves ; so industriously distinguished from our public play-houses, that they should not strike the eye, as now they do, like a copy in miniature, but as the independant sketch of a master who disdains to copy. I can call to mind many noble halls and stately apartments in the great houses and castles of our nobility, which would give an artist ample field for fancy, and which with proper help would be disposed into new and striking shapes for such a scene of action, as should become the dignity of the performers. Halls and saloons, flanked with interior columns and surrounded by galleries, would, with the aid of proper draperies or scenery in the intercolumnations, take a rich and elegant appearance, and at the same time the music might be so disposed in the gallery, as to produce a most animating effect. A very small elevation of stage should be allowed of, and no contraction by side scenes to huddle the speakers together

together and embarrass their deportment;
no shift of scene whatever, and no curtain
to draw up and drop, as if puppets were to
play behind it; the area, appropriated to the
performers, should be so dressed and fur-
nished with all suitable accommodations, as
to afford every possible opportunity to the
performers of varying their actions and pos-
tures, whether of sitting, walking or standing, as their situations in the scene, or their
interest in the dialogue may dictate; so as
to familiarize and assimilate their whole conduct and conversation through the progress
of the drama, to the manners and habits of
well-bred persons in real life.

Prologues and epilogues in the modern
stile of writing and speaking them I regard
as very unbecoming, and I should blush to
see any lady of fashion in that silly and un-
seemly situation : They are the last remaining corruptions of the antient drama; reliques of servility, and only are retained in
our London theatres as vehicles of humili-
ation at the introduction of a new play, and
traps for false wit, extravagant conceits and
female flippancy at the conclusion of it :
Where authors are petitioners, and players

H   servants

fervants to the public thefe condefcenfions muft be made, but where poets are not fui-tors, and performers are benefactors, why fhould the free Mufe wear fhackles? for fuch they are, though the fingers of the brave are employed to put them on the limbs of the fair.

As I am fatisfied nothing ought to be ad-mitted from beginning to end, which can provoke comparifons, I revolt with indigna-tion from the idea of a lady of fafhion being trammelled in the trickery of the ftage, and taught her airs and graces, till fhe is made the mere *fac-fimile* of a mannerift, where the moft fhe can afpire to is to be the copy of a copyift: Let none fuch be confulted in dref-fing or drilling an honorary novitiate in the forms and fafhions of the public ftage; it is a courfe of difcipline, which neither perfon will profit by; a kind of barter, in which both parties will give and receive falfe airs and falfe conceits; the fine lady will be dif-qualified by copying the actrefs, and the actrefs will become ridiculous by apeing the fine lady.

As for the choice of the drama, which is fo nice and difficult a part of the bufinefs,

I fcarce

I fcarce believe there is one play upon the
lift, which in all it's parts and paffages is
thoroughly adapted to fuch a caft as I am
fpeaking of: Where it has been in public
ufe I am fure it is not, for there comparifons
are unavoidable. Plays profeffedly wrote for
the ftage muft deal in ftrong charaƈter, and
ftriking contraft: How can a lady ftand forward in a part, contrived to produce ridicule
or difguft, or which is founded upon broad
humour and vulgar buffoonery?

> *Nempe ipfa videtur,*
> *Non perfona loqui.*

" 'Tis fhe herfelf, and not her mafk which fpeaks."

I doubt if it be altogether feemly for a
gentleman to undertake, unlefs he can reconcile himfelf to cry out with Laberius—

> *Eques Romanus ean e egregus ruo*
> *Domum revertam mimus.*

" Efquire I fign'd myfelf at noon,
" At night I counterfign'd Buffoon."

The drama therefore muft be purpofely
written for the occafion; and the writer
muft not only have local knowledge of every
arrangement

arrangement preparatory for the exhibition, but perſonal knowledge alſo of the performers, who are to exhibit it.   The play itſelf, in my conception of it, ſhould be part only of the projected entertainment, woven into the device of a grand and ſplendid *fête*, given in ſome noble country houſe or palace: Neither ſhould the ſpectators be totally excuſed from their ſubſcription to the general *gala*, nor left to doſe upon their benches through the progreſs of five tedious acts, but called upon at intervals by muſic, dance or refreſhment, elegantly contrived, to change the ſameneſs of the ſcene and relieve the efforts of the more active corps, employed upon the drama.

And now let me ſay one word to qualify the irony I ſet out with and acquit myſelf as a moraliſt.

There are many and great authorities againſt this ſpecies of entertainment, and certainly the danger is great, where theatrical propenſities are too much indulged in young and inexperienced minds.   Tertullian ſays, (but he is ſpeaking of a very licentious theatre) *Theatrum ſacrarium eſt Veneris* —" A playhouſe is the very ſacriſty of Ve-

" nus."

" nus." And Juvenal, who wrote in times of the groffeſt impurity, maintains that no prudent man will take any young lady to wife, who has ever been even within the walls of a theatre—

> *Cuneis an habent ſpeƈtacula totis*
> *Quod ſecurus ames, quodque inde excerpere poſſis ?*

" Look round, and ſay if any man of ſenſe
" Will dare to ſingle out a wife from hence ?"

Young women of humble rank and ſmall pretenſions ſhould be particularly cautious how a vain ambition of being noticed by their ſuperiors betrays them into an attempt at diſplaying their unprotected perſons on a ſtage, however dignified and reſpeƈtable. If they have talents, and of courſe applauſe, are their underſtandings and manners proof againſt applauſe ? If they miſtake their talents, and merit no applauſe, are they ſure they will get no contempt for their ſelf-conceit ? If they have both aƈting talents and attraƈtive charms, I tremble for their danger ; let the fooliſh parent, whoſe itching ears tingled with the plaudits, that reſounded through the theatre, where virgin mo-
deſty

defly depofited its blufhes, beware how his aching heart fhall throb with forrow, when the daughter, *quæ pudica ad theatrum accef-ferat, inde revertetur impudica. (Cyprian. ad Donatum.)*

So much by way of caution to the guardians and protectors of innocence; let the offence light where it may, I care not, fo it ferves the caufe for which my heart is pledged.

As for my opinion of private plays in general, though it is a fafhion, which hath kings and princes for it's nurfing fathers and queens and princeffes for its nurfing mothers, I think it is a fafhion, that fhould be cautioufly indulged and narrowly confined to certain ranks, ages and conditions in the community at large. Grace forbid! that what the author of my motto faid fcoffingly of the Greeks fhould be faid prophetically of this nation; emulate them in their love of freedom, in their love of fcience; rival them in the greateft of their actions, but not in the verfatility of their mimic talents, till it fhall be faid of us by fome future fatirift—

Natio comæda eft. Rides? majore cachinno
Concutitur: flet, fi lacrymas afpexit amici,

Nec

Nec dolet.   Igniculum brumæ fi tempore pofcas,
Accipit cndromidem : Si dixeris, æfluo, fudat.
Nm fumus ergo pares ; melior, qui femper et omni
Nocte dieque poteft alienum fumere vultum.

" Laugh, and your merry echo burfts his fides ;
" Weep, and his courteous tears gufh out in tides :
" Light a few fticks you cry, 'tis wintry—Lo !
" He's a furr'd Laplander from top to toe ;
" Put out the fire, for now 'tis warm—He's more,
" Hot, fultry hot, and fweats at every pore :
" Oh ! he's beyond us ; we can make no race
" With one, who night and day maintains his pace,
" And faft as you fhift humours ftill can fhift his face."

Before I clofe this paper I wifh to go
back to what I faid refpecting the propriety
of new and occafional dramas for private exhibition : Too many men are in the habit of
decrying their contemporaries, and this dif-
couraging practice feems more generally levelled at the dramatic province, than any
other ; but whilft the authors of fuch tragic
dramas as *Douglas, Elfrida* and *Caractacus,*
of fuch comic ones as *The School for Scandal,*
The Jealous Wife, The Clandeftine Marriage
and *The Way to Keep Him,* with others in
both lines, are yet amongft us, why fhould
we fuppofe the ftate of genius fo declined
as not to furnifh poets able to fupport and

to

to supply their honorary reprefentatives?
Numbers there are no doubt, unnamed and
unknown, whom the fiery trial of a public
ftage deters from breaking their obfcurity:
Let difinterefted fame be their prize and
there will be no want of competitors.

Latet anguis in herba,

There is a ferpent in the grafs, and that ferpent is the emblem of wifdom; the very
fymbol of wit upon the watch, couching for
a while under the cover of obfcurity, till the
bright rays of the fun fhall ftrike upon it,
give it life and motion to erect itfelf on end
and difplay the dazzling colours of it's bur-
nifhed fcales.

" Though thou, vile cynic, art the age's fhame,
  " Hope not to damn all living fame;
  " True wit is arm'd in fcales fo bright,
  " It dazzles thy dull owlifh fight;
  " Thy wolfifh fangs no entrance gain,
  " They gnaw, they tug, they gnafh in vain,
" Their hungry malice does but edge their pain.

" Avaunt, profane! 'tis confecrated ground:
  " Let no unholy foot be found
" Where the Arts mingle, where the Mufes haunt,
" And the Nine Sifters hymn their facred chaunt,

" Where

" Where freedom's nymph-like form appears,
" And high 'midſt the harmonious ſpheres
" Science her laurel-crowned head uprears.

" Ye moral maſters of the human heart!
" And you advance, ye ſons of Art!
" Let Fame's far-echoing trumpet ſound
" To ſummon all her candidates around;
" Then bid old Time his roll explore,
" And ſay what age preſents a ſtore
" In merit greater or in numbers more.

" Come forth, and boldly ſtrike the lyre,
" Break into ſong, poetic choir!
" Let Tragedy's loud ſtrains in thunder roll:
" With Pity's dying cadence melt the ſoul;
" And now provoke a ſprightlier lay;
" Hark! Comedy begins to play,
" She ſmites the ſtring, and Dullneſs flits away.

" For envious Dullneſs will eſſay to fling
" Her mud into the Muſe's ſpring,
" Whilſt critic curs with pricking ears
" Bark at each bard as he appears;
" Ev'n the fair dramatiſt, who ſips
" Her Helicon with modeſt lips,
" Sometimes alas! in troubled water dips.

" But ſtop not, fair one, faint not in thy taſk,
" Slip on the ſock and ſnatch the maſk,
" Poliſh thy clear reflecting glaſs,
" And catch the manners as they paſs;
" Call home thy playful Sylphs again,
" And chear them with a livelier ſtrain:
" Fame weaves no wreath that is not earn'd with pain.

" And

" And thou, whofe happy talent hit
" The richeft vein of Congreve's wit,
" Ah! fickle rover, falfe ingrateful loon,
" Did the fond eafy Mufe confent too foon,
" That thou fhould'ft quit Thalia's arms
" For an old *Begum*'s tawny charms,
" And fhake us, not with laughter, but alarms?

" Curft be ambition! Hence with mufty laws!
" Why pleads the bard but in Apollo's caufe?
" Why move the Court and humbly apprehend
" But as the Mufe's advocate and friend?
" She taught his faithful fcene to fhow
" All that man's varying paffions know,
" Gay-flafhing wit and heart-diffolving woe.

" Thou too, thrice happy in a *Jealous Wife*,
" Comic interpreter of nuptial life,
" Know that all candid hearts deteft
" Th' unmanly fcoffer's cruel jeft,
" Who for his jibes no butt could find
" But what cold palfy left behind,
" A fhaking man with an unfhaken mind.

" And ye, who teach man's lordly race,
" That woman's wit will have its place,
" Matrons and maidens who infpire
" The fcenic flute or fweep the Sapphic lyre,
" Go, warble in the fylvan feat,
" Where the Parnaffian fifters meet,
" And ftamp the rugged foil with female feet.

" 'Tis ye, who interweave the myrtle bough
" With the proud palm that crowns Britannia's brow.

I 5.   " Who,

" Who, to the age in which ye live
" It's charms, it's graces and it's glories give;
" For me, I feek no higher praife,
" But to crop one fmall fprig of bays,
" And wear it in the funfhine of your days."

No. CIII.

I DO not know a man in England better received in the circles of the great than
Jack Gaylefs : Though he has no one quality
for which he ought to be refpected, and
fome points in his character for which he
fhould be held in deteftation, yet his manners are externally fo agreeable, and his temper generally fo focial, that he makes a holiday in every family where he vifits. He lives
with the nobility upon the eafieft footing,
and in the great houfes where he is in habits of intimacy, he knows all the domef-
tics by name, and has fomething to fay to
every one of them upon his arrival : He has
a joke with the butler at the fide-board during dinner, and fets the footman a tittering
behind his chair, and is fo comical and fo
familiar—He has the beft receipt book in
England,

England, and recommends himfelf to the
cook by a new fauce, for he is in the fecrets of the King's kitchen at Verfailles :
He has the fineft breed of fpaniels in Europe, and is never without a puppy at the
command of a friend : He knows the theory
of hunting from top to bottom, is always in
with the hounds, can develop every hit in a
check, and was never known to chear a
wrong dog in a cover, when he gives his
tongue: If you want an odd horfe to match
your fet, Jack is your man; and for a neat
travelling carriage, there is not an item that
he will not fuperintend, if you are defirous
to employ him; he will be at your door with
it, when the builder brings it home, to fee
that nothing is wanting, he is fo ready and
fo obliging : No man canvaffes a county or
borough like Jack Gaylefs; he is fo pleafant with the freeholders, and has fo many
fongs and fuch facetious toafts, and fuch
a way with him amongft their wives and
daughters, that flefh and blood cannot hold
out againft him : In fhort, he is the beft
leader of a mob, and of courfe *the honeftest
fellow in England.*

A merchant's daughter of great fortune

married

married him for love; he ran away with her
from a boarding-fchool, but her father after
a time was reconciled to his fon-in-law, and
Jack, during the life of the good man, paffed his time in a fmall country houfe on
Clapham Common, fuperintending the concerns of about fix acres of ground; being
very expert however in the gardens and
grape-houfe, and a very fociable fellow over
a bottle with the citizen and his friends on
a Saturday and Sunday, he became a mighty
favourite: All this while he lived upon the
beft terms with his wife; kept her a neat
little palfrey, and regularly took his airing on
the common by her fide in the moft uxorious manner: She was in fact a moft excellent creature, of the fweeteft temper and
mildeft manners, fo that there feemed no
interruption to their happinefs, but what
arofe from her health, which was of a delicate nature. After a few years the citizen
died, and Jack, whofe conviviality had given
him a helping hand out of the world,
found himfelf in poffeffion of a very handfome fum of money upon cafting up his
affairs at his deceafe.

Jack Gaylefs having no further purpofe

to

to ferve, faw no occafion to confult appearances any longer, and began to form connexions, in which he did not think it neceffary for his wife to have a fhare. He now fet out upon the purfuit of what the world calls pleafure, and foon found himfelf in the company of thofe whom the world calls the Great. He had the addrefs to recommend himfelf to his new acquaintance, and ufed great difpatch in getting rid of his old ones; His wife was probably his greateft incumbrance on this occafion; but Jack poffeffed one art in perfection, which ftood him in great ftead; he had the civilleft way of infulting that could be imagined; and as the feelings of his wife were thofe of the fondeft fufceptibility, operating upon a weak and delicate conftitution, he fucceeded to admiration in tormenting her by neglect, at the fame time that he never gave her a harfh expreffion, and in particular, when any body elfe was prefent, behaved himfelf towards her in fo obliging a manner, that all his acquaintance fet him down as the beft tempered fellow living, and her as a lady, by his report, rather captious and querulential. When he had thus got the world on

his

his fide, he detached himfelf more and more
from her fociety, and became lefs ftudious
to difguife the infults he put upon her: She
declined faft in her health, and certain fymptoms began to appear, which convinced
Jack that a perfeverance in his fyftem would
in a fhort time lay her in the grave, and
leave him without any further moleftation.
Her habit was confumptive, for where is
the human frame that can long refift the
agony of the heart? In this extremity fhe
requefted the affiftance of a certain phyfician, very eminent in thefe cafes: This little gentleman has a way of hitting off the
complaints of his patients, which is not always fo convenient to thofe expectant parties, who have made up their minds and
reconciled themfelves to the call of nature.
As Jack had one object, and the Doctor
another, they did not entirely agree in their
procefs, and fhe was fent down by her hufband into a diftant county for the benefit
of the air, in a low fituation and a damp
houfe. Jack and the phyfician had now a
fcene of altercation, in which it was evident that the leaft man of the two had the
greateft fpirit and the largeft heart, and

3   Jack

Jack certainly put up with some expressions, which could only be passed over by perfect innocence or absolute cowardice: The little Doctor, who had no objection to send Jack out of the world, and a very longing desire to keep his lady in it, spoke like a man who had long been in the practice of holding death at defiance; but what Jack lost in argument he made up in address, and after professing his acquiescence in the measures of his antagonist, he silently determined to pursue his own, and the Doctor's departure was very soon followed by that of his patient. The dying wife made a feeble stand for a while, but what can a broken heart do against a hardened one ?

After Jack had taken such zealous pains to over-rule the Doctor's advice, it is not to be supposed but he would have accompanied his wife to the place of her destination, if it had been only for the satisfaction of contemplating the effects of his own greater sagacity in her case; and he protested to her, in the kindest manner, that nothing should have robbed him of the pleasure of attending her on the journey, but the most indispensable and unexpected business: He had just

then

then received letters from two friends, which would be attended with the greateſt breach of honour, if neglected ; and ſhe knew his nicety of principle in thoſe affairs : He would not read them to her, as ſhe was in too weak a condition (he obſerved) to attend to buſineſs, but ſhe might reſt aſſured, he would, if poſſible, overtake her on the way, or be with her in a few hours after her arrival, for he ſhould be impatient to be a witneſs of her recovery, which he perſuaded himſelf would ſoon take place, when ſhe had made experiment of the place he had choſen for her. When he had finiſhed his apology, his wife raiſed her eyes from the ground, where ſhe had fixed them whilſt he was ſpeaking, and with a look of ſuch mild languor, and ſuch dying ſoftneſs, as would almoſt have melted marble into pity, mournfully replied—*farewell !*—and reſigning herſelf to the ſupport of her maid and a nurſe, was lifted into her carriage, and left her huſband to purſue his buſineſs without reproach.

Jack Gayleſs now loſt no further time in fulfilling the promiſe he had made to his wife, and immediately began to apply himſelf

felf to the letters, which had fo indifpen-
fably prevented him from paying her thofe
kind offices, which her fituation was in fo
much need of. Thefe letters I fhall now
infert, as fome of my readers may probably
think he wants a juftification on this occafion. The firft was from a great lady of
unblemifhed reputation, who has a character for public charity and domeftic virtues,
which even malice has not dared to impeach.
Her ladyfhip was now at her country feat,
where fhe prefided at a table of the moft
fplendid hofpitality, and regulated a princely
eftablifhment with confummate judgment
and decorum : In this great family Jack
had long been a welcome vifiter, and as he
had received a thoufand kindneffes at her
hands, gratitude would difpofe him to confider her requefts as commands the moft
preffing. The important contents were as
follows, viz,

> *Dear Jack,*
>
> *I am forry your wife's fo fick; but methinks
> you'd do well to change the fcene, and come
> amongft us, now home's fo dull. You'll be
> griev'd to hear I have clapp'd Tom Jones in
> the*

the back finews : Ned has put a charge to
him, but he is fo cruelly let down, I am afraid
he muſt be fcor'd with a fine iron, and that
will be an eye-fore, to fay no worſe on't. My
lord you know hates writing, fo he bids me tell
you to bring Moll Roſs with you, as he thinks
there is a young man here will take her off your
hands ; and as you have had the beſt of her,
and ſhe is rather under your weight, think you'll
be glad to get well out of her. Would you believe it, I was eight hours in the faddle yeſter-
day : We dug a fox in Lady Tabby's park :
The old Dowager goes on fetting traps ; all the
country round cries out upon it : Thank the
fates, ſhe had a py'd peacock and a whole
brood of Guinea fowls carried off laſt night :
My lord fays 'tis a judgment upon her. Don't
forget to bring your Highland tarrier, as I
would fain have a croſs with my bitch Cruel.

Dear Jack, your's,

*.

As Jack Gaylefs was not one of thofe
milkfops, who let family excufes ſtand in the
way of the more amiable office of obliging
his friends, and faw in its juſt light the ridicule he would naturally expofe himfelf to,

if

if he sheltered himself under so silly a pretence as a wife's sickness, he would infallibly
have obeyed her ladyship's commands, and
set out with the Highland tarrier instead of
Mrs. Gaylefs, if he had not been divided by
another very pressing attention, which every
man of the world will acknowledge the importance of. There was a certain young
lady of easy virtue, who had made a tender
impression on his heart as he was innocently
taking the air in Hyde Park : He had prevailed so far with her as to gain her consent
to an appointment for that day : not foreseeing, as I should suppose, or perhaps not just
at that moment recollecting his wife's journey, and the call there would be upon him
on that account. This young lady, who
was wanting in no other virtue but chastity,
had learnt some particulars of Mr. Gaylefs,
which she had not been informed of when
she yielded to the assignation, and in conse-
quence had written him the following per-
plexing billet :

    Sir,

    *I am sorry it is not possible for me to receive
the honour of your visit, and the more so, as I*
am

am afraid my reason for declining it, though insuperable with me, will not appear a sufficient one in your opinion.   I have just now been informed that you are a married man ; this would have been enough, if I had not heard it with the addition, that your Lady is one of the most excellent and most injured women living—if indeed she be yet living, for I learn from the same authority that she is in the last stage of a rapid decline.

In what light must I regard myself, if I was to supply you with a motive for neglecting that attention, which her situation demands of you ? Don't let it surprize you, that a woman who has forfeited her claim to modesty, should yet retain some pretensions to humanity : If you have renounced both the one and the other, I have a double motive for declining your acquaintance.

I am, &c.

**

The stile of this letter seemed so extraordinary to Jack, and so unlike what he had been used to receive from correspondents of this lady's description, that it is not to be wondered at, if it threw him into a profound meditation : Not that the rebuke made any other impression on him, than as it seemed to
involve

involve a myſtery which he could not ex-
pound ; for it never entered into his head to
ſuppoſe that the writer was it earneſt. In
this dilemma he imparted it to a friend, and
with his uſual gaiety deſired his help to
unriddle it : His friend peruſed it, and with
a ſerious countenance told him he was acquainted with the lady, and gave her perfect
credit for the ſincerity of the ſentiments it
contained : She was a romantic girl, he told
him, and not worth a further thought ; but
as he perceived he was chagrined with the
affair, he adviſed him to take poſt for the
country, and attend the ſummons of his
noble correſpondent, for that he himſelf had
always found the diſſipation of a journey
the beſt remedy in all caſes of vexation, like
the preſent. This friendly advice was immediately followed by an order for the journey,
and Jack Gayleſs put himſelf into his poſt-
chaiſe, with his tarrier by his ſide, ordering
his groom to follow with Moll Roſs by eaſy
ſtages.

Whilſt Jack was rapidly poſting towards
the houſe of jollity and diſſipation, his
ſuffering and forſaken wife by ſlow ſtages
purſued her laſt melancholy journey : Sup-
ported

ported in her coach by her two women, and
attended by an old man-fervant of her father's, fhe at laft reached the allotted houfe,
where her miferies were to find a period.
One indifcretion only, a ftolen and precipi-
tate marriage, had marked her life with a
blemifh, and the hufband, who in early
youth had betrayed her artlefs affection into
that fatal miftake, was now the chofen in-
ftrument of chaftifement. She bore her
complicated afflictions with the moft patient refignation; neither ficknefs nor forrow forced a complaint from her; and
Death, by the gentlenefs of his advances,
feemed to lay afide his terrors, and approach
her with refpect and pity.

Jack was ftill upon his vifit, when he received the news of her death: This event
obliged him to break off from a moft agreeable party, and take a journey to London;
but as the feafon had happened to fet in for
a fevere froft, and the fox-hounds were confined to their kennel, he had the confolation
to reflect that his amufements were not fo
much interrupted as they might have been.
He gave orders for a handfome funeral, and
deported himfelf with fuch outward propriety

priety on the occafion, that all the world gave him credit for his behaviour, and he continues to be the fame popular character amongft his acquaintance, and univerfally careffed : In fhort, Jack Gaylefs (to ufe the phrafe of fafhion) is *the honefteft fellow in England*, and—a difgrace to human nature.

No. CIV.

THE conduct of a young lady, who is the only daughter of a very worthy father, and fome alarming particulars refpecting her fituation which had come to my knowledge, gave occafion to me for writing my Paper, No. XXVII. in which I endeavour to point out the confequences parents have to apprehend from novels, which though written upon moral plans, may be apt to take too ftrong a hold upon young and fufceptible minds, efpecially in the fofter fex, and produce an affected character, where we wifh to find a natural one.

As the young perfon in queftion is now happily extricated from all danger, and has

feen

feen her error, I fhall relate her ftory, not
only as it contains fome incidents which are
amufing, but as it tends to illuftrate by example the feveral inftructions, which in
my Paper before mentioned I endeavoured
to convey.

  Sappho is the only child of *Clemens*, who
is a widower; a paffionate fondnefs for this
daughter, tempered with a very fmall fhare
of obfervation or knowledge of the world,
determined Clemens to an attempt (which
has feldom been found to fucceed) of ren-
dering Sappho a miracle of accomplifh-
ments, by putting her under the inftructions
of mafters in almoft every art and fcience
at one and the fame time: His houfe now
became an academy of muficians, dancing-
mafters, language-mafters, drawing-mafters,
geographers, hiftorians, and a variety of inferior artifts male and female; all thefe ftudies appeared the more defirable to Clemens, from his own ignorance of them,
having devoted his life to bufinefs of a very
different nature. Sappho made juft as much
progrefs in each, as is ufual with young ladies fo attended; fhe could do a little of
moft of them, and talk of all: She could
play

play a concerto by heart with every grace her mafter had taught her, note for note, with the precife repetition of a barrel-organ: She had ftuck the room round with drawings, which Clemens praifed to the fkies, and which Sappho affured him had been only *touched up a little* by her mafter: She could tell the capital of every country, when he queftioned her, out of the newfpaper, and would point out the very fpot upon the terreftrial globe, where Paris, Madrid, Naples and Conftantinople actually were to be found: She had as much French as puzzled Clemens, and would have ferved her to buy blond-lace and Paris netting at a French milliner's; nay, fhe had gone fo far as to pen a letter in that language to a young lady of her acquaintance, which her mafter, who ftood over whilft fhe wrote it, declared to be little inferior in ftile to Madame Sevigné's: In hiftory, both antient and modern, her progrefs was proportionable, for fhe could run through the twelve Cæfars in a breath, and reckon up all the kings from the conqueft upon her fingers without putting one out of place; this appeared a prodigy to Clemens, and in the

warmth of his heart he fairly told her fhe
was one of the world's wonders; Sappho
aptly fet him right in this miftake, by affuring him that there were but feven wonders in the world, all of which fhe repeated
to him, and only left him more convinced
that fhe herfelf was defervedly the eighth.

There was a gentleman about fifty years
old, a friend of Clemens, who came frequently to his houfe, and, being a man of
talents and leifure, was fo kind as to take
great pains in directing and bringing Sappho
forward in her ftudies: This was a very acceptable fervice to Clemens, and the vifits
of *Mufidorus* were always joyfully welcomed
both by him and Sappho herfelf: Mufidorus declared himfelf overpaid by the delight
it gave him to contemplate the opening talents of fo promifing a young lady; and as
Sappho was now of years to eftablifh her
pretenfions to tafte and fentiment, Mufidorus made fuch a felection of authors for
her reading, as were beft calculated to ac-
complifh her in thofe particulars: In fet-
tling this important choice, he was careful
to put none but writers of delicacy and fenfibility into her hands; interefting and affecting

fecting tales or novels were the books he chiefly recommended, which, by exhibiting the faireft patterns of female purity (fuffering diftrefs and even death itfelf from the attacks of licentious paffion in the groffer fex) might infpire her fympathetic heart with pity, and guard it from feduction by difplaying profligacy in its moft odious colours.

Sappho's propenfiy to thefe ftudies fully anfwered the intentions of her kind director, and fhe became more and more attached to works of fentiment and pathos. Mufidorus's next folicitude was to form her ftile, and with this view he took upon himfelf the trouble of carrying on a kind of probationary correfpondence with her; this happy expedient fucceeded beyond expectation, for as two people, who faw each other every day, could have very little matter to write upon, there was fo much the more exercife for invention; and fuch was the copioufnefs and fluency of expreffion which fhe became miftrefs of by this ingenious practice, that fhe could fill four fides of letter paper with what other people exprefs upon the back of a card: Clemens once, in the exultation

K 2   of

of his heart, put a bundle of thefe manu-
fcripts into my hands, which he confeffed
he did not clearly underftand, but neverthe-
lefs believed them to be the moft elegant
things in the language; I fhall give the
reader a fample of two of them, which I drew
out of the number, not by choice, but by
chance; they were carefully folded, and
labelled at the back in Sappho's own hand as
follows, *Mufidorus to Sappho of the* 10*th of*
June; underneath fhe had wrote with a pen-
cil thefe words :

PICTURESQUE !

ELEGANT !

HAPPY ALLUSION TO THE SUN !

KING DAVID NOT TO BE COMPARED TO

MUSIDORUS.

Here follows the note, and I cannot doubt
but the reader will confefs that its contents
deferve all that the label expreffes.

" *June the* 10*th* 1785.
" As foon as I arofe this morning, I di-
" rected my eyes to the eaft, and demanded
" of the fun, if he had given you my good-
" morrow: This was my parting injunc-
" tion laft night, when I took leave of him
" in

" in the weſt, and he this moment plays his
" beams with ſo particular a luſtre, that I am
" ſatisfied he has fulfilled my commiſſion,
" and ſaluted the eyelids of Sappho : If he
" is deſcribed to *come forth as a bridegroom*
" *out of his chamber*, how much rather may
" it be ſaid of him, when he comes forth
" out of *your's ?* I ſhall look for him to per-
" form his journey this day with a peculiar
" glee ; I expeĉt he will not ſuffer a cloud
" to come near him, and I ſhall not be
" ſurprized, if through his eagerneſs to
" repeat his next morning's ſalutation, he
" ſhould *whip his fiery-footed ſteeds to the*
" *weſt* ſome hours before their time ;
" unleſs indeed you ſhould walk forth
" whilſt he is deſcending, and he ſhould
" delay the wheels of his chariot to look
" back upon an objeĉt ſo pleaſing. You ſee
" therefore, moſt amiable Sappho, that
" unleſs you fulfil your engagement, and
" conſent to repeat our uſual ramble in the
" cool of the evening, our part of the
" world is likely to be in darkneſs before it
" is expeĉted, and that nature herſelf will be
" put out of courſe, if Sappho forfeits her
" promiſe to Muſidorus."

K 3 " SAPPHO

"SAPPHO IN REPLY TO MUSIDORUS."

" If nature holds her course till Sappho
" forfeits her word to Musidorus, neither
" the setting nor the rising sun shall vary
" from his appointed time.   But why does
" Musidorus ascribe to me so flattering an
" influence, when, if I have any interest
" with Apollo, it must be to his good
" offices only that I owe it ? If he bears the
" messages of Musidorus to me, is it not
" a mark of his respect to the person who
" sends him, rather than to her he is sent
" to ? And whom should he so willingly
" obey, as one whom he so copiously in-
" spires ? I shall walk as usual in the cool
" hour of even-tide, listening *with greedy*
" *ear* to that discourse, which, by the re-
" fined and elevated sentiments it inspires,
" has taught me to look down with silent
" pity and contempt upon those frivolous
" beings, who talk the mere language of
" the senses, not of the soul, and to whose
" silly prattle I neither condescend to lend
" an ear, or to subscribe a word. Know then
" that Sappho will reserve her attention for
                              " Musidorus,

" Mufidorus, and if Apollo *fhall delay the*
" *wheels of his chariot* to wait upon us in
" our evening ramble, believe me he will
" not ftop for the unworthy purpofe of
" looking back upon Sappho, but for the
" nobler gratification of liftening to Mufi-
" dorus."

The evening walk took place as ufual,
but it was a walk in the dufty purlieus of
London, and Sappho fighed for a cottage
and the country: Mufidorus feconded the
figh, and he had abundance of fine things
to fay on the occafion: Retirement is a
charming fubject for a fentimental enthu-
fiaft; there is not a poet in the language,
but will help him out with a defcription;
Mufidorus had them all at his fingers ends,
from *Hefperus that led the ftarry hoft*, down
to a glow-worm.

The paffion took fo ftrong a hold of Sappho's mind, that fhe actually affailed her
father on the fubject, and with great energy
of perfuafion moved him to adopt her ideas:
It did not exactly fuit Clemens to break
up a very lucrative profeffion, and fet out
in fearch of fome folitary cottage, whofe,

romantic

romantic fituation might fuit the fpiritu-
alized defires of his daughter, and I am
afraid he was for once in his life not quite
fo refpectful to her wifhes, as he might
have been : Sappho was fo unufed to con-
tradiction, that fhe explained herfelf to
Mufidorus with fome afperity, and it became the fubject of much debate between
them : Not that he held a contrary opinion
from her's; but the difficulty which embar-
raffed both parties was, where to find the
happy fcene fhe fighed for, and how to obtain it when it was found. The firft part
of this difficulty was at laft furmounted,
and the chofen fpot was pointed out by
Mufidorus, which according to his defcription was the very bower of felicity ; it was
in a northern county at a diftance from the
capital, and its fituation was moft delectable :
The next meafure was a ftrong one ; for the
queftion to be decided was, if Sappho fhould
abandon her project or her father; fhe
called upon Mufidorus for his opinion, and
he delivered it as follows : —" If I was not
" convinced, moft amiable Sappho, that a
" fecond application to Clemens would be
" as unfuccefsful as the firft, I would ad-
                                    " vife

" vife you to the experiment; but as
" there is no doubt of this, it muft be the
" heighth of imprudence to put that to a
" trial, of which there is no hope : It comes
" therefore next to be confidered, if you
" fhall give up your plan, or execute it with-
" out his privity; in other words, if you
" fhall or fhall not do that, which is to
" make you happy : If it were not confif-
" tent with the ftricteft purity of character,
" I fhould anfwer no; but when I reflect
" upon the innocence, the fimplicity, the
" moral beauty of the choice you make,
" I then regard the duty you owe to yourfelf
" as fuperior to all others, which are falfely
" called natural; whereas, if you follow this in
" preference, you obey nature herfelf: If you
" were of an age too childifh to be allow-
" ed to know what fuits you beft, or, if
" being old enough to be intitled to a
" choice, you wanted wit to make one,
" there would be no doubt in the cafe;
" nay, I will go fo far as to fay, that if
" Clemens was a man of judgment fuperior
" to your own, I fhould be ftaggered with
" his oppofition; but if truth may ever be
" fpoken, it may on this occafion, and who

K 5   " is

" is there that does not fee the weaknefs of
" the father's underftanding; who but muft
" acknowledge the pre-eminence of the
" daughter's? I will fpeak yet plainer, moft
" incomparable Sappho, it is not fitting
" that folly fhould prefcribe to wifdom:
" The queftion therefore is come to an
" upfhot, Shall Sappho live a life fhe de-
" fpifes and detefts, to humour a father,
" whofe weaknefs fhe pities, but whofe
" judgment fhe cannot refpect?"

" No," replied Sappho, " that point is
" decided; pafs on to the next, and fpeak
" to me upon the practicability of exe-
" cuting what I am refolved to attempt."
" The authority of a parent," refumed
" Mufidorus, " is fuch over an unpro-
" tected child, that reafon will be no de-
" fence to you againft obftinacy and coer-
" cion. In the cafe of a fon, profeffion
" gives that defence: new duties are im-
" pofed by a man's vocation, which fuper-
" fede what are called natural ones; but
" in the inftance of a daughter, where fhall
" fhe fly for protection againft the impe-
" rious controul of a parent, but to the
" arms—? I tremble to pronounce the
      " word;

" word ; your own imagination muſt com-
" plete the ſentence"—" Oh ! horrible !"
cried Sappho, interrupting him, " I will
" never marry ; I will never ſo contaminate
" the ſpotleſs luſtre of my incorporeal pu-
" rity : No, Muſidorus, no—*I'll bear my*
" *bluſhing honours ſtill about me.*"—" And fit
" you ſhould," cried Muſidorus, " what
" dæmon dare defile them ? Periſh the man,
" that could intrude a ſenſual thought with-
" in the ſphere of ſuch repelling virtue !—
" But marriage is a form ; and forms are pure;
" at leaſt they may be ſuch; there's no pollu-
" tion in a name ; and if a name will ſhelter
" you, why ſhould you fear to take it ?"—
" I perceive," anſwered Sappho, " that I
" am in a very dangerous dilemma; ſince
" the very expedient, which is to protect
" me from violence of one ſort, expoſes
" me to it under another ſhape too odious
" to mention."—" And is there then,"
ſaid Muſidorus ſighing, " is there no hu-
" man being in your thoughts in whom
" you can confide ? Alas for me ! if you
" believe you have no friend who is not
" tainted with the impurities of his ſex :
" And what is friendſhip ? what, but the
" union

"union of fouls? and are not fouls thus
" united already married? For my part,
" I have long regarded our pure and fpiritu-
" alized connection in this light, and I
" cannot forefee how any outward ceremony
" is to alter that inherent delicacy of fenti-
" ment, which is infeparable from my foul's
" attachment to the foul of Sappho : If we
" are determined to defpife the world, we
" fhould alfo defpife the conftructions of
" the world : If retirement is our choice,
" and the life and habits of Clemens are
" not to be the life and habits of Sappho,
" why fhould Mufidorus, who is ready to
" facrifice every thing in her defence, not
" be thought incapable of abufing her con-
" fidence, when he offers the protection of
" his name ? If a few words muttered over
" us by a Scotch blackfmith will put all
" our troubles to reft, why fhould we refort
" to dangers and difficulties, when fo eafy a
" remedy is before us ? But why fhould I
" feek for arguments to allay your appre-
" henfions, when you have in me fo natural
" a fecurity for my performance of the
" ftricteft ftipulations ?"—" And what is
" that fecurity ?" fhe eagerly demanded.

Mufidorus

Mufidorus now drew back a few paces, and with the moſt ſolemn air and action, laying his hand upon his heart, replied, " My " age, madam !"—" That's true," cried Sappho; and now the converſation took a new turn, in the courſe of which they agreed upon their plan of proceeding, ſettled their rendezvous for the next day, and Mufidorus departed to prepare all things neceſſary for the ſecurity of their expedition.

CV.

Tange Chloën ſemel arrogantem.

(HORAT.)

" O Cupid, touch this rebel heart !"

UPON the day appointed, Sappho, with her father's conſent, ſet out in a hired poſt-chaiſe upon a pretended viſit to a relation; who lived about twenty miles from town on the northern road : At the inn where ſhe was to change horſes, ſhe diſmiſſed her London poſtillion with a ſhort note to

her

her father, in which she told him she should write to him in two or three days time: Here she took post for the next stage upon the great road, where she was met by Musidorus, and from thence they pressed forward with all possible expedition towards Gretna Green.

The mind of Sappho was visited with some compunctions by the way; but the eloquence of her companion, and the respectful delicacy of his behaviour, soon reconciled her conscience to the step she had taken: The reflections which passed in Musidorus's breast, were not so easily quieted: The anxiety of his thoughts, and the fatigues of the journey, brought so violent an attack upon him, that when he was within a stage or two of his journey's end, he found himself unable to proceed; the gout had seized upon his stomach, and immediate relief became necessary: The romantic visions, with which Sappho hitherto had indulged her imagination, now began to vanish, and a gloomy prospect opened upon her; in place of a comforter and companion by the way to sooth her cares, and fill her mind with soft healing sentiments, she had a

wretched

wretched object before her eyes, tormented with pain and at the point of death.

The houfe, in which fhe had taken fhelter, was of the meaneft fort, but the good people were humane and affiduous, and the village afforded a medical affiftant of no contemptible fkill in his profeffion: There was another confolation attended her fituation, for in the fame inn was quartered a dragoon officer with a fmall recruiting party; this young cornet was of a good family, of an engaging perfon and very elegant addrefs; his humanity was exerted not only in confoling Sappho, but in nurfing and cheering Mufidorus. Thefe charitable offices were performed with fuch a natural benignity, that Sappho muft have been moft infenfible if fhe could have overlooked them; her gentle heart on the contrary overflowed with gratitude, and in the extremity of her diftrefs fhe freely confeffed to him, that but for his fupport fhe muft have funk outright. Though the extremity of Mufidorus's danger was now over, yet he was incapable of exertion; and Sappho, who was at leifure to reflect upon her fituation, began to waver in her refolution, and

to

to put some questions to herself, which
reason could not readily answer. Her
thoughts were so distracted and perplex-
ed, that she saw no resource but to unbur-
then them, and throw herself upon the honour and discretion of Lionel, for so this
young officer was called. This she had frequently in mind to do, and many opportunities offered themselves for it, but still her
sensibility of shame prevented it. The constant apprehension of pursuit hung over her,
and sometimes she meditated to go back to
her father; in one of these moments she had
begun to write a letter to Clemens to prepare him for her return, when Lionel entered the room and informed her that he perceived so visible an amendment in Musidorus, that he expected to congratulate her
on his recovery in a very few days—" and
" then, Madam," added he, " my sorrows
" will begin where your's end; be it so! if
" you are happy, I must not complain:.
" I presume this gentleman is your father
" or near relation?"—" Father!" exclaimed Sappho:—She cast her eyes upon the
letter she was inditing, and burst into tears.
Lionel approached, and took her hand in his;
                                    she

she raised her handkerchief to her eyes
with the other, and he proceeded—" If
" my anxious folicitude for an unknown
" lady, in whofe happinefs my heart is
" warmly interefted, expofes me to any
" hazard of your difpleafure, ftop me before
" I fpeak another word; if not, confide in
" me, and you fhall find me ready to de-
" vote my life to ferve you.　The myftery
" about you and the road you are upon,
" (were it not for the companion you are
" with) would tempt me to believe you was
" upon a generous errand, to reward fome
" worthy man, whom fortune and your pa-
" rents do not favour; but this poor object
" above ftairs makes that impoffible.　If
" however there is any favoured lover, wait-
" ing in fecret agony for that expected mo-
" ment, when your releafe from hence may
" crown him with the beft of human bleffings,
" the hand, which now has hold of your's,
" fhall be devoted to his fervice: Command
" me where you will; I never yet have forfeited
" my honour, and cannot wrong your con-
" fidence."—" You are truly generous," replied Sappho; " there is no fuch man; the
" hand you hold is yet untainted, and till
　　　　　　　　　　　　　　　" now

" now has been untouched; releafe it there-
" fore, and I will proceed.—My innocence
" has been my error; I have been the dupe
" of fentiment: I am the only child of a fond
" father, and never knew the blefling of a
" mother; when I look back upon my edu-
" cation, I perceive that art has been ex-
" haufted, and nature overlooked in it.
" The unhappy object above ftairs has been
" my fole advifer and director; for my fa-
" ther is immerfed in bufinefs: From him,
" and from the duty which I owe him, I
" confefs I have feceded, and my defign
" was to devote myfelf to retirement.   My
" fcheme I now perceive was vifionary in
" the extreme; left to my own reflections,
" reafon fhews me both the danger and the
" folly of it: I have therefore determined
" upon returning to my father, and am
" writing to him a letter, which I fhall fend
" by exprefs, to relieve him from the ago-
" nies my filly conduct has occafioned."—
" What you have now difclofed to me,"
faid Lionel, " with a fincerity that does
" equal honour to yourfelf and me, demands
" a like fincerity on my part, and I muft
" therefore confefs to you, that Mufidorus,
                              " believing

" believing himself at the point of death,
" imparted to me not only every thing
" that has paffed, but all the future pur-
" pofes of this treacherous plot, from
" which you have fo providentially efcaped ;
" thefe I fhall not explain to you at pre-
" fent, but you may depend upon it, that
" this attack upon his life has faved his
" confcience. I cannot as a man of honour
" oppofe myfelf to your refolution of re-
" turning home immediately ; and yet when
" I confider the ridicule you will have to
" encounter from the world at large, the
" reflections that will arife in your mind,
" when there is perhaps no friend at hand to
" affuage them, but above all when I thus
" contemplate your charms, and recollect
" that affectation is expelled, and nature
" reinftated in your heart, I cannot refift
" the impulfe nor the opportunity of ap-
" pealing to that nature againft a fepara-
" tion fo fatal to my peace : Yes, lovelieft
" of women, I muft appeal to nature ; I
" muft hope this heart of your's, where
" fuch refined fenfations have refided, will
" not be fhut from others of a more gene-

                              " rous

" rous kind. What could the name of
" Mufidorus do, which Lionel's cannot ?
" Why fhould you not replace an un-
" worthy friend with one of fairer princi-
" ples ? with one of honourable birth, of
" equal age, and owner of a heart that
" beats with ardent paffion towards you ?
" Had you been made the facrifice of this
" chimæra, this illufion, what had your
" father fuffered ? If I am honoured with
" your hand in marriage, what can he com-
" plain of ? My conduct, my connections
" and my hopes in life will bear the fcru-
" tiny : Suffer me to fay you will have a
" protector, whofe character can face the
" world, and whofe fpirit cannot fear it.
" As for worldly motives, I renounce them ;
" give me yourfelf and your affections;
" give me poffeffion of this hand, thefe eyes,
" and the foul which looks through them ;
" let your father withhold the reft. Now,
" lovelieft and moft beloved, have you the
" heart to fhare a foldier's fortune ? Have
" you the noble confidence to take his
" word ? Will you follow, where his honour
" bids him go, and whether a joyful victory

" or

" or a glorious death attends him, will you
" receive him living, or entomb him dying
" in your arms ?"

Whilst Lionel was uttering these words,
his action, his emotion, and that honest
glow of passion, which nature only can as-
sume and artifice cannot counterfeit, had so
subdued the yielding heart of Sappho, that
he must have been dull indeed, if he could
have wanted any stronger confirmation of
his success, than what her looks bestowed :
Never was silence more eloquent ; the labour of language and the forms of law had
no share in this contract : A sigh of speech-
less ecstasy drew up the nuptial bond ; the
operations of love are momentary : Tears
of affection interchangeably witnessed the
deed, and the contracting parties sealed it
with an inviolable embrace.

Every moment now had wings to waft
them to that happy spot, where the unholy
hand of law has not yet plucked up the
root of love : Freedom met them on the
very extremity of her precincts ; Nature
held out her hand to welcome them, and
the Loves and Graces, though exiled to a
desart, danced in her train.

Thus

Thus was Sappho, when brought to the very brink of deftruction, refcued by the happy intervention of Providence. The next day produced an interview with Clemens, at the houfe to which they returned after the ceremony in Scotland: The meeting, as might well be expected, was poignant and reproachful; but when Sappho, in place of a fuperannuated fentimentalift, prefented to him a fon-in-law, in whofe martial form and countenance he beheld youth, honour, manly beauty, and every attractive grace that could juftify her choice, his tranfports became exceffive; and their union, being now fanctified by the bleffing of a father, and warranted by love and nature, has fnatched a deluded victim from mifery and error, and added one conjugal inftance to the fcanty records of unfafhionable felicity.

Let not my young female readers believe that the extravagance of Sappho's conduct is altogether out of nature, or that they have nothing to apprehend from men of Mufidorus's age and character; my obfervation convinces me to the contrary. *Gravity*, fays Lord Shaftefbury, *is the very effence of*

of impofture; and fentimental gravity, var-
niſhed over with the experienced artifice of
age and wifdom, is the worſt of its fpecies.

No. CVI.

I THINK the ladies will not accufe me of
bufying myfelf in impertinent remarks
upon their drefs and attire, for indeed it
is not to their perfons my fervices are devoted, but to their minds: If I can add to
them any thing ornamental, or take from
them any thing unbecoming, I ſhall gain
my wiſh ; the reſt I ſhall leave to their mil-
liners and mantua-makers.

Now if I have any merit with them for
not intruding upon their toilets, let them
ſhew me fo much complaifance, as not to
read this paper, whilſt they are engaged in
thofe occupations, which I have never before interrupted; for as I intend to talk with
them a little metaphyfically, I would not
wiſh to divide their attention, nor ſhall I be
contented with lefs than the whole.

In the firſt place I muſt tell them, gentle
though

though they be, that human nature is fubject to a variety of paffions, fome of thefe
are virtuous paffions, fome on the contrary
I am afraid are evil; there are however a
number of intermediate propenfities, moft
of which might alfo be termed paffions,
which by the proper influence of reafon
may become very, ufeful allies to any one
fingle virtue, when in danger of being overpowered by a hoft of foes: At the fame
time they are as capable of being kidnap-
ped by the enemies of reafon, and, when
enlifted in the ranks of the infurgents, feldom fail to turn the fate of the battle, and
commit dreadful havock in the peaceful
quarters of the invaded virtue. It is ap-
parent then that all thefe intermediate propenfities are a kind of balancing powers,
which feem indeed to hold a neutrality in
moral affairs, but, holding it with arms in
their hands, cannot be fuppofed to remain
impartial fpectators of the fray, and therefore muft be either with us, or againft us.

J fhall make myfelf better underftood
when I proceed to inftance them, and I will
begin with that, which has been called the
univerfal paffion, *The love of Fame.*

I prefume

I prefume no lady will difavow this propenfity; I would not wifh her to attempt it;
let her examine it however; let her firft enquire to what point it is likely to carry her
before fhe commits herfelf to it's conduct:
If it is to be her guide to that fame only,
which excels in fafhionable diffipation,
figures in the firft circles of the gay world,
and is the loadftone to attract every liber-
tine of high life into the fphere of it's acti-
vity, it is a traitorous guide, and is feduc-
ing her to a precipice, that will fooner or
later be the grave of her, happinefs: On the
contrary, if it propofes to avoid thefe dangerous purfuits, and recommends a progrefs
through paths lefs tempting to the eye perhaps, but terminated by fubftantial comforts, fhe may fecurely follow a propenfity,
which cannot miflead her, and indulge a paffion, which will be the moving fpring of all
her actions, and but for which her nature
would want energy, and her character be no
otherwife diftinguifhed than by avoidance
of vice without the grace and merit of any
pofitive virtue. I can hardly fuppofe, if it
was put to a lady's choice at her out-fet into
life which kind of fame fhe would be diftin-

guiſhed for, good or evil, but that ſhe would at once prefer the good; I muſt believe ſhe would acknowledge more gratification in being ſignalized as the beſt wife, the beſt mother, the moſt exemplary woman of her time, than in being pointed out in all circles ſhe frequents as the moſt faſhionable rake, the beſt dreſſed voluptuary in the nation: If this be rightly conjectured, why will not every woman, who has her choice to make, direct her ambition to thoſe objects, which will give her moſt ſatisfaction when attained? There can be no reaſon but becauſe it impoſes on her ſome ſelf-denials by the way, which ſhe has not fortitude to ſurmount; and it is plain ſhe does not love fame well enough to be at much pains in acquiring it; her ambition does not reach at noble objects, her paſſion for celebrity is no better than that of a buffoon's, who for the vanity of being conſpicuous ſubmits to be contemptible.

Friendſhip is a word which has a very captivating ſound, but is by no means of a decided quality; it may be friend or foe as reaſon and true judgment ſhall determine for it. If I were to decry all female friend-
ſhips

ships in the lump it might seem a harsh
sentence, and yet it will seriously behove
every parent to keep strict watch over this
propensity in the early movements of the
female mind.   I am not disposed to expa-
tiate upon it's dangers very particularly;
they are sufficiently known to people of experience and discretion; but attachmnets must
be stemmed in their beginnings; keep off correspondents from your daughters as you would
keep off the pestilence: Romantic misses,
sentimental novelists and scribbling pedants
overturn each others heads with such eter-
nal rhapsodies about friendship, and refine
upon nonsense with such an affectation of en-
thusiasm, that if it has not been the parent's
study to take early precautions against all
such growing propensities, it will be in vain
to oppose the torrent, when it carries all before it, and overwhelms the passions with
its force.

Sensibility is a mighty favourite with the
fair sex; it is an amiable friend or a very
dangerous foe to virtue: Let the female,
who professes it, be careful how she makes
too full a display of her weakness; for this
is so very soft and insinuating a propensity,

L 2   that

that it will be found in moft female gloffa-
ries as a fynonymous term for love itfelf; in
fact it is little elfe than the *nomme-de-guerre*,
which that infidious adventurer takes upon
him in all firft approaches; the pafs-
word in all thofe fkirmifhing experiments,
which young people make upon each other's
affections, before they proceed to plainer
declarations; it is the whetftone, upon
which love fharpens and prepares his arrows:
If any lady makes a certain fhow of fenfibility in company with her admirer, he muft
be a very dull fellow, if he does not know
how to turn the weapon from himfelf to her.
Now fenfibility affumes a different character
when it is taken into the fervice of benevolence, or made the centinel of modefty; in
one cafe it gives the fpring to pity, in the
other the alarm to difcretion; but whenever it affails the heart by foft feduction to
beftow that pity and relief, which difcretion
does not warrant and purity ought not to
grant, it fhould be treated as a renegado
and a fpy, which, under the mafk of charity,
would impofe upon credulity for the vileft
purpofes, and betray the heart by flattering
it to it's ruin.

Vanity

Vanity is a paffion, to which I think I am very complaifant, when I admit it to a place amongft thefe convertible propenfities, for it is as much as I can do to find any occupation for it in the family-concerns of virtue ; perhaps if I had not known *Vaneffa* I fhould not pay it even this fmall compliment : It can however do fome under-offices in the houfehold of generofity, of chearfulnefs, hofpitality, and certain other refpectable qualities : It is little elfe than an officious, civil, filly thing, that runs on errands for it's betters, and is content to be paid with a fmile for it's good-will, by thofe who have too much good fenfe to fhew it any real refpect : When it is harmlefs, it would be hard to wound it out of wantonnefs ; when it is mifchievous, there is merit in chaftifing it with the whip of ridicule : A lap-dog may be endured, if he is inoffenfive and does not annoy the company, but a fnappifh, barking pett, though in a lady's arms, deferves to have his ears pulled for his impertinence.

Delicacy is a foft name, and fine ladies, who have a proper contempt for the vulgar, are very willing to be thought endowed with

fenfes

senses more refined and exquisite than nature ever meant to give them; their nerves
are susceptible in the extreme, and they are of
constitutions so irritable, that *the very winds of
heaven* must not be allowed to *visit their face
too roughly*. I have studied this female favourite with some attention, and I am not yet able
to discover any one of it's good qualities; I
do not perceive the merit of such exquisite
fibres, nor have I observed that the slen-
derest strings are apt to produce the sweetest
sounds, when applied to instruments of harmony; I presume the female heart should
be such an harmonious instrument, when
touched by the parent, the friend, the husband; but how can these expect a concert
of sweet sounds to be excited, from a thing
which is liable to be jarred and put out of
tune by every breath of air? It may be
kept in it's case, like an old-fashioned virgi-
nal, which nobody knows, or even wishes to
know, how to touch: It can never be
brought to bear it's part in a family concert, but must hang by the wall, or at best
be a solo instrument for the remainder of it's
days.

Bashfulness, when it is attached to modesty,

defty, will be regarded with the eye of can-
dor, and cheared with the fmile of encou-
ragement; but bafhfulnefs is a hireling, and
is fometimes difcovered in the livery of
pride, oftentimes in the caft-off trappings of
affectation; pedantry is very apt to bring it
into company, and fly, fecret confcioufnefs
will frequently *blufh becaufe it underftands*.
I do not fay I have much to lay to it's
charge, for it is not apt to be troublefome in
polite focieties, nor do I commonly meet it
even in the youngeft of the female fex.
There is a great deal of blufhing I confefs
in all the circles of fine ladies, but then it is
fo univerfal a blufh and withal fo permanent,
that I am far from imputing it always to
bafhfulnefs, when the cheeks of the fair are
tinged with rofes. However, though it is
fometimes an impoftor, and for that reafon
may deferve to be difmiffed, I cannot help
having a confideration for one, that has in
paft times been the handmaid of beauty,
and therefore as merit has taken modefty
into her fervice, I would recommend to
ignorance to put bafhfulnefs into full pay
and employment.

Politenefs is a charming propenfity, and
L 4   I would

I would wiſh the fine ladies to indulge it, if
it were only by way of contraſt between
themſelves and the fine gentlemen they con-
ſort with. I do not think it is altogether
becoming for a lady to plant herſelf in the
center of a circle with her back to the fire,
and expect every body to be warmed by the
contemplation of her figure or the reflection of her countenance; at the ſame time
I am free to confeſs it an attitude, by which
the man of high breeding is conſpicuouſly
diſtinguiſhed, and is charming to behold,
when ſet off with the proper accompaniments of leather breeches,' tight boots and a
jockey waiſtcoat. I will not deny however
but I have ſeen this practiſed by ladies, who
have acquitted themſelves with great ſpirit
on the occaſion; but then it cannot be done
without certain male accoutrements, and
preſuppoſes a ſlouched hat, half-boots, ſhort
waiſtcoat and riding dreſs, not to omit
broad metal buttons with great letters en-
graved upon them, or the ſignature of ſome
hunt, with the indiſpenſable appendage of
two long dangling watch-chains, which ſerve
to mark the double value people of faſhion
put upon their time, and alſo ſhew the en-

couragement

couragement they beftow upon the arts: With thefe implements the work may be done even by a female artift, but it is an art I wifh no young lady to ftudy, and I hope the prefent profeffors will take no more pupils, whilft the academies of *Humphries* and *Mendoza* are kept open for accomplifh-ments, which I think upon the whole are altogether as becoming. Politenefs, as I conceive, confifts in putting people at their eafe in your company, and being at your eafe in their's; modern practice I am afraid is apt to mifplace this procefs, for I obferve every body in fafhionable life polite enough to ftudy their own eafe, but I do not fee much attention paid to that part of the rule, which ought to be firft obferved: It is well calculated for thofe, who are adepts in it, but if ever fuch an out-of-the-way thing as a modeft perfon comes within it's reach, the awkward novice is fure to be diftreffed; and whilft every body about him feems repofing on a bed of down, he alone is picket-ted upon a feat of thorns: 'Till this fhall be reformed by the ladies, who profefs to under-ftand politenefs, I fhall turn back to my red-book of forty years ago, to fee what re-

L 5   lifts

licts of the old court are yet amongst us,
and take the mothers for my models in preference to their daughters.

No. CVII.

Alter in obsequium plus aquo pronus, et imi
Derisor lecti, sic nutum divitis horret,
Sic iterat voces, et verba cadentia tollit.

HORAT.

I AM bewildered by the definitions, which
metaphysical writers give us of the human passions: I can understand the characters of *Theophrastus*, and am entertained by
his sketches; but when your profound
thinkers take the subject in hand, they appear to me to dive to the bottom of the
deep in search of that which floats upon
it's surface: if a man in the heat of anger
would describe the movements of his mind,
he might paint the tempest to the life; but
as such descriptions are not to be expected,
moral essayists have substituted personifica-
tion in their place, and by the pleasing introduction

duction of a few natural incidents form a
kind of little drama, in which they make
their fictitious hero defcribe thofe follies,
foibles and paffions, which they who really
feel them are not fo forward to confefs.

When Mr. Locke in his *Effay on the
Human Underftanding* defcribes all pity as
partaking of contempt, I cannot acknowledge that he is fpeaking of pity, as I feel
it : when I pity a fellow-creature in pain,
(a woman, for inftance, in the throes of
childbirth) I cannot fubmit to own there is
any ingredient of fo bad a quality as contempt in my pity; but if the metaphyficians
tell me that I do not know how to call my
feelings by their right name, and that my
pity is not pity properly fo defined, I will
not pretend to difpute with any gentleman
whofe language I do not underftand, and
only beg permiffion to enjoy a fenfation,
which I call pity, without indulging a propenfity which he calls contempt.

The flatterer is a character, which the
moralifts and wits of all times and all nations have ridiculed more feverely and more
fuccefsfully than almoft any other; yet it
ftill exifts, and a few pages perhaps would

L 6   not

not be mifapplied, if I was. to make room
for a civil kind of gentleman of this defcription, (by name *Billy Simper*) who, having
feen his failings in their proper light of ridicule, is willing to expofe them to public
view for the amufemént, it is hoped, if not
for the ufe and benefit, of the reader.

I beg leave therefore to introduce *Mr.*
Billy Simper to my candid friends and protectors, and fhall leave him to tell his ftory
in his own words.————

I am the younger fon of a younger brother:
my father qualified himfelf for orders in the
univerfity of Aberdeen, and by the help of
an infinuating addrefs, a foft counter-tenor
voice, a civil fmile and a happy flexibility in
the vertebræ of his back-bone, recommended
himfelf to the. good graces of a right reverend patron, who, after a due courfe of attendance and dependance, prefented him to
a comfortable benefice, which enabled him
to fupport a pretty numerous family of children. The good bifhop it feems was paf-
fionately fond of the game of chefs, and my
father, though the better player of the two,
knew how to make a timely move fo as to
throw the victory into his lordfhip's hand

after

after a hard battle, which was a triumph very grateful to his vanity, and not a little ferviceable to my father's purpofes.

Under this expert profeffor I was in-ftructed in all the fhifts and movements in the great game of life, and then fent to make my way in the world as well as I was able. My firft object was to pay my court to my father's elder brother, the head of our fami-ly; an enterprize not lefs arduous than im-portant. My uncle Antony was a widower, parfimonious, peevifh, and reclufe, he was rich however, egregioufly felf-conceited, and in his own opinion a deep philofopher and metaphyfician; by which I would be under-ftood to fay that lie doubted every thing, dif-puted every thing and believed nothing. He had one fon, his only child, and him he had lately driven out of doors and difinherit-ed for nonfu; ing him in an argument upon the immortality of the foul: here then was an opening no prudent man could mifs, who fcorned to fay his foul was his own, when it ftood in the way of his intereft: and as I was well tutored beforehand, I no fooner gained admiffion to the old philofopher, than I fo far worked my way into his good graces,

graces, as to be allowed to take poffeffion
of a truckle-bed in a fpare garret of the family manfion: envy muft have owned (if
envy could have looked afquint upon fo
humble a fituation as mine was) that con-
fidering what a game I had to play, I ma-
naged my cards well; for uncle Antony was
an old dog at a difpute, and as that cannot
well take place, whilft both parties are on
the fame fide, I was forced at times to make
battle for the good of the argument, and
feldom failed to find Antony as compleatly
puzzled with the zig-zaggeries of his meta-
phyfics, as uncle *Toby* of more worthy memory was with the horn-works and counter-
fcarps of his fortifications.

Amongft the various topics, from which
Antony's ingenuity drew matter of difpute,
fome were fo truly ridiculous, that if I were
fure my reader was as much at leifure to
hear, as I am juft now to relate them, I
fhould not fcruple the recital. One morning having been rather long-winded in defcribing the circumftances of a dream, that
had difturbed his imagination in the night,
I thought it not amifs to throw in a remark
in the way of confolation upon the fallacy

of

of dreams in general. This was enough for
him to turn over to the other fide, and fupport the credit of dreams *totis viribus* : I
now thought it advifable to trim, and took
a middle courfe between both extremes, by
humbly conceiving dreams might be fometimes true and fometimes falfe: this he con-
tended to be nonfenfe upon the face of it,
and if I would undertake to fhew they were
both true and falfe, he would engage to
prove by found logic they could be neither
one nor the other :—" But why do we be-
" gin to talk," added he, " before we fettle
" what we are to talk about ? What kind
" of dreams are you fpeaking of, - and
" how do you diftinguifh dreams?"—" I
" fee no diftinction between them," I replied; " Dreams vifit our fancies in fleep, and
" are all, according to Mr. Locke's idea,
" made up of the waking man's thoughts."
—" Does Mr. Locke fay that ?" exclaimed
my uncle. " Then Mr. Locke's an impoftor
" for telling you fo, and you are a fool for
" believing him : wifer men than Mr.
" Locke have fettled that matter many cen-
" turies before he was born or even *dreamt*
" of; but perhaps Mr. Locke forgot to tell
                                    " you

" you how many precife forts of dreams there
" are, and how to denominate and define
" them; perhaps he forgot that I fay." I confeffed that I neither knew any thing of the
matter myfelf, nor did I believe the author
alluded to had left any clue towards the difcovery.

" I thought as much," retorted my uncle
Antony in a tone of triumph, " and yet this
" is the man who fets up for an inveftigator
" of the human underftanding; but I will
" tell you, Sir, though he could not, that
" there are neither more nor lefs than five
" feveral forts of dreams particularly diftin-
" guifhed, and I defy even the feven fleepers
" themfelves to name a fixth. The firft of
" thefe was by the Greeks denominated
" *Oneiros*, by the Latins *Somnium*, (fimply
" a *Dream*) and you muft be afleep to dream
" it."   " Granted," quoth I.   " What is
" granted;" rejoined the philofopher, " Not
" that fleep is in all cafes indifpenfable to
" the man who dreams."—" Humph!"
quoth I.—My uncle proceeded.

" The fecond fort of dreams you fhall
" underftand was by the aforefaid Greeks
" called *Orama*, by the Latins *Vifio*, or as we
                                    " might

" might fay a *vifion*; in this cafe take notice
" you may be afleep, or you may be awake,
" or neither, or as it were between both;
" your eyes may be fhut, or they may be
" open,' looking inwards or outwards or
" upwards, either with fight or without
" fight, as it pleafes God, but the *vifion* you
" muft fee, or how elfe can it rightly be
" called a vifion?" "True," replied I, "there
" is a fect who are particularly favoured with
" this kind of vifions." " Prythee, don't
" interrupt me," faid my uncle, and again
went on.

" The third fort of dreams, to fpeak ac-
" cording to the Greeks, we fhall call *Chre-*
" *matifmos*, according to the Latins we muft
" denominate it *Oraculum*, (an *oracle*); now
" this differs from a *vifion*, in as much as it
" may happen to a man born blind as well
" as to Argus himfelf, for he has nothing for
" it but to liften, underftand and believe,
" and whatever it tells him fhall come true,
" though it never entered into his head to
" preconceive one tittle of what is told him:
" and where is Mr. Locke and his waking
" thoughts here?"—" He is done for," I
answered,

answered, " there is no difputing againft
" an oracle."

" The fourth fort," refumed he, " is the
" *Enuption* of the aforefaid Greeks, and an-
" fwers to the Latin *Infomnium*, which is in
" fact a dream and no dream, a kind of
" *refverie,* when a man dofes between fleep-
" ing and waking, and builds caftles (as we
" fay) in the air upon the ramblings of his
" own fancy.

" The fifth and laft fort of dreams is, by
" Greeks and Latins, mutually ftiled *Phan-*
" *tafma,* a word adopted into our own lan-
" guage by the greateft poet who ever wrote
" in it : now this *phantafma* is a vifitation
" peculiar to the firft mental abfence or
" flumber, when the man fancies himfelf
" yet waking, and in fact can fcarce be called
" afleep ; at which time ftrange images and
" appearances feem to float before him and
" terrify his imagination.   Here then you
" have all the · feveral denominations of
" dreams perfectly diftinguifhed and de-
" fined," quoth the old fophift, and throwing himfelf back in his chair with an air
of triumph, waited for the applaufe, which

I was

I was not backward in beſtowing upon this pedantic farrago of dogmatizing dull-neſs.

It will readily be believed that my uncle Antony did not fail to revive his favorite controverſy, which had produced ſuch fatal conſequences to his diſcarded ſon: in faⱦ he held faſt with thoſe antient philoſophers, who maintained the eternity of this material world, and as he ſaw no period when men would not be in exiſtence, no moment in time to come when mortality ſhall ceaſe, he by conſequence argued that there could be no moment in time, when mortality ſhall commence.   There were other points re-ſpeⱦing this grand ſtumbling block of his philoſophy, the human ſoul, upon which he was equally puzzled, for he ſided with Ari-ſtotle againſt Plato in the unintelligible con-troverſy concerning its power of motion: but whilſt my uncle Antony was thus un-luckily wedded to the wrong ſide in all caſes, where reaſon ought to have been his guide, in points of mere quibble and ſophiſtry, which reaſon has nothing to ſay to, and where a wiſe man would take neither ſide, he regularly took both, or hung ſuſ-

pended

pended between them like Socrates in the baſket.

Of this fort was the celebrated queſtion—*Ovumne prius fuerit, an gallina*—viz: "Whether the egg was anterior to the hen, "or the hen to the egg?"—This enquiry never failed to intereſt his paſſions in a peculiar degree, and he found fo much to fay on both fides, that he could never well determine which fide to be of: at length however, hoping to bring it to fome point, he took up the caufe of Egg verfus Hen, and having compofed a learned eſſay, publiſhed it in one of the monthly magazines, as a lure to future controverfialiſts. This eſſay he had fo often avowed in my hearing, and piqued himſelf fo highly upon it, that I muſt have been dull indeed not to have underſtood how to flatter him upon it : but when he had found month after month flip away, and no body mounting the ſtage upon his challenge, he felt angry at the contempt with which his labours were paſſed over, and without imparting to me his purpofe, furniſhed the fame magazine with a counter-eſſay, in which his former argument was handled with an afperity truly controverfial, and the hen was triumphantly

made

made to cackle over the new-laid egg, decidedly pofterior to herfelf.

I am inclined to think that if Antony had any partiality, it was not to this fide; but as the fecond effay was clearly pofterior to the firft, (whatever the egg may have been to the hen) it had the advantage of being couched in all the fpirit of a reply, with an agreeable tinge of the malice of one, fo that when at length it came down printed in a fair type, and refpectfully pofted in the front of the long-wifht-for magazine, his heart beat with joy, and calling out to me in a lofty tone of counterfeited anger, as he run his eye over it—" By the horns of Jupiter " Ammon," quoth he, " here is a fellow " has the confidence to enter the lifts againft " me in the notable queftion of the egg."— " Then I hope you will break that egg about " his ears," replied I.—" Hold your tongue, " puppy, and liften," quoth the fophift, and immediately began to read.

At every paufe I was ready with a pooh! or pifh! which I hooked in with every mark of contempt I could give it both by accent and action. At the conclufion of this effay my uncle Antony fhut the book, and demanded

manded what I thought of the author.—
" Hang him," I exclaimed, " poor Grub-
" ſtreet Garretteer ; the fellow is too con-
" temptible for your notice ; he can neither
" write nor reaſon; he is a mere ignora-
" mus, and does not know the commoneſt
" rules of logic ; he has no feature of a
" critic about him, but the malice of one."
—" Hold your tongue," cried Antony, no
longer able to contain himſelf, " you are a
" booby ; I will maintain it to be as fine an
" eſſay as ever was written."—With theſe
words he ſnatched up the magazine and departed : I ſaw no more of him that night,
and early next morning was preſented by a
ſervant with the following billet :—" The
" Grub-ſtreet Garretteer finds himſelf no
" longer fit company for the ſagacious *Mr.*
" *William Simper* ; therefore deſires him
" without loſs of time to ſeek out better
" ſociety than that of a *mere ignoramus, who*
" *does not know the common rules of logic :* one
" rule however he makes bold to lay down,
" which is, Never again to ſee the face of an
" impertinent upſtart, called William Sim-
" per, whilſt he remains on this earth."

A. S.

No. CVIII.

Sunt verba et voces, quibus hunc lenire dolorem
Possis, et magnam morbi deponere partem.

HORAT.

DRIVEN from my uncle Antony's doors by my unlucky miftake between the hen and her egg, my cafe would have been defperate, but that I had yet one ftring left to my bow, and this was my aunt *Mrs. Sufanna Simper*, who lived within a few miles of my uncle, but in fuch declared hoftility, that I promifed myfelf a favourable reception, if I could but flatter her animofity with a fufficient portion of invective; and for this I deemed myfelf very tolerably qualified, having fo much good-will towards the bufinefs, and no flight inducements to fpur me to it.

My aunt, who was an aged maiden, and a valetudinarian, was at my arrival clofeted with her apothecary: upon his departure I was admitted to my audience, in which I acquitted myfelf with all the addrefs I was mafter of: my aunt heard my ftory through
without

without interrupting me by a single word;
at last, fixing her eyes upon me, she said,
" 'Tis very well, child; you have said
" enough : your uncle's character I perfectly
" underftand; look well to your own, for
" upon that will depend the terms you and
" I shall be upon."—She now took up a
phial from the table, and surveying it for
some time, said to me—" Here is a nof-
" trum recommended by my apothecary,
" that promises great things, but perhaps
" contains none of the wondrous properties
" it profeffes to have : the label fays it is a
" carminative, fedative mixture; in other
" words, it will expel vapours and fpafms, and
" quiet the mind and fpirits : Do you think
" it will make good what it promifes ?"—
So whimfical a queftion put to me at fuch
a moment confounded me not a little, and
I only murmured out in reply, that I hoped
it would—" Take it then," faid my aunt,
" as you have faith in it; fwallow it yourself,
" and when 1 fee how it operates with you,
" I may have more confidence in it on my
" own account."—I was now in a more
awkward dilemma than ever, for fhe had
emptied the dofe into a cup, and tendered

it

it to me in fo peremptory a manner, that, not knowing how to excufe myfelf, and being naturally fubmiffive, I filently took the cup with a trembling hand, and fwallowed it's abominable contents.

"Much good may it do you, child," cried fhe, " you have done more for me than " I would for any doctor in the kingdom : " Don't you find it naufeous to the palate ?" —I confefs that it was very naufeous.—" And did you think yourfelf in need of fuch " a medicine ?"—" I did not perceive that " I was." " Then you did not fwallow it " by your own choice, but my defire ?"— I had no hefitation in acknowledging that— " Upon my word, child," fhe replied, " you have a very accommodating way with " you." I was now fighting with the curfed drug, and had all the difficulty in life to keep it where it was. My aunt faw my diftrefs, and fmiling at it, demanded if I was not fick : I confefs I was rather difcompofed in my ftomach with the draught. —" I don't doubt it," fhe replied ; " but " as you have fo civilly made yourfelf fick " for my fake, cannot you flatter me fo far " as to be well when I requeft it ?" I was

juſt then ſtruggling to keep the nauſea
down, and though I could not anſwer,
put the beſt face upon the matter in my
power.

A maid-ſervant came in upon my aunt's
ringing her bell.—" Betty," ſaid ſhe, " take
" away theſe things; this doctor will poiſon
" us with his doſes."—" Foh !" cried the
wench, " how it ſmells !"   " Nay, but
" only put your lips to the cup," ſaid the
miſtreſs, " there is enough left for you to
" taſte it."—" I taſte it ! I'll not touch it,
" I want none of his naſty phyſic !"—
" Well, but though you don't want it,"
rejoined the miſtreſs, " taſte it nevertheleſs,
" if it be only to flatter my humour."—
" Excuſe me, madam," replied Betty, " I'll
" not make myſelf ſick to flatter any body."
—" Humph !" cried my aunt, " how this
" wench's want of manners muſt have
" ſhocked you, nephew William ! you ſwal-
" lowed the whole doſe at a word, ſhe, though
" my ſervant, at my repeated command,
" would not touch it with her lips; but theſe
" low-bred creatures have a will of their
" own !"—There was ſomething in my
aunt's manner I did not underſtand; ſhe

                                        puzzled

puzzled me, and I thought it beſt to keep myſelf on the reſerve, and wait the further developement of her humour in ſilence.

We went down to ſupper; it was elegantly ſerved, and my aunt particularly recommended two or three diſhes to me; her hoſpitality embarraſſed me not a little, for my ſtomach was by no means reconciled; yet I felt myſelf bound in good manners to eat of her diſhes and commend their cookery; this I did, though ſorely againſt the grain, and, whilſt my ſtomach roſe againſt it's food, I flattered what I nauſeated.

A grave, well-looking perſonage ſtood at the ſide-board, with whom my aunt entered into converſation.—" Johnſon," ſaid ſhe, " I think I muſt lodge my nephew in " your room, which is warm and well-aired, " and diſpoſe of you in the tapeſtry cham- " ber, which has not lately been ſlept in."— " Madam," replied Johnſon, " I am ready " to give up my bed to Mr. William at your " command; but as to ſleeping in the tape- " ſtry chamber, you muſt excuſe me," " Why?" replied my aunt, " what is your " objection?" " I am almoſt aſhamed to " tell you," anſwered Johnſon, " but every

" body

" body has his humour; perhaps my objec-
" tion may be none to the young gentle-
" man, but I confefs I don't chufe to pafs
" the night in a chamber that is under an
" ill name." " An ill name for what ?" demanded the lady. " For being haunted,"
anfwered the butler, " for being vifited by
" noifes, and rattling of chains and appari-
" tions; the gentleman no doubt is a fcho-
" lar, and can account for thefe things ;. I
" am a plain man, and don't like to have
" my imagination difturbed, nor my reft
" broken, though it were only by my own
" fancies." "What then is to be done ?" faid
my aunt, directing her queftion to me;
" Johnfon don't chufe to truft himfelf in a
" haunted chamber ; I fhall have my houfe
" brought into difcredit by thefe reports:
" Now nephew if you will encounter this
" ghoft, and exorcife the chamber by fleep-
" ing in it a few nights, I dare fay we fhall
" hear no more of it. Are you willing to
" undertake it ?"

I was afhamed to confefs my fears, and
yet had no ftomach to the undertaking ; I
was alfo afraid of giving umbrage to my
aunt, and impreffing her with an unfavour-
                                        able

able opinion of me; I therefore affented upon the condition of Johnfon's taking part of the bed with me: upon which the old lady, turning to her butler, faid, " Well, " Johnfon, you have no objection to this " propofal." " Pardon me, madam," faid he, " I have fuch objections to that cham- " ber, that I will not fleep in it for any body " living." " You fee he is obftinate," faid my aunt, " you muft even undertake it " alone, or my houfe will lie under an ill " name for ever." " Sooner than this fhall " be the cafe," I replied, " I will fleep in " the chamber by myfelf." " You are very " polite," cried my aunt, " and I admire " your fpirit: Johnfon, light my nephew " to his room." Johnfon took up the candle, but abfolutely refufed to march before me with the light, when we came into the gal- lery, where, pointing to a door, he told me that was my chamber, and haftily made his retreat down the ftairs.

I opened the door with no fmall degree of terror, and found a chamber comfortably and elegantly furnifhed, and by no means of that melancholy caft, which I had pictured to myfelf from Johnfon's report of it. My

M 3

firft

firſt precaution was to ſearch the cloſet; I
then peeped under the bed, examined the
.hangings; all was as it ſhould be; nothing
ſeemed to augur a ghoſt, or (which I take
to be worſe) the counterfeit of a ghoſt. I
plucked up as good a ſpirit as I could, ſaid
my prayers and turned into bed: With the
darkneſs my terrors returned; I paſt a ſleepleſs night, though neither ghoſt, nor noiſe
of any ſort moleſted me.

"Why," ſaid I within myſelf, "could
"not I be as ſincere and peremptory as
"Johnſon? He takes his reſt and is at peace,
"I am ſleepleſs and in terrors: Though a
"ſervant by condition, in his will he is in-
"dependant; I, who have not the like call
"of duty, have not the ſame liberty of
"mind: he refuſes what he does not chuſe
"to obey, I obey all things whether I chuſe
"them or not: And wherefore do I this?
"Becauſe I am a flatterer: And why did I
"ſwallow a whole nauſeous doſe to humour
"my aunt's caprice, which her own cham-
"ber-maid, who receives her wages, would
"not touch with her lips? Becauſe I am a
"flatterer: And what has this flattery done
"for me, who am a ſlave to it? what did
"I gain

" I gain by it at my uncle's? I was the echo
" of his opinions, fhifted as they fhifted,
" fided with him againft truth, demonftra-
" tion, reafon, and even the evidence of my
" own fenfes: Abject wretch, I funk myfelf
" in my own efteem firft, then loft all fha-
" dow of refpect with him, and was finally
" expelled from his doors, whilft I was in
" the very act of proftituting my own judg-
" ment to his grofs abfurdities: And now
" again, here I am at my aunt's, devoted to
" the fame mean flattery, that has already fo
" fhamefully betrayed me. What has flat-
" tery gained for me here? A bitter harveft
" truly I have had of it; poifoned by an in-
" fernal dofe, which I had no plea for fwal-
" lowing; furfeited by dainties I had no ap-
" petite to tafte, and now condemned to
" fleeplefs hours within a haunted chamber,
" which her own domeftic would not con-
" fent even to enter: Fool that I am to be
" the dupe of fuch a vapor as flattery! defpi-
" cable wretch, not to affert a freedom of will,
" which is the natural right of every man,
" and which even fervants and hirelings ex-
" ercife with a fpirit I envy, but have not
" the heart to imitate: I am afhamed of

M 4 " my

" my own meannefs : I blufh for myfelf in
" the comparifon, and am determined, if I
" furvive till to-morrow, to affert the dig-
" nity of a man, and abide by the confe-
" quences."

In meditations like thefe night paft away,
and the dawn of morning called me from my
bed : I rofe and refrefhed my fpirits with a
walk through a moft charming plantation :
I met a countryman at his work—" Friend,"
faid I, you are early at your labour."—
" Yes," anfwered he, " 'tis by my labour I
" live, and whilft I have health and ftrength
" to follow it, I have nothing to fear but
" God alone." So ! thought I, here is a
leffon for me; this man is no flatterer;
then why do I worfhip what a clown de-
fpifes?

I found my aunt ready for breakfaft;
fhe queftioned me about my night's reft :
I anfwered her with truth that I had enjoyed
no reft, but had neither feen nor heard any
thing to alarm me, and was perfuaded there
were no grounds for the report of her chamber being haunted. " I am as well per-
" fuaded as yourfelf of that," fhe replied ;
" I know 'tis only one of Johnfon's whims ;
" but

" but people you know will have their
" whims, and it was great courtefy in you
" to facrifice a night's reft to his humour :
" my fervants have been fpoilt by indul-
" gence, but it is to be hoped they will
" learn better fubmiffion by your example."
There was a farcaftic tone in my aunt's manner of uttering this, which gave it more
the air of ridicule than compliment, and I
blufht to the eyes with the confcioufnefs of
deferving it.

After breakfaft fhe took me into her clofet, and, defiring me to fit down to a writing table, " Nephew," fays fhe, " I know
" my brother Antony full well ; he is a ty-
" rant in his nature, a bigot to his opinions,
" and a man of a moft perverted under-
" ftanding, but he is rich, and you have your
" fortune to make ; he can infult, but you
" can flatter ; he has his weakneffes, and you
" can avail yourfelf of them ; fuppofe you
" write him a penitential letter."—I now faw
the opportunity prefent for exerting my
new-made refolution, and felt a fpirit rifing
within me, that prompted me to deliver
myfelf as follows : " No, madam, I will
" neither gratify my uncle's pride, nor
" lower

" lower my own felf-efteem, by making him
" any fubmiffion : I defpife him for the in-
" fults he has put upon me, and myfelf for
" having in fome fort deferved them; but
" I will never flatter him or any living crea-
" ture more.; and if I am to forfeit your
" favour by refifting your commands, I
" muft meet the confequences, and will
" rather truft to my own labour for fupport,
" than depend upon the caprice of any
" perfon living; leaft of all on him."
" Heyday," cried my aunt, " you refufe to
" write !—you will not do as I advife you ?"
" In this particular," I replied, " permit
" me to fay, I neither can nor will obey
" you." " And you are refolved to think
" and act for yourfelf ?" " In the prefent
" cafe I am, and in all cafes, let me add,
" where my honour and my confcience tell
" me I am right." " Then," exclaimed
my aunt, " I acknowledge you for my
" nephew : I adopt you from this hour;"
and with that fhe took me by the hand moft
cordially ; " I faw," faid fhe, " or thought
" I faw, the fymptoms of an abject fpirit in
" you, and was refolved to put my fufpi-
" cions to the teft; all that has paft herè
" fince

" fince your coming has been done in con-
" cert and by way of trial; your haunted
" chamber, the pretended fears of my but-
" ler, his blunt refufal, all have been expe-
" riments to found your character, and I
" fhould totally have defpaired of you, had
" not this laft inftance of a manly fpirit re-
" ftored you to my efteem : you have now
" only to perfift in the fame line of conduct
" to confirm my good opinion of you, and
" enfure your own profperity and happi-
" nefs."

Thus I have given my hiftory, and if the
example of my reformation fhall warn others
from the contemptible character, which I
have fortunately efcaped from, I fhall be
moft happy, being truly anxious to approve
myfelf the friend of mankind, and the *Obferver's* very fincere wellwifher.

WILL. SIMPER.

CIX.

Οὐδὲν γαρ οὕτως ἡδὺ ἀνθρώποις ἔφυ
Ὡς τὸ λαλέειν τ'αλλότρια.

(MENANDER.)

" Still to be tattling, ftill to prate,
" No luxury in life fo great."

THE humours and characters of a populous county town at a diftance from
the capital, furnifh matter of much amufement to a curious obferver. I have now
been fome weeks refident in a place of this
defcription, where I have been continually
treated with the private lives and little fcan-
dalizing anecdotes of almoft every perfon of
any note in it. Having pafled moft of my
days in the capital, I could not but remark the
ftriking difference between it and thefe fub-
ordinate capitals in this particular : in London we are in the habit of looking to our
own affairs, and caring little about thofe,
with whom we háve no dealings : here every
body's bufinefs feems to be no lefs his neighbour's concerns than his own : A fet of
tattling

tattling goffips (including all the idlers in the place male as well as female) feem to have no other employment for their time or tongue, but to run from houfe to houfe, and circulate their filly ftories up and down. A few of thefe contemptible impertinents I fhall now defcribe.

Mifs Penelope Tabby is an antiquated maiden of at leaft forty years ftanding, a great obferver of decorum, and particularly hurt by the behaviour of two young ladies, who are her next door neighbours, for a cuftom they have of lolling out of their windows and talking to fellows in the ftreet: The charge cannot be denied, for it is certainly a practice thefe young ladies indulge themfelves in very freely; but on the other hand it muft be owned Mifs Pen Tabby is alfo in the habit of lolling out of her window at the fame time to ftare at them, and put them to fhame for the levity of their conduct: They have alfo the crime proved upon them of being unpardonably handfome, and this they neither can nor will attempt to contradict. Mifs Pen Tabby is extremely regular at morning prayers, but fhe complains heavily of a young ftaring fellow

in

in the pew next to her own, who violates the
folemnity of the fervice by ogling her at her
devotions: He has a way of leaning over the
pew, and dangling a white hand ornamented
with a flaming pafte-ring, which fometimes
plays the lights in her eyes, fo as to make
them water with the reflection, and Mifs
Pen has this very natural remark ever
ready on the occafion—" Such things, you
" know, are apt to take off one's atten-
" tion."

Another of this illuftrious junto is *Billy
Bachelor*, an old unmarried petit-maitre:
Billy is a courtier of antient ftanding; he
abounds in anecdotes not of the frefheft
date, nor altogether of the moft interefting
fort; for he will tell you how fuch and
fuch a lady was dreffed, when he had the
honour of handing her into the drawing-
room: he has a court-atalantis of his own,
from which he can favour you with fome hints
of fly doings amongft the maids of honour,
particularly of a certain dubious duchefs now
deceafed, (for he names no names) who appeared at a certain mafquerade *in puris natu-
ralibus*, and other valuable difcoveries, which
all the world has long ago known, and long
ago

ago been tired of. Billy has a fmattering in the fine arts, for he can nett purfes, and make admirable coffee and write fonnets; he has the beft receipt in nature for a dentifrice, which he makes up with his own hands, and gives to fuch ladies as are in his favour, and have an even row of teeth: He can boaft fome fkill in mufic, for he plays Barberini's minuet to admiration, and accompanies the airs in the Beggar's Opera on his flute in their original tafte: He is alfo a playhoufe critic of no mean pretenfions, for he remembers Mrs. Woffington, and Quin and Mrs. Cibber; and when the players come to town, Billy is greatly looked up to, and has been known to lead a clap, where nobody but himfelf could find a reafon for clapping at all. When his vanity is in the cue, Billy Bachelor can talk to you of his amours, and upon occafion ftretch the truth to fave his credit: particularly in accounting for a certain old lamenefs in his knee-pan, which fome, who are in the fecret, know was got by being kicked out of a coffee-houfe, but which to the world at large he afferts was incurred by leaping out of a window to fave

a lady's

a lady's reputation, and escape the fury of an enraged husband.

Dr. Pyeball is a dignitary of the church, and a mighty proficient in the *belles lettres :* He tells you Voltaire was a man of some fancy and had a knack of writing, but he bids you beware of his principles, and doubts if he had any more christianity than Pontius Pilate : He has wrote an epigram against a certain contemporary historian, which cuts him up at a stroke. By a happy jargon of professional phrases, with a kind of Socratic mode of arguing, he has so bamboozled the dons of the cathedral as to have effected a total revolution in their church music, making Purcell, Crofts and Handel give place to a quaint, quirkish stile, little less capricious than if the organist was to play cotillions, and the dean and chapter dance to them. The doctor is a mighty admirer of those ingenious publications, which are intitled *The flowers* of the several authors they are selected from : this short cut to Parnassus not only saves him a great deal of round-about riding, but supplies him with many an apt couplet for off-hand quota-
tions,

tions, in which he is very expert, and has besides a clever knack of weaving them into his pulpit essays (for I will not call them sermons) in much the same way as *Tiddy-Doll stuck* plums *on his short pigs and his long pigs and his pigs with a curley tail.* By a proper sprinkling of these spiritual nosegays, and the recommendation of a soft insinuating address, doctor Pyeball is universally cried up as a very pretty genteel preacher, one who understands the politeness of the pulpit, and does not surfeit well-bred people with more religion than they have stomachs for. Amiable Miss *Pen Tabby* is one of the warmest admirers, and declares Doctor Pyeball in his gown and cassock is quite the man of fashion : The ill-natured world will have it she has contemplated him in other situations with equal approbation.

Elegant Mrs. *Dainty* is another ornament of this charming coterie : She is separated from her husband, but the eye of malice never spied a speck upon her virtue; his manners were insupportable, she, good lady, never gave him the least provocation, for she was always sick and mostly confined to her chamber in nursing a delicate constitution :

Noise

Noifes racked her head, company fhook her
nerves all to pieces; in the country fhe
could not live, for country doctors and apo-
thecaries knew nothing of her cafe: in London fhe could not fleep, unlefs the whole
ftreet was littered with ftraw.   Her hufband
was a man of no refinement ; *all the fine feelings of the human heart* were heathen Greek to
him ; he loved his friend, had no quarrel
with his bottle, and, coming from his club
one night a little fluftered, his horrid dal-
liances threw Mrs. Dainty into ftrong hyfte-
rics, and the covenanted truce being now
broken, fhe kept no further terms with
him, and they feparated.   It was a ftep of
abfolute neceffity, for fhe declares her life
could no otherwife have been faved; his
boifterous familiarities would have been her
death.   She now leads an uncontaminated
life, fupporting a feeble frame by medicine,
fipping her tea with her dear quiet friends
every evening, chatting over the little news
of the day, fighing charitably when fhe
hears any evil of her kind neighbours, turning off her femme-de-chambre once a week
or thereabouts, fondling her lap-dog, who
is a dear fweet pretty creature and fo fenfible,

fible, and taking the air now and then on a pillion behind faithful John, who is fo careful of her and fo handy, and at the fame time one of the ftouteft, handfomeft, beft-limbed lads in all England.

Sir *Hugo Fitz-Hugo* is a decayed baronet of a family fo very antient, that they have long fince worn out the eftate that fupported them: Sir Hugo knows his own dignity none the lefs, and keeps a little fnivelling boy, who can fcarce move under the load of worfted lace, that is plaiftered down the edges and feams of his livery: He leaves a vifiting card at your door, ftuck as full of emblems as an American paper dollar. Sir Hugo abominates a tradefman; his olfactory nerves are tortured with the fcent of a grocer, or a butcher, quite acrofs the way, and as for a tallow-chandler he can wind him to the very end of the ftreet; thefe are people, whofe vifits he cannot endure; their very bills turn his ftomach upfide down. Sir Hugo inveighs againft modern manners as feverely as Cato would againft French cookery; he notes down omiffions in punctilio as a merchant does bills for protefting: and in cold weather Sir Hugo is of fome ufe,

ufe, for he fuffers no man to turn his back
to the fire and fcreen it from the company
who fit round : He holds it for a folecifm
in good-breeding for any man to touch a
lady's hand without his glove : This as a
general maxim Mifs *Pen Tabby* agrees to,
but doubts whether there are not fome cafes
when it may be waved : He anathematizes
the herefy of a gentleman's fitting at the
head of a lady's table, and contends that
the honours of the upper difh are the una-
lienable rights of the miftrefs of the family :
In fhort, Sir Hugo Fitz-Hugo has more
pride about him than he knows how to difpofe of, and yet cannot find in his heart to
beftow one atom of it upon honefty : From
the world he merits no other praife but that
of having lived fingle all his life, and being
the laft of his family ; at his deceafe the
Fitz-Hugos will be extinct.

This fociety may alfo boaft a tenth mufe
in the perfon of the celebrated *Rhodope:*
Her talents are multifarious : poetical, bio-
graphical, epiftolary, mifcellaneous : She can
reafon like Socrates, difpute like Ariftotle
and love like Sappho; her magnanimity
equals that of Marc Antony, for when the
world

world was at her feet, she sacrificed it *all for love*, and accounted it *well lost*. She was a philosopher in her leading-strings, and had travelled geographically over the globe ere she could set one foot fairly before the other: Her cradle was rocked to the Iambic measure, and she was lulled to sleep by singing to her an ode of Horace. Rhodope has written a book of travels full of most enchanting incidents, which some of her admirers say was actually sketched in the nursery, and only filled up with little temporary touches in her riper years: I know they make appeal to her stile as internal evidence of what they assert about the nursery; but though I am ready to admit that it has every infantine charm, which they discover in it, yet I cannot go the length of thinking with them, that a mere infant could possibly dictate any thing so nearly approaching to the language of men and women : We all know that *Goody Two-shoes*, and other amusing books, though written for children, were not written by children. Rhodope has preserved some singular curiosities in her museum : She has a bottle of coagulated foam, something like the congealed blood of Saint Januarius :

Januarius: this she maintains was the veri- .
table foam of the tremendous Minotaur of.
Crete of immortal memory; there are some,
indeed, who profess to doubt this, and affert that it is nothing more than the flaver
of a noble English maſtiff, which went tame
about her houſe, and, though formidable
to thieves and interlopers, was ever gentle
and affectionate to honeſt men. She has
a lyre in fine preſervation, held to be the
identical lyre which *Phaon* played upon,
when he won the heart of the amorous *Sappho*; this alſo is made matter of diſpute
amongſt the *cognoſcenti*; theſe will have it to
be a common Italian inſtrument, ſuch as
the ladies of that country play upon to this
day; this is a point they muſt ſettle as they
can, but all agree it is a well-ſtrung inſtrument, and *diſcourſes ſweet muſic*. She has
in her cabinet an evergreen of the cypreſs
race, which is ſuppoſed to be the very individual ſhrub, that led up the ball when
Orpheus fiddled and the groves began a
vegetable dance; and this they tell you was
the origin of all country dances, now in
ſuch general practice. ˙ She has alſo in her
poſſeſſion the original epiſtle which king
Agenor

Agenor wrote to *Europa*, diffuading her from her ridiculous partiality for her favorite bull, when Jupiter in the form of that animal took her off in fpite of all *Agenor's* remonftrances, and carried her acrofs the fea with him upon a tour, that has immortalized her name through the moft enlightened quarter of the globe : Rhodope is fo tenacious of this manufcript, that fhe rarely indulges the curiofity of her friends with a fight of it ; fhe has written an anfwer in *Europa's* behalf after the manner of Ovid's epiftle, in which fhe makes a very ingenious defence for her heroine, and every body, who has feen the whole of the correfpondence, allows that *Agenor* writes like a man who knew little of human nature, and that *Rhodope* in her reply has the beft of the argument.

No. CX.

Homo extra eſt corpus ſuum cum iraſcitur.

(P. SYRUS.)

IT is wonderful to me that any man will surrender himself to be the slave of peevish and irascible humours, that annoy his peace, impair his health and hurt his reputation. Who does not love to be greeted in society with a smile? Who lives that is insensible to the frowns, the sneers, the curses of his neighbours? What can be more delightful than to enter our own doors amidst the congratulations of a whole family, and to bring a chearful heart into a chearful house? Foolish, contemptible self-tormentors ye are, whom every little accident irritates, every slight omission piques! Surely we should guard our passions as we would any other combustibles, and not spread open the inflammable magazine to catch the first spark that may blow it and ourselves into the air.

Tom

Tom Tinder is one of thefe touchy block-heads, whom nobody can endure : The fellow has not a fingle plea in life for his ill temper; he does not want money, is not married, has a great deal of health to fpare, and never once felt the flighteft twinge of the gout. His eyes no fooner open to the morning light than he begins to quarrel with the weather; it rains, and he wanted to ride; it is funfhine, and he meant to go a fifhing; he would hunt only when it is a froft, and never thinks of fkaiting but in open weather; in fhort the wind is never in the right quarter with this tefty fellow; and though I could excufe a man for being a little out of humour with an eafterly wind, Tom Tinder fhall box the whole compafs, and never fet his needle to a fingle point of good humour upon the face of it.

He now rings his bell for his fervant to begin the operation of dreffing him, a tafk more ticklifh than to wait upon the toilette of a monkey : As Tom fhifts his fervants about as regularly as he does his fhirt, 'tis all the world to nothing if the poor devil does not ftumble at ftarting; or if by happy infpiration he fhould begin with the right

foot foremoft, Tom has another infpiration
ready at command to quarrel with him for
not fetting forward with the left: To a cer-
tainty then the razor wants ftrapping, the
fhaving water is fmoaked, and the devil's
in the fellow for a dunce, booby and block-
head.

Tom now comes down to breakfaft, and
though the favage has the ftomach of an
oftrich, there is not a morfel paffes down
his blafpheming throat without a damn to
digeft it; 'twould be a lefs dangerous tafk
to ferve in the morning mefs to a fafting
bear. He then walks forth into his garden;
there he does not meet a plant, which his
ill-humour does not engraft with the bitter
fruit of curfing; the wafps have pierced his
nectarines; the caterpillars have raifed contributions upon his cabbages, and the infernal blackbirds have eaten up all his cher-
ries: Tom's foul is not large enough to
allow the denizens of creation a tafte of
Nature's gifts, though he furfeits with the
fuperabundance of her bounty.

He next takes a turn about his farm;
there vexation upon vexation croffes him at
every corner: The fly, a plague upon't,
has

has got amongst his turnips; the smut has
seized his wheat, and his sheep are falling
down with the rot: All this is the fault of his
bailiff, and at his door the blame lies with a
proportionable quantity of bleſſings to recommend it. He finds a few dry ſticks
pickt out of his hedges, and he blaſts all
the poor in the neighbourhood for a ſet of
thieves, pilferers and vagabonds. He meets
one of his tenants by the way, and he has
a petition for a new gate to his farm-yard, or
ſome repairs to his dove-houſe, or it may be
a new threſhing-floor to his barn—Hell and
fury! there is no end to the demands of
theſe curſed farmers—His ſtomach riſes at
the requeſt, and he turns aſide ſpeechleſs
with rage, and in this manner pays a viſit
to his maſons and carpenters, who are at
work upon a building he is adding to his
offices : Here his choler inſtead of ſubſiding
only flames more furiouſly, for the idle raſ-
cals have done nothing; ſome have been
making holiday, others have gone to the
fair at the next town, and the maſter work-
man has fallen from the ſcaffold, and keeps
his bed with the bruiſes : Every devil is conjured up from the bottomleſs pit to come

on earth and confound thefe dilatory mif-
creants; and now let him go to his dinner
with what ftomach he may. If an humble
parfon or dependant coufin expects a peaceful meal at his table, he may as well fit
down to feed with Thyeftes or the Centaurs.
After a meal of mifery and a glafs of wine,
which ten to one but the infernal butler has
clouded in the decanting, he is fummoned
to a game at back-gammon: The parfon
throws fize-ace, and in a few more cafts
covers all his points; the devil's in the dice!
Tom makes a blot, and the parfon hits it;
he takes up man after man, and all his
points are full, and Tom is gammoned paft
redemption—Can flefh and blood bear this?
Was ever fuch a run of luck? The dice-
box is flapt down with a vengeance; the
tables ring with the deafening crafh, the
parfon ftands aghaft, and Tom ftamps
the floor in the phrenzy of paffion—Defpi-
cable paffion! miferable dependant!—

Where is his next refource? the parfon
has fled the pit; the back-gammon table is
clofed; no chearful neighbour knocks at his
unfocial gate; filence and night and folitude
are his melancholy inmates; his boiling
bofom

bosom labours like a turbid sea after the winds are lulled; shame stares him in the face; conscience plucks at his heart, and, to divert his own tormenting thoughts, he calls in those of another person, no matter whom —the first idle author that stands next to his hand: he takes up a book; 'tis a volume of comedies; he opens it at random; 'tis all alike to him where he begins; all our poets put together are not worth a halter; he stumbles by mere chance upon *The Choleric Man*; 'twas one to a thousand he should strike upon that blasted play—What an infernal title! What execrable nonsense! What a canting, preaching puppy of an author!—Away goes the poet with his play, and half a dozen better poets than himself bound up in the same luckless volume, the innocent sufferers for his offence.

Tom now sits forlorn, disgusted, without a friend living or dead to chear him, gnawing his own heart for want of other diet to feed his spleen upon: At length he slinks into a comfortless bed; damns his servant as he draws the curtains round him, drops asleep and dreams of the devil.

Major Manlove is a near neighbour, but

no intimate of Tom Tinder's: With the enjoyments that refult from health, the major is but rarely bleft, for a body-wound, which he received in battle, is apt upon certain changes of the climate to vifit him with acute pains. He is married to one of the beft of women; but fhe too has impaired her health by nurfing him when he was wounded, and is fubject to fevere rheumatic attacks. Love however has an opiate for all her pains, and domeftic peace pours a balfam into the hufband's wound. It is only by the fcrutinizing eye of affection, that either can difcover when the other fuffers, for religion has endowed both hearts with patience, and neither will permit a complaint to efcape, which might invite the fympathizing friend to fhare it's anguifh. Difabled for fervice, major Manlove has retired upon half-pay, and as he plundered neither the enemy's country nor his own during the war, he is not burthened with the fuperfluities of fortune; happily for him thefe are not amongft his regrets, and a prudent œconomy keeps him ftrait with the world and independant.

One brave youth, trained under his own

eye

eye in the same regiment with himself, is all the offspring Heaven hath bestowed upon this worthy father, and in him the hearts of the fond parents are centered; yet not so centered, as to shut them against the general calls of philanthropy, for in the village where they live they are beloved and blessed by every creature. The garden furnishes amusement to Mrs. Manlove, and when the sharp north-east does not blow pain into the major's wound, he is occupied with his farm: His trees, his crops, his cattle are his nurselings, and the poor that labour in his service are his children and friends. To his superiors major Manlove deports himself with that graceful respect, that puts them in mind of their own dignity without diminishing his; to his inferiors he is ever kind and condescending: To all men he maintains a natural sincerity, with a countenance so expressive of the benevolence glowing in his heart, that he is beloved as soon as known, and known as soon as seen. With a soul formed for society, and a lively flow of spirits, this amiable man no sooner enters into company, than his presence diffuses joy and gladness over the whole circle:

N 4

Every

Every voice bids him welcome; every hand
is reached out to greet him with a cordial
shake. He fits down with a complacent
smile; chimes in with the converfation as it
is going, hears all, overbears none, damps
nobody's jeft, if it is harmlefs; cuts no
man's ftory, if it is only tedious, and is the
very life and foul of the table.

According to annual cuftom I paffed
fome days with him laft autumn : There is a
tranquillity, which tranfpires from the mafter
and miftrefs of this family through every
member belonging to it; the fervants are
few, but fo affiduous in their refpective fta-
tions, that you can no where be better
waited on : The table is plain, but elegant,
and though the major himfelf is no fportf-
man, and has done carrying a gun, the kindnefs of his neighbours keeps him well fupplied with game, and every fort of rural
luxury, that their farms and gardens can
furnifh. Nothing can be more delightful
than the face of the country about him,
and I was charmed with his little ornamented farm in particular: The difpofition
of the garden, and the abundance of it's
fruits and flowers befpeak Mrs. Manlove no
                                    common

common adept in that fweet and captivating fcience.

One day as my friend and I were riding through the fields to enjoy the weftern breeze of a fine September morning, our ears were faluted with the full chorus of the hounds from a neighbouring copfe, and as we were croffing one of the paftures towards them, we heard two men at high words behind a thick hedge, that concealed them from our fight, and foon after the found of blows which feemed to be heavily laid on, accompanied with oaths and cries that made us pufh to the next gate with all the fpeed we could mufter. One of the combatants was lying on the ground, roaring for mercy under the cudgel of his conqueror, who was belaboring him at a furious rate: The perfon of the victor was unknown to major Manlove; the vanquifht foon made him recognize the rueful features of Tom Tinder, who called upon the major by name to interpofe and fave him from being murdered.

This was no fooner done than the cudgeller, who was a fturdy clown, gave us to underftand, that he had been doing no more

than

than every Englifhman has a right 'to do,
returning the loan of a blow with proper
intereft to the lender: This the proftrate'
hero did not deny, but afferted that the rafcal had headed the hare as fhe was breaking
cover, and turned her into the wood again,
by which means he had fpoilt the day's
fport.—And did you this defignedly? faid
the major.—Not I, mafter, replied the
countryman, as Heaven fhall judge me! I
love the fport too well to fpoil it wilfully:
But if I was travelling along the road juft
as pufs was popping through the hedge,
could I help it? am I in the fault? And
fhould this gentleman, if he be a gentleman,
ride up to me as if he would have trampled
me like a dog under his horfe's feet, and lay
the butt of his whip upon my fcull? I think
no man can bear that; fo I pulled him out
of the faddle, and banged him well, and I
think no good man, as you appear to be,
will fay otherwife than that he well deferved
it.—If this be fo, anfwered the major, I can
fay nothing to the contrary.—How, Sir,
exclaimed the fquire, who was now upon his
legs, is a rafcal like this to return blow for
blow, and does major Manlove abet him in
fuch

fuch infolence?—I am forry, Sir, replied the
major calmly, you fhould put fuch a queftion to me; but when gentlemen lofe their
temper—Sir, quoth Tom, interrupting him,
I have loft my horfe, and that's the worfe
lofs of the two—'Tis what you are leaft
ufed to, replied the major, and without
more words quietly trotted homewards.

As we jogged along my friend began to
comment with much pleafantry upon this
ridiculous incident, interlarding his difcourfe
every now and then with remarks of a more
ferious fort upon the ill effects of a hafty
temper, and giving me fome traits of his
neighbour's habits of life, which, though
not fo uncommon as I could wifh, were ne-
verthelefs fuch, as, when contrafted with
his benevolent character, may perhaps ferve
to furnifh out no very unedifying topic for
an Effay in *The Obferver.*

No. CXI.

Neque lex eſt juſtior ulla
Quàm necis artifices arte perire ſud.

Wᴇ have heard ſo much of the tragical effects of jealouſy, that I was not a little pleaſed with an account lately given me of a gentleman, who had been happily cured of his jealouſy without any of thoſe melancholy circumſtances, which too frequently reſult from that fatal paſſion, even when it is groundleſs : As this gentleman's jealouſy was of that deſcription, I am the rather tempted to relate the ſtory (under proper caution as to names and perſons) becauſe there is a moral juſtice in its cataſtrophe, which is pleaſing even in fiction, but more ,particularly ſo when we meet it in the real occurrences of life.

Sir Paul Teſty in his forty-eighth year married the beautiful Louiſa in her eighteenth : there are ſome parents, who ſeem to think a good ſettlement can atone for any diſparity of age, and Louiſa's were of this ſort. Sir Paul had a maiden ſiſter ſeveral

years

years younger than himfelf, who had kept
his houfe for fome time before his marriage
with Louifa, and as this lady was in fact an
admirable œconomift, and alfo in poffeffion
of a very confiderable independent fortune,
the prudent baronet took his meafures for
her continuance in his family, where, under
pretence of affifting the inexperience of his
young bride, fhe ftill maintained her government in as abfolute authority as ever: As
Mifs Rachel would have been better pleafed
with her brother, had he chofen a wife with
lefs beauty and more fortune than Louifa
brought into the family, it may well be
doubted if fhe would have remained with
him after his marriage, had fhe not been
pretty far advanced in an affair of the heart
with a certain young gentleman, whofe
attentions, though in fact directed to her
purfe, fhe was willing to believe had been
honourably addreffed to her perfon: This
young gentleman, whom I fhall call Lionel,
was undoubtedly an object well deferving
the regards of any lady in Mifs Rachel's
predicament; with a fine perfon and engaging addrefs he had the recommendation
of high birth, being a younger fon of the Lord
Mortimer,

Mortimer, a venerable old peer, who refided at his family manfion within a few miles of Sir Paul, and lived upon the moft friendly terms with him in a frequent intercourfe of vifits: Lionel had given this worthy father great uneafinefs from his early diffipation and extravagance; confiderable fums had been paid for him to clear his debts, but the old lord's eftate being a moderate one and entailed upon his eldeft fon, Lionel had been obliged to fell out of the army, and was now living at home upon the bounty of his father on a reduced and flender allowance.

It is not to be wondered at that Lionel, who felt his own embarraffments too fenfibly to negleƈt any fair means of getting rid of them, fhould be willing to repair his fhattered fortunes by an advantageous match; and though Mifs Rachel was not exaƈtly the lady he would have chofen, yet he very juftly confidered that his circumftances did not entitle him to chufe for himfelf; he was alfo ftrongly urged to the meafure by his father, to whofe wifhes he held himfelf bound to conform not only on the fcore of duty but of atonement likewife:

At

At this time the affair was in fo promifing a train, that there is little doubt but it would have been brought to a conclufion between the parties, had not Sir Paul's marriage taken place as it did; but as Mifs Rachel, for reafons which are fufficiently explained, determined upon remaining with her brother, the intercourfe between the lovers was renewed, as foon as Sir Paul had brought home his bride, and was fufficiently fettled to receive the vifits of his friends and neighbours on the occafion.

Now it was that the unhappy Rachel became a victim to the moft tormenting of all human paffions: her fifter-in-law had a thoufand charms, and fhe foon difcovered, or fancied fhe difcovered, that Lionel's attentions were directed towards a fairer object than herfelf: She had now the ftrongeft of all motives for keeping a watchful eye upon Louifa's behaviour, and it is the property of jealoufy to magnify and difcolour every thing it looks upon; for fome time however fhe kept herfelf under prudent reftraint; a hint now and then, cautioufly introduced in the way of advice, was all fhe ventured upon; but thefe hints were fo

little

little attended to by Louifa, whofe innocent
gaiety lent no ear to fuch remonftrances, that
they were occafionally repeated in a graver
tone ; as thefe grew more and more peevifh,
Louifa began to take a little mifchievous
pleafure in teazing, and was piqued into a
behaviour, which probably fhe would never
have indulged herfelf in towards Lionel, had
not Rachel's jealoufy provoked her to it ;
ftill it was innocent, but fo far imprudent,
as it gave a handle to Rachel's malice, who
now began to fow the feeds of difcontent
in her brother's irritable bofom.

In one of thofe fparring dialogues, which
now frequently paffed between the fifters,
Rachel, after defcanting upon the old topic
with fome degree of afperity, concluded her
lecture with many profeffions of zeal for
Louifa's happinefs, and obferved to her as an
apology for the freedom of her advice, that
fhe had a right to fome little experience of
the world more than had yet fallen to the
other's lot : To which Louifa replied with
fome tartnefs—" True ! for you have lived
" more years in it than I have."—" A few
" perhaps," anfwered Rachel.—" As few or
" as many as you chufe to acknowledge,"
added

added Louisa: " It is one amongst a variety
" of advantages over me, which you are too
" generous to boast of, and I am too humble
" to repine at."—" Be that as it may," said
the other damsel, " you will give me leave
" to observe that you have a double call
" upon you for discretion; you are a mar-
" ried woman."

" Perhaps that very circumstance may be
" a proof of my indiscretion."

" How so, madam! I may venture to say
" my brother Sir Paul was no unseasonable
" match for your ladyship; at least I can
" witness some pains were employed on your
" part to obtain him."

" Well, my dear sister," replied Louisa
with an affected nonchalance, " after so
" much pains is it not natural I should wish
" to repose myself a little ?"—" Indiscretion
" admits of no repose ; health, honour, hap-
" piness are sacrificed by it's effects ; it saps
" the reputation of a wife ; it shakes the af-
" fections of a husband."

" Be content !" cried Louisa, " if you
" will give no cause for disturbing the affec-
" tions of the husband, I will take care none

" shall

" fhall be given for attainting the reputation
" of the wife."

At this moment Sir Paul entered the
room, and perceiving by the countenances of
the ladies, that they were not perfectly in
good-humour with each other, eagerly demanded of Louifa why fhe looked fo
grave.

" I would look grave, if I could,"- fhe
replied, " out of compliment to my com-
" pany; but I have fo light a confcience and
" fo gay a heart, that I cannot look gravity
" in the face without laughing at it."

This was delivered with fo pointed a
glance at Rachel, that it was not poffible to
miftake the application, and fhe had no
fooner left the room, than an explanation
took place between the brother and fifter,
in the courfe of which Rachel artfully contrived to infufe fuch a copious portion of her
own poifonous jealoufy into the bofom of Sir
Paul, that upon the arrival of lord Mortimer, which was at this crifis announced
to him, he took a fudden determination to
give him to underftand how neceffary it was
become to his domeftic happinefs,   that
                                Lionel

Lionel fhould be induced to difcontinue his
vifits in his family.

Under thefe impreffions and in a very
awkward ftate of mind Sir Paul repaired to
his library, where lord Mortimer was ex-
pecting him in a fituation of no lefs embarraffment, having conned over a fpeech for
the purpofe of introducing a propofal for an
alliance between the families, and with a
view to found how Sir Paul might ftand
affected towards a match between his fon
Lionel and Mifs Rachel.

As foon as the firft ceremonies were over,
which were not very fpeedily difmiffed, as
both parties were ftrict obfervers of the old
rules of breeding, his lordfhip began after
his manner to wind about by way of recon-
noitring his ground, and having compofed
his features with much gravity and deliberation, began to open his honourable trenches
as follows—" In very truth, Sir Paul, I pro-
" teft to you there are few things in life can
" give me more pleafure than to find my fon
" Lionel fo affiduous in his vifits to this fa-
" mily."—The baronet, whofe mind at this
moment was not capable of adverting to any
other idea but what had reference to his own
jealoufy,

jealoufy, ftared with amazement at this unexpected addrefs, and was ftaggered how to
reply to it; at laft with much hefitation, in a
tone of ill counterfeited raillery, he replied,
that he truly believed there was one perfon in
his family, to whom Mr. Lionel's vifits were
particularly acceptable: and as this was a
fubject very near his heart, nay, that alone
upon which the honour and happinefs of
him and his family depended, he affured
his lordfhip that it was with avidity he em-
braced the opportunity of coming to an explanation, which he hoped would be as
confidential on his lordfhip's part, as it
fhould be on his own. There was fomething
in the manner of Sir Paul's delivery, as well
as in the matter of the fpeech itfelf, which
alarmed the hereditary pride of the old peer,
who drawing himfelf up with great dignity
obferved to Sir Paul, that for his fon Lionel
he had this to fay, that want of honour was
never amongft his failings; nay it was never
to be charged with impunity againft any
member of his family, and that to prevent
any imputation of this fort from being
grounded upon his fon's affiduities to a certain lady, he had now fought this interview
                                    and

and explanation with his good friend and neighbour.

This was fo kind a lift in Sir Paul's conception towards his favourite point, that he immediately exclaimed—" I fee your lord-
" fhip is not unapprifed of what is too con-
" fpicuous to be overlooked by any body
" who is familiar in this houfe; but as I
" know your lordfhip is a man of the niceft
" honour in your own perfon, I fhould hold
" myfelf effentially bound to you, if you
" would prevail upon your fon to adopt the
" like principles towards a certain lady un-
" der this roof, and caution him to defift
" from thofe affiduities, which you your-
" felf have noticed, and which, to confefs
" the truth to you, I cannot be a witnefs to
" without very great uneafinefs and difcon-
" tent."

Upon thefe words the peer ftarted from his feat as nimbly as age would permit him, and with great firmnefs replied—" Sir Paul
" Tefty, if this be your wifh and defire, let
" me affure you, it fhall be mine alfo; my
" fon's vifit in this family will never be re-
" peated; fet your heart at reft; Lionel
" Mortimer

" Mortimer will give you and your's no fur-
" ther difturbance."

" My lord," anfwered the baronet, " I
" am penetrated with the fenfe of your very
" honourable proceedings, and the warmth
" with which you have expreffed yourfelf on
" a fubject, fo clofely interwoven with my
" peace of mind; you have eafed my heart
" of its burthen, and I fhall be ever moft
" grateful to you for it."

" Sir," replied the peer, " there is more
" than enough faid on the fubject; I dare
" fay my fon will furvive his difappoint-
" ment."—" I dare fay he will," faid Sir
Paul, " I cannot doubt the fuccefs of Mr.
" Lionel's attentions; I have only to hope
" he will direct them to fome other ob-
" ject."

Lord Mortimer now muttered fomething
which Sir Paul did not hear, nor perhaps
attend to, and took a hafty leave. When
it is explained to the reader that Mifs Rachel had never, even in the moft diftant
manner, hinted the fituation of her heart
to her brother, on the contrary had induf-
trioufly concealed it from him, this *mal-
entendu*

entendu will not appear out of nature and pro-
bability. Lionel, whofe little gallantries with
Louifa had not gone far enough ferioufly to
engage his heart, was fufficiently tired of his
mercenary attachment to Mifs Rachel; fo
that he patiently fubmitted to his difmiffion,
and readily obeyed his father's commands by
a total difcontinuance of his vifits to Sir
Paul: To the ladies of the family this behaviour appeared altogether myfterious; Sir
Paul kept the fecret to himfelf, and watched
Louifa very narrowly; when he found fhe
took no other notice of Lionel's neglect,
than by flightly remarking that fhe fuppofed
he was more agreeably engaged, he began to
difmifs his jealoufy and regain his fpirits.

It was far otherwife with the unhappy
Rachel; her heart was on the rack; for
though fhe naturally fufpected her brother's
jealoufy of being the caufe of Lionel's abfence, yet fhe could not account for his
filence towards herfelf in any other way than
by fuppofing that Louifa had totally drawn
off his affections from her, and this was
agony not to be fupported; day after day
paffed in anxious expectation of a letter to
explain this cruel neglect, but none came;
all

all communication with the whole family of
lord Mortimer was at a ftop; no intelligence could be obtained from that quarter,
and to all fuch inquiries as fhe ventured to
try upon her brother, he anfwered fo drily,
that fhe could gather nothing from him:
In the mean time, as he became hourly better reconciled to Louifa, fo he grew more
and more cool to the miferable Rachel, who
now too late difcovered the fatal confequences of interfering between hufband and
wife, and heartily reproached herfelf for her
officioufnefs in aggravating his jealoufy.

Whilft fhe was tormenting herfelf with
thefe reflections, and when Louifa feemed
to have forgotten that ever fuch a perfon as
Lionel exifted, a report was circulated that
he was about to be married to a certain lady
of great rank and fortune, and that he had
gone up with lord Mortimer to town for
that purpofe. There wanted only this blow
to make Rachel's agonies compleat; in a
ftate of mind little fhort of phrenfy fhe
betook herfelf to her chamber, and there
fhutting herfelf up, fhe gave vent to her paffion in a letter fully charged with complaints and reproaches, which fhe committed

to

to a trusty messenger, with strict injunctions
to deliver it into Lionel's own hand, and
return with his answer: This commission
was faithfully performed, and the following
is the answer she received in return.—

    " Madam,

" I am no less astonished than affected
" by your letter : If your brother has not
" long since informed you of his conference
" with my father and the result of it, he has
" acted as unjustly by you as he has by lord
" Mortimer and myself: When my father
" waited upon Sir Paul for the express pur-
" pose of making known to him the hopes
" I had the ambition to entertain of render-
" ing myself acceptable to you upon a pro-
" posal of marriage, he received at once so
" short and peremptory a dismission on my
" behalf, that, painful as it was to my feel-
" ings, I had no part to act but silently to
" submit, and withdraw myself from a fa-
" mily, where I was so unacceptable an in-
" truder.

    " When I confirm the truth of the report
" you have heard, and inform you that my
" marriage took place this very morning,

" you will pardon me if I add no more
" than that I have the honour to be,

 " Madam, your moſt obedient   .

  " and moſt humble ſervant,   '

   " LIONEL MORTIMER."

Every hope being extinguiſhed by the
receipt of this letter, the diſconſolate Rachel
became henceforth one of the moſt miſer-
able of human beings : After venting a torrent of rage againſt her brother, ſhe turned
her back upon his houſe for ever, and unde-
termined where to fix, whilſt at intervals
ſhe can ſcarce be ſaid to be in poſſeſſion of
her ſenſes, ſhe is ſtill wandering from place
to place in ſearch of that repoſe, which is
not to be found, and wherever ſhe goes
exhibits a melancholy ſpectacle of diſap-
pointed envy and ſelf-tormenting ſpleen.

No. CXII.

"WHAT good do you expect to do by your "Obfervers?" faid a certain perfon to me t'other day: As I knew the man to be a notorious *damper*, I parried his queftion, as I have often parried other plump queftions, by anfwering nothing, without appearing to be mortified or offended : To fay the truth I do not well know what anfwer I could have given, had I been difpofed to attempt it: I fhall fpeak very ingenuoufly upon the fubject to my candid readers, of whofe indulgence I have had too many proofs to hefitate at committing to them all that is in my heart relative to our paft or future intercourfe and connection.

When I firft devoted myfelf to this work, I took it up at a time of leifure and a time of life, when I conceived myfelf in a capacity for the undertaking; I flattered myfelf I had talents and materials fufficient to furnifh a collection of mifcellaneous effays, which through a variety of amufing matter fhould convey inftruction to fome, entertain-

ment

292 THE OBSERVER. No. 112.

ment to moſt, and diſguſt to none of my
readers. To effect theſe purpoſes I ſtudied
in the firſt place to ſimplify and familiarize
my ſtile by all means ſhort of inelegance,
taking care to avoid all pedantry and affectation, and never ſuffering myſelf to be led aſtray
by the vanity of florid periods and laboured
declamation: At the ſame time I reſolved
not to give my morals an auſtere complexion, nor convey reproof in a magi-
ſterial tone, for I did not hold it neceſſary
to be angry in order to perſuade the world
that I was in earneſt: As I am not the age's
Cenſor either by office or profeſſion, nor am
poſſeſſed of any ſuch ſuperiorities over
other men as might juſtify me in aſſuming
a taſk to which nobody has invited me, I
was ſenſible I had no claim upon the public
for their attention but what I could earn by
zeal and diligence, nor any title to their can-
dour and complacency but upon the evidence of thoſe qualities on my own part.
As I have never made particular injuries a
cauſe for general complaints, I am by no
means out of humour with the world, and it
has been my conſtant aim throughout the
progreſs of theſe papers to recommend and
inſtil

inftil a principle of univerfal benevolence; I
have to the beft of my power endeavoured
to fupport the Chriftian character by occafional remarks upon the evidences and benefits of Revealed Religion; and as the fale
and circulation of thefe volumes have exceeded my moft fanguine hopes, I am encouraged to believe that my endeavours are
accepted, and if fo, I truft there is no arro-
gance in prefuming fome good may have
refulted from them.

I wifh I could contribute to render men
mild and merciful towards each other, tole-
rating every peaceable member, who mixes in
our community without annoying, it's eftablifhed church : I wifh I could infpire an
ardent attachment to our beloved country,
qualified however with the gentleft manners
and a beaming charity towards the world at
large : I wifh I could perfuade contemporaries to live together as friends and fellow
travellers, emulating each other without
acrimony, and chearing even rivals in the
fame purfuit with that liberal fpirit of pa-
triotifm, which takes a generous intereft in
the fuccefs of every art and fcience, that
embellifh or exalt the age and nation we be-

long

long to: I wifh I could devife fome means
to ridicule the proud man out of his folly,
the voluptuary out of his falfe pleafures; if
I could find one confpicuous example, only
one, amongft the great and wealthy, of an
eftate adminiftered to my entire content, I
fhould hold it up with exultation; but when
I review their order from the wretch who
hoards to the madman who fquanders, I fee
no one to merit other praife than of a preference upon comparifon; as for the domeftic bully, who is a brute within his own
doors and a fycophant without, the malevo-
lent defamer of mankind, and the hardened
reviler of religion, they are characters fo incorrigible, and held in fuch univerfal deftefla-
tion, that there is little chance of making
any impreffion upon their nature, and no
need for provoking any greater contempt,
than the world is already difpofed to entertain for them: I am happy in believing,
that the time does not abound in fuch characters, for my obfervations in life have not
been fuch as fhould difpofe me to deal in melancholy defcriptions and defponding lamen-
tations over the enormities of the age; too
many indeed may be found, who are lan-
guid

guid in the practice of religion, and not a
few, who are flippant in their converfation
upon it ; but let thefe fenfelefs triflers call
to mind, if they can, one fingle inftance of
a man, however eminent for ingenuity, who
either by what he has written, or by what
he has faid, has been able to raife a well-
founded ridicule at the expence of true religion ; enthufiafm, fuperftition and hypo-
crify may give occafion for raillery, but
againft pure religion the wit of the blaf-
phemer carries no edge ; the weapon, when
ftruck upon that fhield, fhivers in the affaffin's hand, the point flies back upon his
breaft and plunges to his heart.

I have not been inattentive to the interefts of the fair fex, and have done my beft
to laugh them out of their fictitious characters : On the plain ground of truth and nature they are the ornaments of creation,
but in the maze of affectation all their
charms are loft. Where vice corrupts one,
vanity betrays an hundred; out of the many
difgraceful inftances of nuptial infidelity
upon record, few have been the wretches,
whom a natural depravity has made defperate, but many and various are the miferies,

which

which have been produced by vanity, by
refentment, by fafhionable diffipation, by
the corruption of bad example, and moft
of all by the fault and neglect of the hufband.

They have affociated with our fex to the
profit of their underftandings and the prejudice of their morals : We are beholden
to them for having foftened our ferocity and
difpelled our gloom ; but it is to be regretted that any part of that pedantic character,
which they remedied in us, fhould have in-
fected their manners.   A lady, who has
quick talents, ready memory, and ambition
to fhine in converfation, a paffion for reading, and who is withal of a certain age or
perfon to defpair of conquering with her
eyes, will be apt to fend her underftanding
into the field, and it is well if fhe does not
make a ridiculous figure before her literary
campaign is over.   If the old ftock of our
female pedants were not fo bufy in recruiting their ranks with young novitiates, whofe
underftandings they diftort by their train-
ing, we would let them ruft out, and fpend
their fhort annuity of nonfenfe without annoying them, but whilft they will be fedue-

ing

ing credulous and inconfiderate girls into
their circle, and transforming youth and
beauty into unnatural and monftrous fhapes,
it becomes the duty of every knight-errant
in morality to fally forth to the refcue of
thefe hag-ridden and diftreffed damfels.

It cannot be fuppofed I mean to fay that
genius ought not to be cultivated in, one
fex as well as in the other; the object of my
anxiety is the prefervation of the female
character, by which I underftand thofe gentle unaffuming manners and qualities peculiar to the fex, which recommend them to
our protection and endear them to our
hearts; let their talents and acquirements
be what they may, they fhould never be
put forward in fuch a manner as to over-
fhadow and keep out of fight thofe feminine
and proper requifites, which are fitted fo
the domeftic fphere, and are indifpenfable
qualifications for the tender and engaging
duties of wife and mother; they are not
born to awe and terrify us into fubjection
by the flafhes of their wit or the triumphs
of their underftanding: their conquefts are
to be effected by fofter approaches, by
a genuine delicacy of thought, by a

O 5   fimplicity

simplicity and modesty of soul, which
stamp a grace upon every thing they act or
utter. All this is compatible with every
degree of excellence in science or art; in
fact it is characteristic of superior merit, and
amongst the many instances of ladies now
living, who have figured as authors or artists, they are very few, who are not as
conspicuous for the natural grace of character as for talents; prattlers and pretenders
there may be in abundance, who fortunately
for the world do not annoy us any other-
wise than by their loquacity and impertinence.

Our age and nation have just reason to be
proud of the genius of our women; the
advances they have made within a short period are scarcely credible, and I reflect upon
them with surprize and pleasure: It behoves
every young man of fashion now to look well
to himself, and provide some fund of information and knowledge, before he commits
himself to societies, where the sexes mix:
Every thing that can awaken his ambition,
or alarm his sense of shame, call upon him
for the exertions of study and the improve-
ment of his understanding; and thus it
comes

comes to pass that the age grows more and more enlightened every day.

Away then with that ungenerous praise, which is lavished upon times past for no other purpose than to degrade and sink the time-present upon the comparison!

Plus vetustis nam favet
Invidia mendax, quam bonis præsentibus.

PHÆDRUS.

I conscientiously believe the public happiness of this peaceful æra is not to be paralleled in our annals. A providential combination of events has conspired to restore our national dignity, and establish our internal tranquillity, in a manner which no human foresight could have pointed out, and by means which no political sagacity could have provided. It is a great and sufficient praise to those, in whom the conduct of affairs is reposed, that they have clearly seen and firmly seized the glorious opportunity.

Let us, who profit by the blessing, give proof that we are deserving of it, by being cordially affectioned towards one another, just and generous to all our fellow-creatures, grateful and obedient to our God.

No. CXIII.

ADELISA, poffeft of beauty, fortune, rank, and every elegant accomplifh-ment, that genius and education could beftow, was withal fo unfupportably capri-cious, that fhe feemed born to be the tor-ment of every heart, which fuffered itfelf to be attracted by her charms. Though her coquetry was notorious to a proverb, fuch were her allurements, that very few, upon whom fhe thought fit to practife them, had ever found refolution to refift their power. Of all the victims of her vanity Leander feemed to be that over whom fhe threw her chains with the greateft air of triumph; he was indeed a conqueft to boaft of, for he had long and obftinately defended his heart, and for a time made as many reprifals upon the tender paffions of her fex as fhe raifed contributions upon his: Her better ftar at length prevailed; fhe beheld Leander at her feet, and though her victory was accomplifhed at the expence of more tender glances, than fhe had ever beftowed upon the whole fex collectively,

yet

yet it was a victory, which only piqued Adelifa to render his flavery the more intolerable for the trouble it had cost her to reduce him to it.   After she had trifled with him and tortured him in every way that her ingenious malice could devife, and made fuch public display of her tyranny, as fubjected him to the ridicule and contempt of all the men, who had envied his fuccefs, and every woman, who refented his neglect, Adelifa avowedly difmiffed him as an object which could no longer furnish fport to her cruelty, and turned to other purfuits, with a kind of indifference as to the choice of them, which feemed to have no other guide but mere caprice.

Leander was not wanting to himfelf in the efforts he now made to free himfelf from her chains; but it was in vain; the hand of beauty had wrapped them too clofely about his heart, and love had riveted them too fecurely for reafon, pride, or even the ftrongeft ftruggles of refentment to throw them off; he continued to love, to hate, to execrate and adore her. His firft refolution was to exile himfelf from her fight; this was a meafure of abfolute neceffity, for he was not yet recovered enough to abide the chance of meeting her, and he had neither fpirits nor inclination to ftart a frefh attachment by way of experiment upon her jealoufy. Fortune however befriended him in the very moment of defpair, for no fooner was he out of her fight, than the coquettifh Adelifa found fomething wanting, which had been fo familiar to her; that Leander, though defpifed when poffeft, when loft was regretted. In vain fhe culled her numerous admirers for fome one to replace him; continually peevifh and difcontented, Adelifa became fo intolerable to her lovers, that there feemed to be a fpirit conjuring up amongft them, which threatened her with a general defertion. What was to be done? Her danger was alarming, it was imminent: She determined to recall Leander: She informed herfelf of his haunts, and threw herfelf in the way of a rencontre; but he avoided her: Chance brought them to an interview, and fhe began by rallying him for his apoftacy: There was an anxiety under all this affected pleafantry, that fhe could not thoroughly conceal, and he did not fail

to

to difcover : He inftantly determined upon
the very wifeft meafure, which deliberation
could have formed ; he combated her with
her own weapons ; he put himfelf appa-
rently fo much at his eafe, and counterfeited
his part fo well, as effectually to deceive
her : fhe had now a new tafk upon her hands,
and the hardeft as well as the moft hazard-
ous fhe had ever undertaken : She attempted to throw him off his guard by a pretended
pity for his paft fufferings, and a promife
of kinder ufage for the future : He denied
that he had fuffered any thing ; and affured
her that he never failed to be amufed by her
humours, which were perfectly agreeable to
him at all times,—" then it is plain," replied fhe, " that you never thought of me
" as a wife ; for fuch humours muft be
" infupportable to a hufband."—" Pardon
" me," cried Leander, " if ever I fhould be
" betrayed into the idle act of marriage,
" I muft be in one of thofe very humours
" myfelf : Defend me from the dull uni-
" formity of domeftic life ! What can be
" fo infipid as the tame ftrain of nuptial
" harmony everlaftingly repeated ? What-
" ever other varieties I may then debar
                              " myfelf

" myfelf of, let me at leaft find a variety
" of whim in the woman I am to be fet-
" tered to."—" Upon my word," exclaimed
Adelifa, " you would almoft perfuade me
" that we were deftined for each other."—
This fhe accompanied with one of thofe
looks, in which fhe was moft expert, and
which was calculated at once to infpire and
to betray fenfibility: Leander, not yet fo
certain of his obfervations as to confide in
them, feemed to receive this overture as a
raillery, and affecting a laugh, replied—" I
" do not think it is in the power of def-
" tiny herfelf to determine either of us; for
" if you was for one moment in the humour
" to promife yourfelf to me, I am certain
" in the next you would retract it; and if
" I was fool enough to believe you, I fhould
" well deferve to be punifhed for my cre-
" dulity: Hymen will never yoak us to
" each other, nor to any body elfe; but if
" you are in the mind to make a very
" harmlefs experiment of the little faith I
" put in all fuch promifes, here is my hand;
" 'tis fit the propofal fhould fpring from
" my quarter and not your's; clofe with it
" as foon as you pleafe, and laugh at me as
                                    " much

" much as you pleafe, if I vent one mur-
", mur 'when you break the bargain."—
" Well then," faid Adelifa, " to punifh
" you for the faucinefs of your provoking
" challenge, and to convince you that I do
" not credit you for this pretended indif-
" ference to my treatment of you, here is
" my hand, and with it my promife; and
" now I give you warning, that if ever I do
" keep it, 'twill be only from the convic-
" tion that I fhall torment you more by
" fulfilling it than by flying from it."—
" Fairly declared," cried Leander, " and
" fince my word is paffed, I'll ftand to it;
" but take notice, if I was not perfectly
" fecure of being jilted, I fhould think
" myfelf in a fair way to be the moft egregi-
" ous dupe in nature."

- In this ftrain of mutual raillery they proceeded to fettle the moft ferious bufinefs of
their lives, and whilft neither would venture upon a confeffion of their paffion,
each feemed to rely upon the other for a
difcovery of it. They now broke up their
conference in the gayeft fpirits-imaginable,
and Leander upon parting offered to make

a bett

a bett' of half. his fortune with Adelifa that
fhe did not ftand to her engagement, at the
fame time naming a certain day as the period of its taking place.—" And what fhall
" I gain," faid fhe, " in that cafe by half
" your fortune, when I fhall have a joint
" fhare in poffeffion of the whole ?"—
" Talk not of fortune," cried Leander,
giving loofe to the rapture which he could
no longer reftrain, " my heart, my happinefs, my life itfelf is your's"—So faying he
caught her in his arms, preffed her eagerly
in his embrace, and haftily departed.

No fooner was he out of her fight than
he began to expoftulate with himfelf upon
his indifcretion: in the ecftafy of one unguarded moment he had blafted all his
fchemes, and by expofing his weaknefs
armed her with frefh engines to torment
him. In thefe reflections he paffed the remainder of the night; in vain' he ftrove
to find fome juftification for his folly; he
could not form his mind to believe that the
tender looks fhe had beftowed upon him
were any other than an experiment upon his
heart to throw him from his guard, and re-
eftablifh

eftablifh her tyranny. With thefe impreffions he prefented himfelf at her door next
morning, and was immediately admitted;
Adelifa was alone, and Leander immediately began by faying to her—" I am now
" come to receive at your hands the pu-
" nifhment, which a man who cannot keep
" his own fecret richly deferves; I furrender
" myfelf to you, and I expeſt you will ex-
" ert your utmoft ingenuity in tormenting
" me; only remember that you cannot give
" a ftab to my heart without wounding your
" own image, which envelopes every part,
" and is too deeply impreft for even your
" cruelty totally to extirpate."—At the
conclufion of this fpeech, Adelifa's countenance became ferious; fhe fixt her eyes
upon the floor, and, after a paufe, without
taking any notice of Leander, and as if fhe
had been talking to herfelf in foliloquy, repeated in a murmuring tone—" Well, well,
" 'tis all over; but no matter."—" For the
" love of Heaven," cried Leander in alarm,
" what is all over?"—" All that is moft
" delightful to woman," fhe replied; " all
" the luxury which the vanity of my fex
                                    " enjoys

" enjoys in tormenting your's: Oh Leander!
" what charming projects of revenge had
" I contrived to punish your pretended in-
" difference, and depend upon it I would
" have executed them to the utmost rigour
" of the law of retaliation, had you not in
" one moment disarmed me of my malice
" by a fair confession of your love. Believe
" me, Leander, I never was a coquette but
" in self-defence; sincerity is my natural
" character; but how should a woman of
" any attractions be safe in such a character,
" when the whole circle of fashion abounds
" with artificial coxcombs, pretenders to
" sentiment and professors of seduction?
" When the whole world is in arms against
" innocence, what is to become of the
" naked children of nature, if experience
" does not teach them the art of defence?
" If I have employed this art more particu-
" larly against you than others, why have I
" so done, but because I had more to appre-
" hend from your insincerity than any other
" person's, and proportioned my defences
" to my danger? Between you and me,
" Leander, it has been more a contest of

" cunning

" cunning than an affair of honour, and if
" you call your own conduct into fair re-
" view, truſt me you will find little reaſon
" to complain of mine.   Naturally diſpoſed
" to favour your attentions more than any
" other man's, it particularly behoved me
" to guard myſelf againſt propenſities
" at once ſo pleaſing and ſo ſuſpicious.
" Let this ſuffice in juſtification of what is
" paſt; it now remains that I ſhould ex-
" plain to you the ſyſtem I have laid
" down for the time to come: If ever I
" aſſume the character of a wife, I devote
" myſelf to all its duties; I bid farewell
" at once to all the vanities, the petu-
" lancies, the coquetries of what is falſely
" called a life of pleaſure ; the whole ſyſtem
" muſt undergo a revolution, and be ad-
" miniſtered upon other principles and to
" other purpoſes : I know the world too
" well to commit myſelf to it, when I have
" more than my own conſcience to account
" to ; when I have not only truths but the
" ſimilitudes of truths to ſtudy ; ſuſpicions,
" jealouſies, appearances to provide againſt ;
" when I am no longer ſingly reſponſible on
                                    " the

" the fcore of error, but of example alfo :
" It is not therefore in the public difplay of
" an affluent fortune, in drefs, equipage,
" entertainments, nor even in the fame of
" fplendid charities . my pleafures will be
" found ; they will center in domeftic occu-
" pations ; in cultivating nature and the
" fons of nature, in benefiting the tenants
" and labourers of the foil that fupplies us
" with the means of being ufeful ; in living
" happily with my neighbours ; in availing
" myfelf of thofe numberlefs opportunities,
" which a refidence in the country affords,
" of relieving the untold diftreffes of thofe,
" who fuffer in fecret, and are too humble
" or perhaps too proud to afk."—Here the
enraptured Leander could no longer keep
filence, but breaking forth into tranfports
of love and admiration, gave a turn to
the converfation, which is no otherwife interefting to relate than as it proved the pre-
lude to an union which fpeedily took place,
and has made Leander and Adelifa the
fondeft and the worthieft couple in England.

From Adelifa's example I would willingly

lingly eftablifh this conclufion, that the characters of young unmarried women, who are
objects of admiration, are not to be decided
upon by the appearances, which they are
oftentimes tempted to affume upon the plea
of felf-defence : I would not be underftood
by this to recommend difguife in any fhape,
or to juftify thofe who refort to artifice
upon the pretended neceffity of the meafure ; but I am thoroughly difpofed to believe, that the triflings and diffemblings of
the young and fair do not fo often flow from
the real levity of their natures, as they are
thought to do : Thofe in particular, whofe
fituation throws them into the vortex of
the fafhion, have much that might be faid
in palliation of appearances. Many co-
quettes befides Adelifa have become admirable wives and mothers, and how very
many more might have approved themfelves
fuch, had they fallen into the hands of men
of worth and good fenfe, is a conjecture,
which leads to the moft melancholy reflections. There is fo little honorable love in
the men of high life before marriage, and
fo much infidelity after it, that the hufband

band is almoſt in every inſtance the corrupter
of his wife. A woman (as ſhe is called) of
the world is in many people's notions a pro-
ſcribed animal; a ſilly idea prevails that
ſhe is to lead a huſband into certain ruin
and diſgrace: Parents in general ſeem
agreed in exerting all their influence and
authority for keeping her out of their
families; in place of whom they frequently
obtrude upon their ſons ſome raw and inexperienced thing, whom they figure to
themſelves as a creature of perfect innocence and ſimplicity, a wife who may be
modelled to the wiſhes of her huſband,
whoſe manners are untainted by the vices
of the age, and on whoſe purity, fidelity
and affection he may repoſe his happineſs
for the reſt of his days. Alas! how groſsly
they misjudge their own true intereſts in
the caſe: How dangerous is the ſituation of
theſe children of the nurſery at their firſt
introduction into the world! Thoſe only
who are unacquainted with the deceitfulneſs
of pleaſure can be thoroughly intoxicated by
it; it is the novelty which makes the danger; and ſurely it requires infinitely more
judgment,

judgment, ftronger refolutions and clofer attentions to fteer the conduct of a young wife without experience, than would ferve to detach the woman of the world from frivolities fhe is furfeited with, and by fix-ing her to your interefts convert what you have thought a diffipated character into a domeftic one.

The fame remark applies to young men of private education: you keep them in abfolute fubjection till they marry, and then in a moment make them their own mafters; from mere infancy you expect them to ftep at once into perfect man-hood: the motives for the experiment may be virtuous, but the effects of it will be fatal.

I am now approaching to the conclufion of this my fourth volume, and according to my prefent purpofe fhall difmifs the *Ob-fervers* from any further duty: The reader

and I are here to part. A few words therefore on fuch an occafion I may be permitted
to fubjoin; I have done my beft to merit
his protection, and as I have been favourably heard whilft yet talking with him, I
hope I fhall not be unkindly remembered
when I can fpeak no more : I have paffed a
life of many labours, and now being near it's
end have little to boaft but of an inherent
good-will towards makind, which difap-
pointments, injuries and age itfelf, have not
been able to diminifh. It has been the chief
aim of all my attempts to reconcile and endear man to man : I love my country and
contemporaries to a degree of enthufiafm
that I am not fure is perfectly defenfible;
though to do them juftice, each in their turns
have taken fome pains to cure me of my
partiality. It is however one of thefe ftub-
born habits, which people are apt to excufe
in themfelves by calling it a *fecond nature*.
There is a certain amiable lady in the world,
in whofe interefts I have the tendereft concern, and whofe virtues I contemplate
with paternal pride; to her I have always
wifhed to dedicate thefe volumes; but
when

when I confider that fuch a tribute cannot
add an atom to her reputation, and that no
form of words, which I can invent for the
occafion, would do juftice to what paffes in
my heart, I drop the undertaking and am
filent.

END OF THE FOURTH VOLUME.

www.ingramcontent.com/pod-product-compliance
Lightning Source LLC
Chambersburg PA
CBHW060533030726
47498CB00004B/1176